I0586736

Conglommora
Found

Conglommora
Found

Andy Hunt

Copyright © 2018 by Andy Hunt.

All rights reserved. No part of this publication may be reproduced, stored in a retrieval system, or transmitted, in any form or by any means, electronic, mechanical, photocopying, recording, or otherwise, without the prior written permission of the publisher.

This is a work of fiction. Names, characters, businesses, places, events and incidents are either the products of the author's imagination or used in a fictitious manner. Any resemblance to actual persons, living or dead, or actual events is purely coincidental.

ISBN: 978-0-9992560-2-2 (softcover)

Printed in the United States of America. First Printing, September 2018.

Explore the mysteries online at

http://www.Conglommora.com

Books by Andy Hunt

Science Fiction/Adventure

1. *Conglommora*
2. *Conglommora Found*
3. *Conglommora Defense* (upcoming)

Technical Non-fiction

- *The Pragmatic Programmer: From Journeyman to Master*
- *Programming Ruby*
- *Pragmatic Version Control*
- *Pragmatic Unit Testing in Java*
- *Pragmatic Unit Testing in C#*
- *Practices of an Agile Developer*
- *Pragmatic Thinking & Learning: Refactor Your Wetware*
- *Learn to Program with Minecraft Plugins (Bukkit Edition)*
- *Learn to Program with Minecraft (CanaryMod Edition)*

Acknowledgments

First off, thanks to all the readers of my first novel in this series for your kind encouragement and support.

Thanks to my early reviewers, including Bas Bloembergen, Kerry Buckley, Adam K. Dean, Zach Dennis, Jason Jolly, Charlie Payne, Eustáquio Rangel, Mike Riley, and Bill Tucker.

Thanks also to my copyeditor, Tracey Seybold, who diligently tracked down my errant commas and fat-fingered typos. Any remaining errors are entirely my fault.

And special thanks to my family for their support, suggestions, and patience with me as my attention wandered off into the world of Conglommora.

Dedication

To my wife, Ellie, without whom there be no books, or even a reason to write.

One

I WAS BACK AT MY HOME, the *Neylan*, briefly, just to get a few things I wanted to have with me in Skyville. The screen in the wall lit up in the darkness and chimed at me, and I made an answering gesture.

"Charlie! How are you doing, buddy?" Chalu's warm manner shone right through the screen. Even though he was down on Earth, untold light years from here, you probably could have seen him beaming with the naked eye. Chalu always seemed to glow with an unquenchable joy. The hair helped. Chalu sported multicolored strands of long hair, sometimes down to his waist, braided in parts, and always in a *wide* mix of colors.

"Hey Chalu. I'm well, just on my way back to Skyville for a while. You seem pretty excited for a guy who spends all his time underwater."

There was a pause. Communications over qradio had improved a lot but still wasn't quite real-time. The image froze and jittered a bit. It took a little patience still, but you could pretend to have a conversation. Sort of. A dozen seconds, maybe more, slipped by.

"I *am* excited. Denisova has grown so quickly, we've added so much to the station. It's more like a small city now. And we've really improved the whole docking/surface vessel thing. You really should come visit us. Bring Alain! Ahdom's been asking after him."

Ahdom was Chalu's son. Looked just like him, for the most part, with very similar features and the same burnished brown skin, although Ahdom kept his hair jet black instead of colorful. He and Alain had grown to be friends over the last few years.

Chalu really wanted to get us to visit Denisova. That's what they called the new underwater base on Earth, located in the middle of one of their very large oceans.

It had started as a small research station, built just after our very first visit. But within a few years, it was clear this was an excellent way to visit Earth and avoid any interaction with the natives, our descendants. Arty, our collective AI, approved and considered it perfectly safe for us to visit Denisova.

But the Earth natives—and the Earth itself—were now over 100,000 years ahead of when we'd left, which had only been a couple of generations for us. Strange place, this universe of ours. All evidence of our civilization on Earth was gone; most of it we'd scavenged in our hasty flight from the planet, the rest eroded into dust from time and nature. It wasn't our planet anymore.

A lot of folks seemed to think it was nice to visit, though. There were minimum physical requirements, of course, so not *everyone* was automatically allowed to go. Arty had to approve.

For me, the thought of going back to Earth, and then staying *underwater*, was truly claustrophobic. I barely survived that first historic trip. Chalu was a good friend, and we stayed in touch even through his lengthy sojourns to Denisova, but I felt that was his adventure, not mine. Speaking of adventures…

"You still there?" Chalu asked.

"Oh, sorry. Mind wandered a bit. Yeah, I haven't see Alain in a good long while now. He's still out on his Walk."

"Still?" Chalu's brow furrowed, his head tilted forward, and a few of the multicolored strands of long hair hung into his face. "I thought he was done with all that by now."

"Nope," I said with some resignation. "He's still out there. Still looking. How's your family?"

"Doing well. Sundara is almost old enough to join us; she and my wife are planning on coming down full time next season."

"And Ahdom?"

"My son takes after his father too much, I think." Chalu laughed lightly. "He wants to explore the whole of the planet, pole to pole and everything in between."

"Hah, he's welcome to it."

Chalu nodded to someone off-screen. "Be right there. Hey, I've got to run. But really, I think you and your lady friend should come on down and visit. It's safe; we've had no problems here. Nothing like your first visit to Earth!"

"There's still the joy of being sucked through the resonance wave," I commented dryly.

Chalu winced, slightly. "Yes, well, there is still that. But such a small price to pay." His eternal joy bubbled back up quickly, an irrepressible fountain. "Okay, we'll see you soon one way or another."

The screen went dark, matching the rest of the lighting on the *Neylan*. Had I always kept it so dark here, in the home I grew up in? Skyville seemed so much brighter, so much more open. Granted, it was a big dome instead of a just this small little ship house. But still.

I got up, ambling through the darkened passageway and into the living area. Waved my hand along the wall, a chairform popped out and I slumped into it.

So much had changed.

Maybe it was brighter in the house when Alain still lived here. Ah, probably not. He seemed to always have his head stuck in a game or vr of some sort. Well, not anymore, I guess. Now he's out and about, who knows where. He pinged me every once in a while, let me know where he was and what he was up to. But not often enough, not for me. And here I was, sitting alone in the dark. Waiting for the ghosts of my past, my wife, my life…

I got up in one quick move, quick enough to leave my glum thoughts behind. Enough of this. I had plans to have dinner with my good friends Ronny and Janel, spend the night here, then set off for Skyville again in the morning. Better to be with Ronny than mope around in this empty shell of a former life.

I pulled on a fresh coverall, tossing the old one into the reclaimer, palmed open the hatch and was back into the corridors once again.

Another one of those endless, mostly featureless corridors of the sort that connected all of the original ships together into the Conglommora. Blue and amber lights, and not much else. All these corridors connected our ships, our houses. Ronny and Janel's place wasn't far.

I caught myself going around a junction as the gravity field shifted slightly. Midway up a narrow corridor before it met with a broad, circular tube—this was one of the spots where Eddie used to hang out. *Crazy.* I always thought he was just plain crazy. Ranting, incoherent. But not wrong as it turned out. Eddie had discovered the first readings of a recovered Earth. The Earth that killed him and the others on that first landing.

Guess I hadn't completely left my gloomy thoughts behind at the *Neylan.* The narrow, skinny corridor joined up with a larger, circular tube at the junction, lit in the familiar muted colors of amber and blue from the service lighting. I walked on to the last narrow corridor at the next junction and had arrived. I took a deep breath, determined to leave my shadows behind.

The hatch slid open and Janel Q'tel swept me into their house grandly. "Welcome, Charlie! Oh, man, we haven't seen you in… well, I don't know how long. Too long, for sure. Come on in." That last bit was redundant, as she had maneuvered me halfway into their front room and sealed the hatch by now.

"Hey, Charlie!" Ronny Sullivan called out from the back. "Be right with you. You all sit and make yourselves some drinks."

We did, and I once again had the opportunity to ask Janel what she was up to. Usually, Janel's research and passion was focused on Dead Earth. Or rather, what led up to it. Geopolitics, psychology, history, anthropology, that sort of thing. It was good someone around here knew our history so well, I suppose.

Glad it didn't have to be me.

Janel and Ronny seemed like complete opposites in every respect, starting with their exteriors. Janel was tall and lanky; both her skin and hair were jet black, just like the void itself. Ronny was short, stout, with pearly luminescent white skin. But they were nearly just as opposite on the inside as well; Ronny, frank and even abrasive; Janel, well-studied and thoughtful.

"So, what's new in the annals of Dead Earth?" I asked, after clinking our glasses of sweet-brewed algae in welcoming celebration.

"Dead Earth?" Janel looked askance. "Not so dead as we thought, apparently. I've been looking into that more and more lately, and it just doesn't make any sense." She fanned her hands out in a gesture of frustration. "Green and fertile again, no sign of pollution, radiation… no sign of *us*. No sign of our civilization at all. Nothing Arty can detect. There's no *way* Earth could have recovered so completely, not even in 100,000 years." She leaned back in her chairform. "But here we are."

"Huh," I responded with my usual eloquence. "Well, maybe it was actually longer than that. Maybe things decay faster than we think. Maybe a meteor *did* hit the planet and wiped everything clean!" I grinned. Janel punched my arm and rolled her eyes at the same time, preparing for a retort.

Ronny came in just then, bearing a mouth-watering tray of appetizers of all kinds. Bright primary colors, geometric shapes; it smelled wonderful even if I had literally no idea what it was.

"It's called *plenare*," Ronny said. "The folks in the outer arc are most fond of it."

I tried a bite and found it had a wonderful texture— crispy and salty on the outside, light and creamy in the middle, with a tang I couldn't quite identify.

"What's it made—?" I started.

Ronny waved his hands and grabbed a couple more for his plate.

"Shhhh. Don't ask. Nothing harmful."

I had my doubts, but it was really good. I took another one of the bright, electric blue ones and let it evaporate in my mouth before continuing the conversation.

"So everything on Earth is gone. Well, to be fair, we lost so many records of ancient civilizations—and even more modern ones"

"The Erasures," Janel added.

"That. It wasn't just people, right? Whole fields of knowledge were destroyed? Artifacts as well?"

Janel sighed and hesitated, a *plenare* in her hand. "At first, it was the usual. Politicians would have an opponent assassinated and all records of the victim erased. Then they started in on the scientific records—climate research, even animal and environmental research. We lost the names of whole species, even entire ancient civilizations. Their ruins were destroyed, their names erased. All by the fearful, the superstitious. We don't even know how much was lost by the Erasures. Maybe it doesn't really matter. It's all gone anyway."

"Think of it as a fresh start," I said, trying to lighten the mood a little. Janel could be a little grim at times. I only got a glare for my troubles. Well, might as well really stir things up.

"Any plans to go down to Earth and see for yourselves? Check it out again? Visit Denisova? Chalu keeps after me to come visit," I said.

Janel shot Ronny a look. Their first camping trip to Earth back in the day ended badly, and Ronny had to regrow his arm when they got back. Still a sore point, so I tried to bring it up every so often. Just for fun.

Ronny took a swig of the algae ferment. "No, no plans. I think I've had my fill. Janel talks about it sometimes. Try and get more data on Earth's recovery, find out the real story. But nothing serious."

Janel was put out. "How do you know I'm not serious?"

Ronny looked sideways at her. "Because as I remember it, you said you'd kill me with your bare hands if I ever made you go to Earth again."

"Doesn't count if it's my idea," Janel proclaimed and popped some more *plenare* in her mouth.

"Ah," Ronny acknowledged with a smirk, wisely not continuing the conversation.

Janel brought out the main courses later, and we chatted and ate through the night, like old friends who hadn't seen each other in a while. Which happened to be exactly the case. The hour grew late.

"What's wrong with recolonizing Earth?" Ronny was asking. "Get rid of the damn bears and lions, poisonous snakes and deadly viruses. We could do it, at least for a region at a time. Remake the world to suit us."

"Terraforming isn't that easy," Janel countered. "It's been tried. Remember your grandfather's story about the near-belt asteroid colonies?"

"Well, that was just plain damn stupid," Ronny retorted. "They didn't have nearly enough natural resources, no Arty to keep the minerals and nutrients in balance… nothing. I could have told them they were all going to die." He drained his glass and got up for yet another.

"Okay," Janel played along. "Suppose we get all the tech right, manage to figure out to re-engineer an entire, planet-sized biosphere with all its quirks and subtle nuances. Suppose we get all that perfectly right and remake the planet in our own image. What about the humans who already live there? What about the animals in the food chain who depend on the 'pests' you want to eliminate? What happens to all of that?" Janel asked, with more than a hint of agitation and accusation on her breath. And a fair bit of fermented algae, too.

Ronny sighed. They'd had this conversation before, of course, and despite his hopes, it always ended up the same way. Our large-scale presence wouldn't be fair to the humans on Earth now. Our children. Perhaps cousins, some said. Either way, the Earthans were our kin. And considering how few of us there were in the whole of the cosmos, "don't screw up the humans" was a compelling argument all by itself.

"Besides." Janel drained her glass as well. "Arty wouldn't let you, even if you wanted to."

Ronny pursed his lips. "But Arty let Lucille go down and teach those poor natives God knows what."

The room shrunk a little. Maybe a chill came over us. Over me, certainly. I tried not to dwell on those events, on how I lost Grace, the only love of my life after my wife died, on how Grace somehow became Lucille.

Janel shook her head. "Yes, it did allow that. Arty still thinks it's a reasonable idea to have small teams go down and help the Earthans along. And who knows, maybe it's right. I don't trust Lucille. I know *you* don't trust Lucille," she said, flailing an arm at me. "But Arty runs on quantum logic, not stupid human fears."

Ronny harrumphed. "True enough, I suppose. But fear is a good thing. Keeps us safe. Arty doesn't know fear from waking up in the morning. Not in its programming. It doesn't *know* to be afraid of Lucille."

In the ensuing silence, he got up, swooshed open a panel in the wall, and retrieved an ornate, decorative bottle, covered in a delicate filigree of silver and shiny gems. The good stuff. He poured a round for us.

"It's not worried about Lucille," he continued. "I'm just saying maybe it should be."

I did not disagree.

Two

So. Many. People. The hatch closed behind Alain, and he scanned as much as he could, as quickly as he could, as far as his eyes could see.

Edge to edge, he couldn't even see the floor of the dome, and really not even the walls. Just a sea of people, a giant ocean with waves of humanity of all different colors, heights, and speeds as they flowed their way around. Clothing of dark red, fluorescent green, and watery blue. Skin of shining silver, gold, pink, brown, alabaster white, and iridescent black. And that was just the batch immediately in front of him, elbow to elbow with almost no space in between at all.

Maybe this was a mistake. There's no way I can even get through here. He struggled against the crowd, but only made it a short way inside the dome before the tide pushed him back toward the hatch he'd entered from. He tried again in a slightly different direction but wasn't making much headway.

"Welcome to the Hive! What's your name?" shouted the girl with silver skin and matching hair.

"Alain." He tried for as much volume as he could without actually screaming.

"What?" The girl was trying to make conversation, but it was so loud in the dome. Filled with loud, happy people, going about their daily lives. Trading, cooking, eating, telling stories, all trying to be heard over each other. Hard to hear anything other than the dull, continuous, roar of the crowd.

And the smells! A whole section looked like food shacks, or carts, or both, cooking a vast, mind-numbing variety of offerings. Mostly magnetic cooking, but it smelled like there were some real open fires as well.

"What's your name?" she belted out again while still smiling.

"Alain Neylan," he repeated, as she turned her ear closer to his head.

She noticed the piece attached to his right ear. "You an imager?"

"Yes, that's right." Alain smiled. "I've been all over Conglommora taking images and talking to folks. So much to see." He drew a long breath and looked up at the silver dome—same color as the girl—and back down at the immense sea of people ahead of him.

"But I've never seen a crowd like this," he admitted. "I was hoping to find a place to stay tonight, but I'm not sure I can even get through this crowd."

"Oh, this?" she said dismissively. "This is nothing. You should see it really packed on the local holidays. I'm

Essi." She grinned, wider now. "I've got room. My place is just over there." She gestured vaguely toward the middle of the dome.

"There's a trick to navigating crowds like this. It's just a like a river back on Green Earth. Here, follow me." And with that, she darted farther into the crowd. Alain was startled but dove in after her.

Sure enough, there was a flow of people within the thick of the crowd. Several flows, in fact, rushing and conjoining, losing and gaining members. Essi had a knack for finding the rivers, the eddies, backwashes; the current and flow of the crowd. Alain had a time keeping up, bumping into quite a few people with less grace than he had hoped. They didn't seem to mind or even notice.

Finally, they were swept out of the main crush and up against the hatch of a modest house. Essi palmed the wall and they entered. The sudden seal of the hatch behind them felt like earplugs; the sudden quiet was like a silver blanket, warm, enveloping, comforting.

"Wow." Alain waited a moment before breaking the stillness. "You weren't kidding. River of people, all right."

Essi shook her head, as if to clear it, and Alain noted her long, flowing hair. She motioned for a chairform, and Alain did as well, sitting next to her.

"That's really a great metaphor," Alain continued, then paused a space. "I... I don't usually tell people this, but I've seen a real river, once, back on Earth. Teeming with life, just like the river of people here in Hive."

"You've been?" Essi startled, her eyes widened. "I haven't met anyone who's been down yet."

"I was lucky… I guess." Alain smiled. "I was on the very first ship down with my Dad, Charlie Neylan."

"Neylan. Alain Neylan," she echoed, then chuckled. "Well, I've got a genuine celebrity here for the night! And here I thought you were just another handsome wanderer."

Alain may have blushed, may have simply stood up too quickly as he started to pace.

"Oh, I don't know about that whole *celebrity* business, but thanks for the lodging. I was hoping to stay at Hive for a couple of days, is that okay?"

Essi got up from her chair as well. "Sure… plenty of room here. You can stay as long as you like." She smiled warmly.

"I don't really have any Raw to trade or anything," Alain admitted. "Well, I mean, I did, but then there was that incident back at the Chance Dome and…"

"Not a problem at all," Essi said, undimmed. "You will be *required* to tell me that story, however. And all the others. Tell me about Earth! Your trip there and back, tell me what you've seen of Conglommora, tell me…" She paused for breath, having suddenly run out. "Tell me all of it."

"All?" Alain raised an eyebrow. "Okay, I suppose. Seems a fair trade. But that's a lot of work on an empty stomach. Perhaps we should cook up some dinner first?" He nodded hopefully back toward the galley.

Now it was Essi's turn to look surprised. "What, cook ourselves? Huh. I suppose some folks do that. Not here, though. Come on," she grabbed his arm, "I'll show you how to get a proper dinner here in Hive."

She propelled him out the hatch and into the river of humanity once again, tacking against the current of bodies toward a row of free-standing cooking carts. The most incredible smells wafted past them, richer now and more focused.

Alain thought he might learn to like Hive after all.

————————————

They stood together past the third cart, nibbling on some sort of very spicy food on a stick, cooked over a real open fire with its own oxygen feed. Alain had no idea what it was, but ate gratefully.

"This is fantastic. What is it?" Alain mumbled between mouthfuls.

Essi shrugged. "Food."

He swallowed. "Could you be a *little* more specific?"

"Oh, I don't know what they call it. I think these folks make up new names every day anyway. That old lady over there…" She pointed, "I swear I've never gotten the same thing twice from her. And this guy," she gestured at the most recent stall featuring a very large gentleman with an equally large and bushy mustache, "I get these same things here almost every day, and he still won't tell me what they are. The names don't matter. You learn to get what you like from who you like. And where to get surprises if you want that, too!"

Alain captured a bunch of images of the stalls, of the unending crowd, of Essi.

"I don't think I've ever tasted these particular spices before," he said as they headed for a row of dessert offerings.

"As I hear it, the recipes are all closely-guarded family secrets. Most using descendants of original spice plants rescued from Dead Earth itself. But that's just talk—you've actually *been!*" Essi exclaimed. "Come on, let's grab something cold and sweet and head back to my place, so you can tell me all about it."

"Wow. Just wow." Essi was sitting in her living area, leaning forward, her head in her hands, her legs at an awkward, outward angle, completely enthralled at Alain's tale. They were each sipping a sweet, glowing blue concoction. "What were you thinking when the ship exploded and you were stranded? I would have pissed myself, I think. At least."

"Hah, I'm not sure I didn't." Alain sat back in his chairform, looking rueful. "That was pretty damn terrifying. Stuck in that little lander craft, the ship we came in blown to bits." He shook his head. "But you know, once we landed back on Earth and started gathering supplies, I felt better about the whole thing. I mean, it was a huge, devastating shock at first, of course. All of it. Those first couple of folks on our crew who died on our first landing, that crazy guy Robert blowing up in the ship, and there we were, all alone, in orbit, no food, no water... nothing. But once we started *doing* something,

I felt better. I thought we might really make it after all. My dad was great through the whole thing, too, don't get me wrong. I don't think any of us would have made it back without him."

Essi finished off her dessert drink, leaning back in her chairform. "Incredible. A real, genuine adventure. Arty showed me the summary points back when all that happened, but I really had no idea what you'd been through. And here you are now, wandering all of Conglommora? I would have thought that was enough adventure to last a lifetime!" She laughed.

"Maybe it should have been." Alain pursed his lips, rolling his hands around his drink. "But I've had some pretty wild times in the darker corners out here, too. Nothing quite as dramatic," he added hastily at her worried look. "But I've been threatened, been in trouble, nearly gotten killed a couple of times—mostly accidents."

"Then why do you keep doing it?"

"Hmm." A short puff of a smile, and Alain looked down at his now-empty dessert cup, wistfully. "Why, indeed. A couple of reasons, I guess. I'm looking for something. I'll know it when I find it. And I'm looking for someone. A girl."

"Well, maybe you've found someone," Essi said, leaning in closer and tilting her head to one side, eyes bright and hair flowing.

"Oh!" Alain exclaimed, a little slow on the uptake. "I mean, I'm sort of looking for someone for my father."

Essi raised an eyebrow and moved back. "That's a little weird, don't you think?"

"No, no, not like that," Alain laughed gently. "It's… complicated. Family matters, I guess you could say. Here, here's a picture. Have you seen her?" He held up his shiny and made a few motions until the image came up.

Essi peered over at it.

"Ah. No, can't say I've ever seen her. But I don't wander too far from The Hive, so that's not saying much. But, maybe I'm someone you're looking for, too?" Essi said hopefully.

"Just might be." Alain moved closer to her, leaned in, and kissed her gently.

Essi awoke the next morning, same as any other day. But not exactly the same. She smiled, eyes still closed, vividly remembering Alain the night before. She rolled over to wake him, but he wasn't there. Must be up already.

She slid out of the bedform, still naked, and groggily wandered into the galley. It was dark. No Alain here. Now she was more wide awake and darted to the front of her house. Nothing. His pack was gone.

He was gone.

Damn. She slumped a little in the hatchway. He had seemed so nice. But those wandering types, they did like to wonder. *Well, there goes plans for today.*

Essi meandered back to the bedroom and pulled on a simple coverall, the standard utilitarian clothing popular throughout Conglommora. It was snug, optimized for her particular body type and weight at the moment. On a whim, she asked aloud, "Arty, where is Alain?"

Arty's voice came from the nearest speaker, "Alain Neylan is no longer in The Hive."

At least he's making good time. One other thing to do before she forgot. Essi pulled the shiny out of her pocket, stiffened it, and searched through the contacts. There was no name on this entry, just a stylized icon of a heart. She pinged the contact. A woman with dark golden hair and uncommonly deep, dark green eyes answered.

"Faith?" Essi asked.

A slight eye roll. "I've asked you not to call me that. Or call me, for that matter. What's up?"

"Some guy was through here yesterday, asking about you. Looking for you."

Faith frowned slightly. "What guy? What was his name?"

"Alain Neylan. He and his dad were on that first mission to Earth—"

"Yeah, I got that," Faith interrupted. "What did you tell him?"

"Nothing," Essi answered. "There is nothing to tell."

"Thanks for letting me know." Faith terminated the connection, and Essi's screen went dark.

She stuffed the shiny into a pocket on her coveralls and strode purposefully back to the front of her house, palmed open the hatch, and silently rejoined the massed throng of humanity in the great expanse of The Hive.

Three

AFTER I LEFT RONNY AND JANEL'S, I headed back to Skyville. Where Ronny's place was more or less in my old neighborhood, near the *Neylan*, Skyville was a considerable distance.

On my first few trips, I walked and contorted myself through the several day's worth of corridors, connectors, and hatches. I figured a gravsled would have been more trouble than it was worth, having to stop and constantly recalibrate it every time the gravity field shifted—which was often. But the constant long walks were a little more than I could take, so I started using the gravsled anyway. I got better at the whole quick-recalibrate thing, and it wasn't so bad once you got the knack of it.

I was on approach up the last, long, lonely corridor to Skyville, gliding pretty damn fast up the straightaway. Not as fast as a hyperloop car, but maybe a little faster than I should have. I backed off as I approached the hatch, entered, and headed for the house.

The gravsled ramped its field down, gently settling onto the lush green lawn in the middle of the massive Skyville dome. I took my packages off, and the sled slid up and nestled into the niche right next to the hatch. I went inside.

The house was dark at the moment. But not dark like the *Neylan* had been. That was a dark of energies spent, of a light lost to the past. This was warmer, more comforting. A temporary dark of resting, only. Light was on the way—she'd be back shortly.

I leaned into the hatchway, looked out at the broad expanse of the Skyville dome, with its azure blue ceiling. Kind of like the sky on Earth. Close enough for everyone here, I guess. I was one of the few who'd actually *seen* the color of the sky on Earth. Not just the color, but the breadth, depth, and richness of it all. The sky here was none of that, but it was still very pleasant.

As far as I'd seen, Skyville was pretty unique in Conglommora. Sure, there were plenty of other large domes, dedicated to different aspects of life as our grandparents and great-grandparents found it back on Green Earth. And other biospheres had large animals, too. But Skyville was a little different, because the people lived and worked right alongside the beasts. All together, sharing an endless grassy field under an Earth-like, bright blue sky.

To me, that pretty much summed up Skyville. Kind of like Earth. But not as deadly. Large, peaceful animals going about their business. Folks doing the same. Peace, quiet—but not isolated and lonely. I enjoyed what I thought was the peace and quiet living on the *Neylan*, but in hindsight, I was just disconnected. I withdrew from what friends I had after my wife Haily died and hadn't noticed how cut off I'd become. It wasn't until Arty asked me to spy, and my son Alain and I had that whole adventure through the resonance wave back to Earth, that I really began to appreciate life again. Had to see the dark to appreciate the light, I guess. Like one of those poems I never appreciated as a youth. Some of those you just have to get older to finally understand. You have to live the light, live the dark to appreciate the subtle nuances of real life. And the light on Earth was so much more dazzling than this pale simulacrum. *That* was real light.

So, at some point, I realized that the dark and quiet of the *Neylan*, which I had cherished for so long, wasn't healthy. Especially after Alain had left.

But here in Skyville, walking and working side by side with good friends under a bright blue sky, I found peace and quiet, done properly. This was where I belonged now.

Alain had asked me to go with him a few times, but wandering all of Conglommora on a Walk was a young man's game. Or at least, someone else's game. Not mine. I'd had my share of adventure. Alain was welcome to dig for whatever excitement he could find out here. I did worry about him, though. He'd gotten in a couple tight spots and scrapes already, especially when he first set out. Nothing too bad—Arty was always there to protect against any serious problem, if it could. But still. A parent's worry never ends.

I hadn't heard from him for a while now. What wonders was he exploring today? The joy of surreal fabrication in the Mech Section, wonders of the deep in Sea? Outside of Skyville, those were my favorites. Probably not his. He was probably off with some other wild young people doing who knows what. I guessed I'd hear from him in due course. I always did.

Ah, she was on her way back now. Good timing. Picking her way through the fields of large animals and their droppings. Golden hair flowing behind her, golden skin. Just gold all over. I straightened.

"Charlie! Right on time. I missed you!" We hugged, kissed deeply. I hadn't been gone *that* long, but our relationship was still in the early years. The hatch slid open, and we went inside.

Some folks talk about love at first sight, and I think that was definitely the case when I first met Grace. A strange, rare, electrifying experience. Which made losing Grace—her mind, at least—very hard to take. Maybe you only get one "love at first sight" moment in your life. When Haily and I met and married, it was a slower process. Both Haily and I had a firm goal at the time to find a mate, so it was all very conscious and deliberate but hardly instantaneous.

And now, with the latest love of my life, the process was different yet again. This one had taken some time. In fact, I didn't even like her when we first met. I thought we were far too different, nothing in common. I didn't find it easy to talk to her at all. Maybe I felt out of my league—she remains incredibly beautiful. One of the most beautiful people I've ever seen in real life (vr models don't count). And I'm not, frankly. So, no, we didn't hit it off on our first meeting.

Or our second.

No connection on our third, fourth, and so on.

But I was spending more and more time in Skyville. I got to know some of Grace's friends, where she worked and hung out. She didn't have any family left. Well, there was a sister, Faith, but she'd been on an extended Walk for many, many years now. No one knew where she was or really remembered what she looked look—apparently, she was very shy if you had an imager pointed at her. Didn't like pictures of herself. By now, she was close to passing into myth, or legend even.

I thought getting closer to Grace's world would help me feel closer to Grace, to the Grace I knew, but it didn't. It *did* make me appreciate Skyville more and more, however. And as I spent more of my time there, I, of course, kept running into Käthe. Which wasn't fate, or destiny, or even unusual. Käthe was the coordinator for Skyville, which was as close to a leader as anyone had, so, of course, we had dealings with each other frequently. I still found her hard to talk to, hard to get to know.

Until one night.

There had been an issue with contamination in the dairy process. After milk is extracted from the cows, it is lightly processed to remove any harmful bacteria or other dangerous bits. Well, something had gone wrong and a few children got sick as a result. Nothing dangerous, but that sort of thing wasn't supposed to happen—and hadn't happened in many years.

With some extra hand-scanners and Arty's help, we were checking all aspects of the dairy. Käthe and I happened to end up in the same place, the back of a storage area of one of the barns, filled with pipes, nanophotonic circuits, and mechanical devices.

"Anything yet?" I asked, somewhat redundantly but trying to make conversation.

Käthe put down her scanner and looked right at me. "No. Absolutely nothing. But I will keep on trying."

She was still looking at me, not the scanner. Something in the dim of my brain clicked, and I realized that maybe she wasn't talking about the dairy issue. The rest of my brain, especially the talking part, seemed to go offline and shutdown. I sputtered a little to get it going again, voicing a few nonsense syllables like a useless, damaged life form. A complete do-over. I managed to get a reasonable sentence going, something along the lines of, "You're not talking about the scanner, are you?"

"No, Charlie, I'm not." Käthe took my hand. "Charlie, you're an amazing person. Do you know how many folks I know who've led a mission to Earth? One. Who've survived exploding ships and treacherous natives? One. Who's kind, and funny, witty and fun to be around? One."

My brain exploded at the sudden notion that Käthe *wasn't* out of my league, after all. I leaned in and kissed her passionately.

Let's just say it's a good thing we had the barn to ourselves that evening.

Even then, it took a while for Käthe and I to get comfortable with each other. She loved Skyville so much; she was really dedicated to sharing the beauty of the animals and nature with everyone. She always felt that the nature of Skyville could heal anyone of anything. Especially me. I think in the beginning she took me on as a project in healing. If she could help me, surely she could help anyone.

And maybe she was right. I was healed. It had taken a while, and she probably wasn't done even yet. That night had been a long time ago, and here I was still "moving in."

It may have taken a while, but I felt happy again, and perfectly safe—not like on Earth. Yes, I mused as Käthe was dealing with some late-breaking business on her screen, this was the place for me. I'd live out my years here, no more ridiculous spy missions or planetary expeditions.

I was sure Earth was getting along fine without me.

Four

CRUNCH, CRUNCH, CRUNCH. Nothing but the sound of their feet on Earth's forest floor against the background drone of a valley teeming with insects. The group slowed down a pace. Quiet as they were, they still might be heard. Last thing they needed now was to attract the attention of some large predator.

A snapping stick probably was the least of it. Any halfway awake lion or tiger could probably smell him a full valley's-width away, covered as he was in a permanent layer of sweat, mud, urine, and blood. In that order. The blood came and went, depending on the hazards of the day. But the rest was pretty much constant.

Shoes would have been nice. But those were long gone. He had lost his shoes and much of his clothing within the first day or two here. He hadn't figured on spending the next few years being ripped and shredded by the rough surfaces that indifferently scraped his bare skin.

Years. Had it really been years? How many? He had counted moons, at first. But after maybe twenty-five or thirty he had lost count. The Earthans here counted moons and rainy seasons; one per year. At first, he tried to make sense of the sun's position during its passage each day. Morning, mid-morning, noon, afternoon, dusk, night. Only after a good while did he accept that none of that made any difference at all. But at first, at first...

His people came back for him, once. Just once. But he was injured, lying in a cave–not really a cave; more like a ditch. Hadn't made a fire yet, couldn't signal to them. They never came back. A day, maybe two later, he crawled out from the half-ditch, found some berries, some green plants to eat. One made him throw up. He didn't eat that one again.

Oh, to be dry. Or clean. Hands forever wet and slippery, bare feet slippery, he fell again. Made too much noise. The first few men in line shot a warning look back at him. He waved his hands open; a gesture of apology.

He didn't know how to live here; they still treated him like a child. Just like the small children playing, scampering around the village fires at night. But he knew how to count, knew when the moon would be full and bright. He mashed up the raw food, burned it a little in fire before eating it. Slowly they began to imitate him. And respect him for his unusual abilities. Even if he still couldn't walk through the world in quiet.

The tribes hunted deer, waterbuck, the faster gazelles, and great, horned-cattle-like aurochs. But those often took a coordinated effort with help from your friends.

Those massive horns on some of the cattle species were not to be trifled with. Alone or in smaller numbers, it was easier to dine on turtles, small game like rabbits and such, and bird eggs. Eggs were not created equal, he discovered. One preposterous-looking animal had a fuzzy, ball-like body, skinny legs that bent backward, and a long neck ending with quizzical and accusing eyes in a small head. It could run like the wind, though, and one egg could feed maybe ten people at once.

He'd learned a lot.

But it had taken a long time to get to this point. His first meeting with natives hadn't gone so well. He tried to talk to them, to gesture, but they didn't understand. Those strange noises he made. Was he even of the same kind as them? He sounded different. He looked different. Taller, smaller in the middle. Nose fine and delicate, not broad and flat. Eyes set strangely. Wearing pale skins of some frail animal they didn't know. Whatever he was wearing, it tore easily and was soon gone.

Those first tribesmen he met shook him off in fear and mistrust, and left him to his fate.

And so it was maybe not even a moon later that he met his current companions. So long ago, but he still remembered that day clearly—as clear as the stream from the mountain itself.

It had been a cool, cloudless dawn. The sun just barely edging over the far horizon. Not hot yet, not even bright with the full yellow of the sun. Just a slowly warming blue, the last gasp of night giving way to the day. He was walking with purpose, trying to reach the foothills of the next mountain range. About to cross an open plain—a dangerous move at best, but it couldn't be avoided.

He was just about to move out from under the cover of the canopy when he came across several men crouched ahead of him, spears in hands. They looked up quickly, but quietly, putting both hands to their mouths, palms out. He took that to mean "be quiet." Or maybe "stop," or "freeze." Since they had spears and he didn't, he did all three.

They turned their attention back to the plain, just as a large animal burst out of the grasses in pursuit of some small furry thing. They fell on it with their spears and quickly subdued it. Stone knives came out as they began to carve the animal up. He felt it was maybe safe now to move and began to approach them—slowly, carefully.

The first one looked up sharply from the warm wet meal, and growled something that he took to be words. He didn't try and reply this time, since that seemed to have scared off the first tribesmen he met. He gestured to his throat, then to his stomach.

First man rose from his squat position, looked at him strangely, and barked some "words" again. Second man looked up at this, and rose as well, facing him.

He patted his stomach again, pointed to this throat and shook his head. *Let them assume I'm just mute.*

Second man barked over to one of the others. That one made some sort of gesture and worked the carcass with a knife for a moment. A fresh piece of meat was brought over.

He bowed, opened his hands wide and palms open in a gesture he hoped would be taken as a "thank you." He ate the meat with wild fury. The few berries and plants he'd been chewing hadn't quite been enough so far. He was starving. They grunted something akin to acknowledgment and went back to the meal.

He followed First, Second, and the others in the tribe for a few days like this. They were stopped by a thin ribbon of water—hardly a river, not even a respectable stream. But it must have been larger recently, as a broad, flat bank of not-quite-dry mud ran alongside. He stopped and, using a stick, began to draw figures in the mud.

This was quite a marvel to the tribe. They stopped their march and gathered around to watch this new novelty. It took a while, some prodding and more patience than he could bear, but he finally was able to work out names for his new friends. First man drew a rough, flat outline of a man, and a larger beast next to it. A bear, maybe. First man pointed to the bear, then to himself.

Okay, got it. He drew a great bear in the dirt also, pointed to it, then pointed to the man. Greatbear hopped a few times, wearing a broad smile and pointing to his chest. *Yes, yes!*

Second man took the stick and drew what he guessed was a deer, moving at great speed past stick figure trees. Again, he copied the design, pointed the man, and so would know him as Runningdeer.

He'd been with Greatbear and Runningdeer ever since. He'd met the women of the tribe, the children, many others who had come and gone. Some were killed; some disappeared. But always he stuck with these two, all these moons. Today was another long walk, with a small number of companions, and they had far to go before nightfall. Plenty of time to think.

Oh, there was no shortage of time to think here, in this place. It would almost be mind-numbing boredom except for the sudden, surprising moments of sheer terror from some horrific beast or other threat. It was a wonder he was still alive. Well, he mused, he wouldn't be if it hadn't been for their help.

Back when they first met, and he had learned their names, they of course handed him the stick and pointed directly at him. What was *his* name?

Oh boy, he thought, *that's going to be tough to explain.* How do you convey your name when you aren't named for a beast, mountain, river or flower?

How do I tell them I'm not from here, that I'm from far away?

Far away. Outside, outside the village, outside the fire, outside the world itself. That's it, he realized. He took the stick that Greatbear had offered him, and drew a circle on the ground. He pointed to all of the men around him, and pointed to the circle. They were the circle. Then he drew a line—outside of the circle. Outside. Was it even a concept they could grasp? It took a few more tries, and a lot of pointing, but they seemed to get the idea, and copied the drawing, the O/, the line outside the circle. He was outside. He was O/.

O/ smiled, if only they knew how right they were.

Silentstream was up scouting ahead, following the track of birds in the sky. The birds knew the seasons, knew well the vastness of the planet far beyond what the dirt-crawlers had ever seen firsthand. To know more than the land could tell, follow the birds.

But they could only follow, not fly. The land itself was treacherous, and wild beasts were bad enough. O/ had seen giant beasts, including what he thought was once called a mammoth, and an armored creature with a long snout the size of a hyperloop car. All teeth and fur, and muscles like reinforced cable strands.

But now, apparently, they had to keep an eye open for the other tribes, too. That was new, as near as O/ could tell. All the tribes had always lived in peace almost as long as anyone could remember. But now there were rumors, stories, that one tribe in the middle, the Central Tribe, was causing trouble. O/ couldn't be sure he had the details correct. Something about killing, whether it was other tribesmen or beasts they weren't supposed to have killed, he didn't know. But it was enough that the Edge Tribes started to keep watch.

O/ called his friends Edge Tribe 2. There was another set of neighbors, Edge Tribe 1, that they ran into from time to time. They were friends and helped each other out. Greatbear explained the tribes using one stick for the neighbors and two sticks for themselves, so O/ called them 1 and 2. Both on the inside edge of a circle— the world, maybe?—and the Central Tribe dead center.

He might not have had it exactly right, but it was close enough.

Silentstream was running back toward them and suddenly disappeared—the ground on the bank slipped away and took him down with it unto the muck of an almost-spent stream. Runningdeer slid gracefully down the bank and scooped him up. Silentstream had a nasty cut up his forearm, and bled like a fountain. He sat, cradling his hurt arm, and did not rise when the rest of 2 began moving off, not on the same path they had been on, but off at an angle.

O/ squat down next to Silentstream and made a gesture he hoped would come across as "I help." Some of the tribe were more adept than others at understanding his hand motions. Silentstream didn't move, or scream, so that was a start. O/ took off the pelt he was wearing around his middle. It was fashioned somewhat like a belt, held his stone knife and a stick, and helped keep his larger pelt from hanging on him like a tent. He removed the items and quickly tied the pelt belt tightly around Silentstream's arm, stemming the all-too-quick flow of blood.

O/ took a smaller piece of hide that was wrapped around Silentstream's head and wrapped that around the wound, too. That would help keep it protected, keep it from dripping too much.

Greatbear was trailing the others and looked back to see this strangeness. He made a quick grunt up to the others, who halted. Greatbear turned and came back. He looked with familiar amazement at O/, then grunted a question to Silentstream. Silentstream held up his arm, waved it slightly, and there was no shower of blood to attract predators or signal his slow but inevitable death. Greatbear bent over, looked more closely, and seemed satisfied. He helped Silentstream up, using his good arm, and waved for him to join the others. He then turned and regarded O/.

Greatbear put both hands up, fingers to his forehead, and nodded. O/ smiled, as he knew well what that meant.

Thank you.

They caught up to the others and continued on.

Five

ALAIN CAME UP THE LAST of several long, nondescript corridors, glowing with the customary amber and blue lighting, and palmed open the latest hatch. He stepped through the archway and was immediately punched in the face. Alain was more surprised than hurt—the punch was well executed for maximum theatrical effect with no real damage. The hatch slid silently closed at his back.

The man who punched him was dressed in some bizarre costume that included a circle of large, white, synthetic feathers on his head, some rich, plush fabric of a great coat, and shiny boots that covered nearly the whole of his legs. He was shouting at a woman, similarly attired, except she was wearing an extremely short skirt of some shiny material. Still the feathers and the boots. Both wore large boxy masks, grotesquely over-sized and angular, with many facets and changing colors.

"What the hell, man!" Alain blurted out.

The woman shouted back at the man, "See! He don't know nothing! What you go and try and kill him for? He don't even know Maurice." She eyed Alain a little more closely. "You ain't even from around here, are you, boy?"

Alain warily took his eyes off the man and replied to her, "No, no, I'm not. I'm on a Walk. I just came from The Hive." He jerked a thumb over his shoulder in the general direction he'd just come from.

Despite this intrusion of the outside, non-narrative world, the man was trying to stay in character. He walked away, circling around Alain menacingly. "But he's one of them! I'm sure of it." His eyes narrowed. "Why are you here, really? No lies! Tell the truth for once!"

Alain tried to clarify. "I'm here trying to find somebody. Looking for someone, a girl."

The man leaned back and laughed, a large, over-exaggerated stage laugh. "You should try the cave orgy." He made a gesture, and the wallform to one side slipped away, revealing the rest of the large dome. He waved his hand expansively across the dome and pointed. Up the side wall was a massive stone structure, made to look something like what they thought cliff-face cave dwellers of Green Earth's distant past would have lived in. Alain mused that the set wasn't that far off from Earth's *current* cave dwellers, but the folks here probably didn't know that. The actors in the cave set were a different story. Mostly nude, or nearly so, wearing just a few strips of some rough cloth. *Well, that wasn't quite right*, Alain thought. Skins and furs, maybe, but not cloth. And they definitely weren't wearing enough of it for any sort of protection from the environment. Oh, and then there was the whole orgy aspect. That seemed a unique Conglommoran addition as well.

"Ah, no, sorry—that's not what I'm looking for. I'm looking for a specific person. Name of Faith. Faith Langston. This might be an image of her." He held up the shiny from his pocket, flicked to stiffen it in position. There on the surface was the image of a young woman, with dark golden hair piled up in a braid on top of her head and uncommonly deep, dark-green eyes.

The woman came over to take a closer look and pulled off her elaborate mask. She was on the older side, but not too much so, darker hair just starting to gray. The man shook his head in frustration, "Margie! The narrative!"

"Oh, give it a rest for a minute, Phil. We have all day. Come over here."

Phil, disgruntled at having to break character, popped his mask off and leaned in to look at the image as well. Without the mask, Alain could see that Phil was also an older man, stocky, with a most generous and graying beard. A couple of other folks nearby, dressed in the same bizarre costumes, apparently took this to mean a short break and they also either removed their masks or slumped onto a convenient piece of set decoration, or both.

"I don't know anyone named Faith," Phil said, "but that sure looks like Praeda to me."

"Praeda?" Alain cocked an eyebrow.

"She was here maybe a hundred days or so ago?" Margie looked at Phil, who nodded. "Remarkable young lady. She's a wanderer, like you. But she could do anything—sets, costumes, body mods, writing, singing… She worked on, even starred in a couple of our narratives. In almost everyone's, I think."

Phil nodded in tacit agreement again.

"Do you know where she went after she left here?"

"Don't even know *when* she left, really." Phil said. "She just sort of wasn't around anymore."

Alain put the shiny back in his pocket, thinking for a moment. "What's the biggest, most exciting area nearest to Storyville?"

Phil rubbed his beard thoughtfully, in an apparently practiced manner. "Well, I suppose, for excitement's sake, there's the Miner's Tubes. You know, the folks who go out on expeditions to mine asteroids and small moons. Sometimes even a real planet. Hardcore adventure seekers, they are."

Margie added, "I've known a couple of folks who got bored of the narratives here and decided to go on a 'real' adventure. But it's real danger out there. Accidents happen. Not a lot, but they happen. You're out there in the void, staring the unknown right in the face. Sometimes it stares back at you," she ended with a theatrical flourish.

"How far?" Alain asked.

"Day's walk," Phil replied quickly. "Not far at all. You can stay the night here, if you like. Hey, Carol!" Phil called over to one of the other characters. "You've still got a couple of extra rooms, right?"

Carol sauntered over, mask under her arm. She was younger than the other two, closer to Alain's age, with thick, red lips, and light blue eyes, accentuated with makeup, and stood with her hips cocked to one side. She looked Alain up and down once, quickly, with eyes like a beam scanner. "Sure. You can come on over when we're done here."

"Great!" Phil thumped Alain on the back in a celebratory manner. Alain tried not to wince, with only limited success. Phil gestured and reconstituted the missing wallform of the set, enclosing them in their little box again. "Now can we *please* get back on with this!" Phil stuck his head back under his mask and went back to take his position for the scene.

Carol's house, the *Durflin*, was small and spare. No decoration, no images of family or friends. Bare walls and subdued light.

"So, what brought you to Storyville?" Alain asked, making conversation.

Carol, now dressed in a simple coverall, tossed the bundle of her costume into the corner of the front room. She regarded Alain out of the corner of her eye. "Brought? No. Born. My parents were here, in the *Durflin*, and so… well, here I am, too, I guess."

"Have you ever been to the Miner's Tubes?"

"What?" Carol looked him full on now. "Oh, no." A small nervous laugh. "No, nothing like that. I've been to a couple of other areas of Conglommora. I go to The Hive every now and again, mostly for the food. Not a lot of good food around here, and I'm too lazy to cook myself. Not much point to it when you're just cooking for one." She shrugged.

"Do you like it here?" Alain asked, even though he felt he was prying now. Not very polite.

"Like it?" Carol turned halfway aside again. Again the corner of the eye, as she fiddled with a panel for a moment. She stopped and looked down. "Like it," she repeated softly. "Ha." A mirthless laugh. "I don't think anyone's ever bothered to ask me that."

Alain palmed the wall and sat in the chairform that popped out. "Well, I'm asking, I guess... I'm sorry, I don't mean to be impolite. You don't have to answer if you don't want. It's just... I've been to a lot of places in Conglommora and talked to a lot of people, and I'm curious."

Carol walked back toward him, popped open a chairform from the wall and sat across from him, elbows on knees and chin in hands. She was lanky, with long legs and long arms, and sort of skinny. Alain didn't think she ate at The Hive very often. Most of the folks there seemed a little heftier.

"Do I like it?" she repeated once again. "I guess so. It's the only life I've ever known. I've visited other sections, but none of them felt like home to me. Just too predictable. Here's it's all about imagination and spontaneity. And I think it's more fun to be *in* the narrative, not just watch someone else's. Even in vr, it's not the same as physically being right there, on the set, in the costumes, the makeup, the constantly changing sets. But…" She trailed off.

Alain waited, didn't say anything. Didn't want to pressure her, or make her feel uncomfortable. Let the story—let the narrative—come out in its own time.

"I dunno. Lately, it just seems kinda… stale. We've done new works, of course, and revisited classics. There's always new interpretations, it's not like we're doing the same thing over and over again. But, still. Maybe it's just not enough."

"Come with me to the Miner's Tubes," Alain blurted out suddenly. He didn't know why he said that, why now, why to Carol. They'd only just met, and he wasn't really attracted to her. Not like Essi.

Essi was wonderful, Essi was… comfortable. That was the word. It was harder than he thought to slip out, to leave without saying goodbye. But that was his habit, for now at least. He wasn't *afraid* of relationships, it was just…

Alain felt guilty every time he left someone behind, someone he could care about. There had been enough of them by now that he'd forgotten some of their names. But Essi was different. Essi was worth remembering. Maybe someday, someday he'd go back to Hive and find her. But not now. Comfort, an end to wandering—that wasn't the mission. Not yet. There were things to do still, secrets to unravel. And, frankly, adventures to have. This was one of them.

It was an impulsive act—he didn't know Carol, but there was something about her. Something he'd seen across Conglommora. Potential. Untapped, wasted potential. Something that could be, but wasn't yet. Something he could encourage; something he could set free, maybe.

"Come with me," Alain said again, his grin widening steadily, despite Carol's wide eyes getting even wider. "We'll ride with the miners, go see a real moon, or a gas giant, or a waterworld."

Carol's mouth gaped, trying to form words, but it wasn't happening.

"And then we'll come back. Just a quick trip. It'll be fun. You'll be back before you know it and have had a real adventure. You said it yourself, there's nothing like *being there*."

Carol looked down at the deck. "You're crazy. I just met you, we haven't even had dinner yet, and you want me to come along on some interstellar adventure?"

"Sure!" Alain grinned wide as a docking hatch. "Think of it as just playing a part. An immersive experience. You'll be playing the part of a miner. A smart, rough and tumble explorer of the unknown. It's just a role. But with better costumes and *way* better props."

Carol sat back and stared at the ceiling. "I can't believe I'm doing this." She leveled her gaze at Alain. "Okay. Sure. Why not."

She walked over toward the galley, palmed open a cabinet in the wall, then came back over to Alain and tossed him a dark, hard bar of algae concentrate.

"If nothing else, I bet the miners have better food! We'll leave in the morning, okay? I've got a lot of studying to do for this 'part.'"

Alain grabbed the bar as she threw it, and took a small, hard, tasteless bite. *Yeah*, he thought, *I am doing Carol a kindness. Rescuing her from this meaningless caricature of life in Storyville, and showing her at least a small glimpse of the grand cosmos itself.*

He sat back, self-satisfied. Real adventure again.

At last.

Six

IT WAS HOTTEST AT MIDDAY, with the Earth's sun directly overhead. Any breeze had died down, the grasses in the valley were still, and even the buzzing of the insects quieted from deafening to merely loud.

O/ was napping, fitfully, along with Greatbear and Twomoons. This was their habit: to nap at midday, avoiding the harshest heat, and rise in the fullest darkness of the night to tend a campfire, hunt a sleeping beast, or do whatever else needed doing. It wasn't what he was used to, but then again, neither was anything else here.

Something crashed in the trees nearby. O/ startled awake, but the others didn't seem troubled. They had a far better sense of such things. In this case, some small beast found himself a lunch treat, apparently. Nothing to be alarmed at.

The Earth animals, for the most part, seemed to stand around a lot. Grazing, waiting. Every now and then, a group would break into a trot or play and chase each other. Sometimes, they almost seemed like children playing. How did they know what was play, and what was a genuine threat? Somehow, they knew.

There was almost a social order of some sort, O/ thought. At a watering hole, or even at a fresh kill, creatures would take their portion and yield to others. Stronger or weaker? Was it out of fear or kindness? He couldn't tell. But they could.

A black and white striped horse-like creature snorted, loudly. Neither its coloring nor its snorting seemed good camouflage. It's a wonder it didn't attract every carnivore in the valley.

O/ tried to settle back in. It was just the three of them, which felt lonely and insufficient out here exposed to an entire, savage planet. He hadn't realized until now just how few Earthans there seemed to be here. There were so many people on Conglommora, and even that was nothing compared to massive overpopulation in the last days of Green Earth.

But here, there were only three nearby tribes in this whole valley, as far as he'd seen, and none of them were very large. You didn't need a crowd of people to feel alive. You don't need any of that. No technology, no Arty meddling in your affairs, telling you what you can and can't do, making food for you, keeping you trapped. Trapped in a comfortable, golden, bejeweled cage. Living death, that's what it really was.

Here, at least, death was honest. It didn't hide, didn't play games, didn't stalk you in quiet or in secret. Death was right here in front of you, right by your side. Overhead in the trees, ahead of you in the grasses. In the cool waters of the stream, in the hot rays of the sun. The beasts and birds died all the time—all day long, every day. Accident and beast had taken a few of the tribesmen, too.

And all of that made O/ feel *alive*. Alive, and home. Home to the Earth—the Green Earth—he'd always dreamed of. But it was far from comfortable. Most of the time, conditions were downright miserable. That is, if one had time to consider misery, which wasn't all that often. Pure survival dominated. Desperation, at times. O/ knew he might have to do anything—*anything*—to survive. He'd already done things he never imagined himself doing. Eating the warm flesh ripped from an animal, its heart still beating. Kill. Maim. Survive.

Survive.

Another, farther-off noise. Not a snort this time; it was a particular rustle in the bushes. This got the attention of Greatbear and the much younger Twomoons. They awoke in an instant and stood quickly, scanning the horizon. O/ glanced at them, worried. Greatbear made a hand gesture, wriggling his right hand in a motion over a still left hand, curved into a fist. Wateroverrocks. A member of the other edge tribe, what O/ called Edge Tribe 1.

Sure enough, the figure arriving at a dead run was Wateroverrocks. Breathless, he exchanged guttural greetings with Greatbear and nodded at Twomoons and O/.

They fell into an urgent discussion. O/ could follow none of it, but the tone was alarming. Something bad had happened, was happening, or was perhaps about to happen. Maybe all three. Greatbear made replies, and as quickly as he had come, Wateroverrocks took off back in the direction he came, a quickening shadow darting across the land.

Greatbear explained something to Twomoons, who took off at great speed also, back toward Runningdeer and the rest of the tribe at their current camp. Greatbear then turned to O/ and knelt in the not-quite-mud to explain.

He sketched a couple of symbols, made a few connection gestures, and tried his best to tell O/ the story. O/ was confused, these were new pictures, new symbols— new ideas, or maybe new people he didn't know yet.

Edge Tribe 1 had been attacked. Not by a lion or other wild beast. By another tribe. By fellow Earthans. The stories were true.

O/ had no idea why, perhaps that was a part of the story he didn't understand. But maybe it didn't matter, because the next part was so chilling. The leaders were not *just* killed. Their heads were cut off and taken by the attackers. Greatbear was shaken. This wasn't something that had ever happened before, to anyone, as far as he knew. There was no reason for it; it made no sense.

O/ touched his chest, opened his palms wide. *Who did this?*

Greatbear sketched a new figure. Dog-like, with long legs, very pointed ears, and fangs. Big fangs. O/ nodded. Greatbear added one more feature to the crude creature's profile: over-sized teats. A female. Inside a great circle.

A she-wolf.

To be fair, O/ called it a wolf. Maybe it was more accurately a "she-beast," O/ named animals as best as he could remember and may not have been entirely correct. But clearly, this was some powerful, dangerous, female leader of the central tribes.

O/ sat back on his haunches. He made a sweeping motion from horizon to horizon and pointed to the she-wolf image. *When did she come?* he was trying to ask.

Greatbear replied, indicating the she-wolf showed up, out of nowhere, only a few rains ago. Much had changed with the Central Tribes since then. This she-wolf spoke with sweet words and had made "great changes." Some in the edge tribes thought she was a spider-shadow, an evil spirit from the world beyond who commanded foul, unheard-of powers. Greatbear didn't believe in evil spirits so much. But his friends, the leaders of Edge Tribe 1, were dead. Killed in a raid by the Central Tribe, their heads cut and taken. Sweet words did not match violent intent.

We are too few, Greatbear indicated. *We need help. Beyond the mountain are other tribes, we must tell them and get them to help us. Together we must stop this evil she-wolf, whatever she may be.*

O/ sat fully back and rested on the ground, taking it all in.

War.

The Earthans had discovered—or were just about to discover—war. This didn't fit in with O/'s notion of Earth being a better life, a more *real* living than the one bound by the technological fetters of Conglommora. He stood up slowly, dejected.

Survive.

Whatever it took. If that meant killing Earthans of the Central Tribe, even finding and killing this "she-wolf," then so be it. He nodded grim agreement to Greatbear, and they ran back through the grasslands, back to the camp.

Seven

CAROL AND ALAIN entered the main observation concourse in the Miner's Tube section. It was a long, shallow room, set above a dozen docking tubes, with a deep burgundy-colored deck and what looked like exotic wood paneling, with many comfortable-looking, over-sized lounge chairforms. The outside wall was curved, made of a clear crystal window, deck to ceiling, running the entire length of the room. You could sit here and watch the shuttles, transits, and ore barges come and go.

The shuttles were for the miners. On the smaller side compared to a house ship but enough for a crew of six or so for a typical mining mission. The ore barges themselves were massive. Each was nearly the size of a biodome, but flatter, more disc-like. It was easier for the drones to load and offload the material that way.

Carol pointed out into the black of space. A shuttle was on approach. Very lucky timing—they'd get to see it arrive. Its barge had already docked, and the scavenged planetary material was being offloaded into large, shuttle-sized storage "sacks." Carol moved to the window to watch the shuttle's flight, Alain walked down the concourse to follow the flow from barge to sack. The sacks were then taken by drone to a massive field, a growing sphere of sacked matter off to the side of the docking area. From there, the sacks were gradually brought in for processing, made into bricks of Raw of differing grades and types.

Alain walked back up the concourse just as the latest shuttle was docking. The shuttle did a tidy multi-axis turn to orient its docking ring to the tube, then slid gently into the automatic apparatus. A handful of other folks had been slowly filtering into the concourse to watch—friends, family, and others who were simply curious.

One of many hatches in the rear of the concourse slid open, and the crew of the shuttle came bounding in, filled with enthusiasm. Alain wondered if that was from the trip itself, or the joy at being back at Conglommora, with family and friends. Or both.

Drinks arrived, and trays of snacks, and before they knew it, Carol and Alain were in the middle of a reception party. Having been stuck with just the six of each other for the last hundred days, the crew was understandably eager to see new faces. A tall woman wearing a black flightsuit came over to them and extended her hand. These flightsuits were similar to the coveralls everyone wore, but sturdier, more heavy duty. Able to withstand the rigors of outer space—actual outer space, not our safe cocoon in the confines of all the ships of Conglommora.

"I'm Théron, pilot of the mission. Welcome! What brings you here?"

Alain replied, "Curiosity, mostly. I've been on an extended Walk and hadn't made it round to the Miner's Tube section yet." He looked around. "Glad I could make it! Very impressive setup you have here."

Théron looked around. "Oh this? This is nothing." She made a wrinkled face. "You should see the sights out there." She gestured at the window wall. "We just got back from a ringed gas giant with a dozen moons. One was covered with ice and low-level organics. Real trove of useful stuff."

"No grassy fields to walk on, though," Alain commented.

Théron laughed. "No, not this trip. You'd probably have to ride the quantum wave back to Earth for that."

Alain played his card. "I have, actually. I was on the first ship down."

"No way!" Théron exclaimed. "I want to hear all about. Stay right there." She turned a few paces away and gathered a couple of her crewmates, coming back at a brisk pace with them in tow. Just like a barge.

"We were about to have a proper dinner, please join us. We'd love to hear all about Earth, and we'll tell you about the bodies we've visited. Come on, it will be fun," she finished with an inviting grin.

Carol accepted for them both. "Absolutely, lead on." They followed Théron and crew to the back of the hall, where Théron palmed open one of the hatches and led them into a fair-sized banquet hall with a large dinner table and fantastic artwork on the walls. Barren moonscapes, far-flung asteroid belts, otherworldly caves, weirdly glowing skies, and endless gaseous seas—it was all here. Even a sunset on a world from the closest system, which was more than a few years away using their best electromag drives.

Alain was seated next to Théron, and Carol next to him. The rest of Théron's crew and some assorted friends and family made about twenty people seated at the long tableform. True to Théron's word, a proper dinner came right out. More than just a proper dinner, Alain noted. It was a stunning sampler of some of the very best that Conglommora had to offer. Clearly, the miners had enough to trade beyond even extravagant wants.

Théron was polite and let Alain enjoy most of the first two courses before asking him to tell the tale of rediscovering Earth. Alain laughed gently at the prodding. It certainly wasn't the first time he had told his story. He did try to avoid over-embellishment, which would be easy enough, given the circumstances. But in fact, under-hyping his story, telling it in a very subdued, matter-of-fact style, seemed to give it an even greater, almost mythic power. He didn't *have* to overdo it.

Alain described going through the quantum resonance wave, and what that felt like, as the entire table sat in rapt attention. There were a few shudders. The infinite inside-out, puking from your toes sensation was unique to the quantum wave displacement. The miners' travel by electromag drive was nothing like that; there was very little sense even of acceleration, let alone cellular dismemberment.

Then there were the attacks and capture by the Earthans, the explosion of their ship, the *Uten*, which killed the malicious stranger Robert Brandeis and ended his Conglommoran separatist/Earthist movement, and stranded Alain, his father, and the others on Earth in their little landing craft. Even though dessert was being served, Alain still held everyone's attention as he described their survival strategies and limping out into the solar system to be picked up by the quantum wave—hoping against hope that Arty would fire it up, even though they had no communications.

Théron raised a simple toast when Alain had finished. "To all explorers." They clinked their glasses and drank. Théron went on, "Quite the story. We've had our scrapes, accidents, and cave-ins. No dreadful natives trying to kill us, thankfully! But we've had a few deaths anyway. To the fallen." They raised their glasses again.

General conversation and hubbub resumed, and Alain turned to Théron. "Carol and I were hoping to tag along on a mining mission. One of the shorter ones, not a multi-year trip."

Théron harrumphed. "Well, there's no 'tagging along,' as you put it, even for famous fellow explorers. Everyone on a mining crew works for it."

"Oh, of course," Alain quickly added.

"Well, if you call it work." Théron smiled back. "The drones do all the *actual* work. We humans are mostly there to supervise. I'm sure Arty could do it all without us, in fact. Arty will have to approve you for travel, of course—there's minimum physical requirements. But that's mostly to weed out the wanna-be vr adventurers who come from the Pod Racks. They'd have trouble even in standard gravity."

She snorted a derisive laugh. "You two look to be in good enough shape, and since you," she pointed to Alain, "have already been to Earth, I don't think you'll have any problem at all."

Théron leaned back, nodding her head, and swept her arm to include all the artwork along the walls. "This is our chance to see some small part of the cosmos. Even if most actual systems are too far away. We stick to what's floating around locally; asteroid belts, a couple of rogue planetoids, a comet every now and then. Those are fun to land on." She grew wistful for a moment.

"And you're in luck, timing-wise. My friend Pel—and a great pilot—is making a simple, quick run to a nearby rogue planetoid. It's pretty rich in heavy metals, and you can be out and back in just about seventy days."

"Perfect!" Alain exclaimed with genuine enthusiasm.

Carol smiled and visibly seemed to relax a little in apparent relief. *I really can do this,* she thought. Only seven tens of days, mostly button pushing, and she'd get a chance to see an actual alien landscape plus a view of Conglommora from the *outside.* Her smile grew wide and a long-lost sparkle returned to her eyes. *This is going to be great.*

"I'll introduce you to Pel tomorrow," Théron promised. "Meantime, there's a bunch of spare quarters here, so I suggest everyone get a good night sleep."

Good night's sleep, Alain mused. That was probably the *last* good night's sleep he'd had since they left Conglommora. The incessant hum of the drive engines was driving him nuts. The experienced miners said you got used to it. After all, everyone's grandparents had lived most—if not all—of their lives on ships like this one, and they survived. Maybe, Alain admitted. But the generational house ships were a lot larger than the mining ships. The *Ycham* was spacious for six people, not twenty families. There was little chance of getting away from that continuous low hum. Never really quiet.

Until you put on a pressure suit and went outside. Then it was so quiet that the sound of blood beating in your ears was deafening. Alain, Carol, Pel and the rest of the crew had spent maybe a tenday out on the surface of the planetoid named X756-J1. A remarkably catchy name; Arty probably had made it up.

Alain sealed his suit and gave a thumbs-up to Carol, who checked her seals and returned the signal. The airlock cycled, and they stepped out onto the alien planetscape. Alain took a deep breath and tried to take it all in. The pure black of space overhead, the dull gray of the rocky, jumbled, broken, and dusty surface, punctuated with the glint of shiny rock shards. There was no sun nearby, only the dim light of distant stars and the blinding beams from their suits. Alain walked in front, headed to their destination for the day. So strange to not hear your own footsteps. Surely, they were making a loud crunching noise. But with no atmosphere, you'd never know. Nothing to carry the sound.

He wondered what the planet smelled like. Oh, you could guess based on chemical analysis. One moon with a sulfur content surely must have smelled like rotten eggs. But there was no way to tell for sure—he certainly wouldn't take his helmet off to check. Strange to be here, to be present, and yet to be so cut off, so separated. Your own air, your own water, your own smells, even. Forever sealed off from the environment you were in.

Carol pinged him. "Almost there." And sure enough, just up over the next rise was a darker opening in an already dark cliff face. They finished the last bit of alien hill as the lights from their suits stabbed into the depths. They entered.

The cave was a treasure, filled with all sorts of exposed bits of various minerals, gemstones, and just plain weird formations. Weird by Earth standards, anyway. They passed through the entrance chamber and continued hiking through a dig tube from an earlier mission, filled with even more outcroppings of exotic metals. No organics though, not on this trip. But Carol was thrilled anyway.

They crossed this larger chamber, past a dazzle of outcroppings, to the other side where a small pit opened up in the floor. "Thanks, Alain," Carol said as they climbed down a ladder into an adjoining, lower dig tube.

"For what?" Alain asked, looking down as he descended and joined her on the lower level.

"For making me come out here. I would never have done it if you hadn't suggested it. I don't think I've ever worked so hard for a part! But I've learned a lot, and this is incredible! I'm glad you talked me into it."

"Well, you didn't take much convincing," Alain reminded her, as they picked their way through some loose, glittering hardscrabble. "I bet you would have come out here eventually, on your own."

"Maybe," Carol said, as she stooped to examine an intricate outcropping of some kind of crystalline structure. Her headlamps drenched it with brilliant light, making small diffraction rainbows all around the cave.

Alain wished he could stop time, right there. It was a magical moment, being on an alien world again. No natives trying to attack you here. Just cool rocks and good friends.

They continued on. Alain thought that one moment would probably stick with him as the highlight of the whole trip. It was just so perfect.

But surface time went all too quickly, and their suits alerted them they needed to head back to the ship now. They did. Carol was in front, striding purposefully. Alain lagged behind a little, trying to really get into the moment.

Alain liked this little planetoid, filled with its sparkling prizes. A drone silently soared overhead, carrying a load of minerals to the ore barge. He could see another one approaching over the horizon from his right side. A reminder that they weren't *just* here to sight-see. In theory, they were mining. Théron had been right; there really wasn't much actual "mining" work to do.

They approached the airlock, and Carol palmed it open, waiting for Alain to catch up. He stepped through the hatch and turned to watch the last of the dark gray planetscape disappear as the hatch silently slid shut.

There was the familiar blast of compressed air, quickly vacuumed away. Not re-pressurization yet, this was just the start of the cleaning cycle. First, the blast of air to remove fine particulate matter. Next, a shot of ionizing radiation and a quick shower of some incredibly toxic solution guaranteed to turn any remaining organic matter into a disassociated liquid. You really didn't want to take your helmet off too soon. Another rinse and drain. Finally, the slow pressure build-up of one atmosphere's worth of air.

It took longer than Alain would have liked, more patience than he had, but it was standard protocol, every time. And that was just to get back into the *Ycham*. They were finishing up the mission, and now he had to be patient through the long, anticlimactic return to Conglommora.

Still many days to go, and Alain was growing restless. *This is fun*, he tried to tell himself. *What would you do if you were on Conglommora anyway?* He'd talk to people, he'd... *Card game, that's the ticket.*

Sitting around the galley table of the *Ycham*, the crew was now in its third day of a non-stop card game. The game was *Lavor*, and at the moment, Alain was losing. Badly.

"So, how'd you come to be a miner anyway," he asked Pel, as Alain put down a purple, six-sided card.

"A-ha! Gotcha!" Pel pounced with a yellow circle, which Alain hadn't seen coming. Another 47 points in the hole. He grimaced. Pel sat back in the chairform and looked at the ceiling, half basking in his small victory, half remembering his origins. He tugged thoughtfully on his large black beard.

"I was born into it, I guess. My parents, my brother Karn, my sister Jal. It was all we did growing up. I've always liked the idea of going somewhere. Even if it's just out to a hunk of black rock in the middle of a black and empty void," he added with a touch of poetry. He sat back up straight at the table. "I've never cared for the idea of just sitting in a ship in Conglommora. Ships are supposed to go places. Somewhere. Anywhere." He played his next card.

"I think most folks who do this come from a mining family. Not all, but most. Some adventurers like yourselves come through every so often, but they don't stay long. Couple of trips to the nearby sights and they move on. Especially for the long trips. There's a four-year and seven-year round trip to two neighboring systems—

proper systems, with a sun, couple of planets each. Those are almost always just the old mining families."

Arthur played his hand next, a disastrous move that cost him the game. He sat back to leave the table, and his friend Maur played the next hand.

"What about you, Arthur? What brings you out here into the void?" Alain asked.

Arthur walked over to the galley wall, palmed the smooth surface to open it up, and took out a bottle of fine brewed algae. He took a swig and turned back.

"Me? Boredom, I suppose. I've seen a lot of Conglommora. Not all of it, by any means, but all the local sections. I hung out in The Hive a lot. Great food there. But too many people. Just too much." He came back to the table and sat. "I like the quiet out here."

"Quiet?!" Alain exclaimed, trying a green square. Not too bad, it kept him in the game for now. Pel wrinkled his eyes at the move. "The damn noise from the engines is driving me crazy. I can hardly sleep at night, and that's with noise canceling on in the room."

"Oh, that." Arthur took a drink. "That's nothing. Drive engines don't bother me. That's a different kind of noise from people noise. That's a constant drone, always the same. People though, that's harder to ignore. All those thoughts, all the conversation, loud and soft, ebb and flow, constantly changing. Harder to ignore all that. Simpler out here."

"Have you been on many missions?" Alain asked.

"Yeah," Arthur admitted. "Not nearly as many as old Pel here, I came to this later in life. Wasn't born to it. But

I'm heading out on a year-and-a-half mission almost as soon as we get back from this one."

"Finally!" Pel exclaimed with a bellow, playing his last and most triumphant cards. He'd won, handily. Alain wasn't sure what hit him.

"Okay, enough of that kid's game," Arthur said, leaning forward. "Let me teach you a real game. Who knows how to play *Pitch*?"

———————

They were so close. Alain was as ready to bust as an over-inflated pressure suit. Only another twenty-eight hours and they'd be docked back at Conglommora. He was in his quarters, flying through a vr sim of Earth. Disappointing. Still nothing like the real thing. He could do a better one, he was sure. Maybe when they get back, and he...

Pel's voice came out of the wall, "Everyone please get up to the bridge, now. We've got a problem."

It was only on hearing Pel's voice that Alain realized how quiet it was. An alarming silence, a quiet that shouldn't be.

No hum.

No drive engines.

"What happened?" Alain asked breathlessly when he reached the bridge. Pel was standing in front of a display, and Arthur and Maur were seated at the console, frantically swiping and typing. Carol came in just behind him.

"Not sure," Pel admitted. "Drive engines are out. Life support is damaged—we have heat and light, but the air processors are offline."

Carol looked at the display of the *Ycham*'s position, a small dot still headed for the massive outline of Conglommora and the Miner's Tube section. "Okay, so the drive is down, but we're still headed for the docking tubes, right? We're close enough that momentum should carry us anyway?" She looked hopefully to Pel.

Arthur answered, "Actually that's the problem. At this stage in the flight, we need the drive engines to slow us down. We're coming in too hot. We'll tear into the mining section and right through the other side. Pieces of us, anyway."

"Arthur!" Pel admonished.

Alain asked, "What about the maneuvering thrusters? Can't we use them to decelerate?"

Pel turned his glare from Arthur and softened. "No. Not enough power, not at this speed. It'd be like trying to stop a hyperloop car with your hand."

"Because that's a great metaphor," Arthur muttered under his breath.

Pel resumed his glare but said nothing.

Carol spoke up. "Well, better call ahead let Arty know we're in trouble. Maybe it can send a ship or a couple of drones."

The usually quiet Maur spoke up, "Forgot to mention. Comms down as well. Qradio, standard," she slapped the board in frustration, "I've got nothing."

Pel took a deep breath. "Okay, so we're coming in hot, no way to decelerate, no way to communicate with Arty or anyone in Conglommora, and oh, by the way, we're running out of air, too?"

Arthur addressed that last point, "The recyclers are down. But there's only six of us, and it's not that tiny of a ship. We probably have three or four days or air before we suffocate. We'll crash into Conglommora and explode in a little under twenty-eight hours. So, at least air isn't the problem."

There was no reply to that.

Eight

AHDOM AND CHALU HAD JUST DOCKED their amphibious shuttle to a ring on the Denisova station. Early on, they'd nicknamed these shuttles "tadpoles," because they resembled the larval stage of several amphibious Earth species. A sort of ovaloid shape, narrow at the front, wide in the middle, with a long taper to an even narrower back, ending with a drive column that looked like a skinny tail. Along the sides, two thick cable-like strands ran along the body. In flight, the space between the cable and the hull filled with an energized plasma film, which acted as a dynamic wing. Very high tech, and yet very organic looking at the same time. Nature knew her stuff.

They'd been out in the upper ocean layers, studying a migrating pod of mammals with large top dorsal fins, a species they hadn't seen before. The tadpole docked, and they waited for the water to flush and the cycle to finish.

Denisova was far enough below the mixed ocean layer so as to not be affected by surface storms, but still well within the upper ten percent of the ocean. Sunlight was plentiful and the vast majority of ocean species lived in these layers, from the largest mammals to the smallest planktons.

Chalu had spearheaded the construction of Denisova himself. It started as a simple, single ship, similar to any of the millions of house ships in Conglommora, but modified to withstand the pressure of the ocean instead of the vacuum of space. Additional modules arrived over time, and eventually they were able to start building their own sections locally. His son Ahdom joined him after they had developed enough family housing and improved transportation to and from the surface, and his wife Chrys split time between Denisova and Conglommora.

The purge cycle finished. Chalu palmed open the hatch and they stepped through the airlock, still dripping with warm ocean water, smelling of salt and fish. Ahdom held his hand out and caught a drip as they passed through the airlock into the warm confines of the Denisova station.

Ahdom wiped his hand on his coverall and asked his father, "Oh, did you talk to Uncle Charlie? Ask him to bring Alain and come visit us? I'd love to show them the pods."

Chalu smiled. Ahdom had only been pestering him for a few tens of days on the subject. "I asked." He shrugged his shoulders. "But you know Charlie, he's pretty happy over at Skyville, doesn't really want to travel again."

"Why not?" asked ever-curious Ahdom, looking up at his father. "Lots of people do it. We get visitors here all the time." He waved his hand at the grand hall in the middle of the station. It really was a grand hall: a central terminus of a dozen different corridors branching off to different sections of Denisova. You could see fish swimming overhead through the domed ceiling of thick crystal, backlit by filtered sunbeams. A fair number of people went to and fro, not quite a crowd, but far from the isolated research station it started off as.

"Well, remember the troubles he and Alain ran into on their maiden voyage here. They had a much harder time, being the first ones down. And they were on land, with the Earthans. That's something we strictly avoid."

They walked across the grand hall toward the living quarters section. Ahdom asked, "Will we always? I've heard you and your friends talk about a shore expedition someday. Can I come?" He stopped and turned excitedly.

Just then a young woman with vivid green hair arranged in a single stalk came up to them. "Chalu, when you have a moment, we need to talk about the algae problem on the surface processor arrays."

Chalu stopped. "Kaia, hi. Sure, I just got in, let me take care of a couple of things and I'll meet you in the upper lab area."

Kaia nodded and continued on across the hall.

"Ahdom, we've talked about this," Chalu said, turning with a tinge of weariness. "Yes, we are considering limited shore missions, well away from the Earthans if we can help it. We need some coastline samples, but we do *not* need to terrorize the Earthans or be their targets. Any mission near them will be very, very dangerous. I don't even want to take some of my best colleagues, let alone my son." He realized he looked exasperated, pulled some composure onto his face, and asked Ahdom, "Why are you so determined to go on land? Is not even a whole planet's oceans enough?"

"It's a start," Ahdom said with a twinkle in his eye. Even their most heated arguments still included a touch of humor. "I want to know. To see. To experience. Land, sea, air—all of it. It... it calls to me."

Chalu raised a suspicious eyebrow.

"There's *so* much to explore. We've seen so much even just from here. Think about how much more there is. *A whole planet.*"

A group of people came through the nearby archway and flowed around the two; a stream around a rock. They paid them no attention.

Chalu finally crossed his arms and said, "Very well. First things first. We have a deepsea mission coming up; we're taking a new high-pressure submersible down one of the deeper trenches. You will come along, and be a valuable member of the crew. Then, and *only* then, will we talk about your role in the shore expedition, if there is one. We will not be going inland, mind you." Chalu had to resist the urge to wag his finger at Ahdom.

"Thanks!" Ahdom said and bounded off to find his friends.

Chalu shook his head, and headed on to his quarters.

"You're back early," Chalu's wife Chrys said, smiling. "How were your dorsal fins?"

"The wh… oh, right." Chalu had almost forgotten the day's adventure. "Excellent, we got some wonderful image captures, really clear sensor logs, even some DNA samples. Couldn't have gone better."

Chrys came over and hugged him. "And you're all preoccupied because…" Chalu hugged her back, then crossed over the front room and sat heavily in a chairform under their extra-large picture window. A large school of silvery fish flashed by, glittering in the dwindling sunlight at the end of the day. "Oh, it's just Ahdom. He's so restless here."

Chrys looked concerned. "Does he want to go back to Conglommora and stay with Sundara instead?" Their older daughter had decided to stay behind; she hadn't come with them to Denisova.

"No, no, it's not that. That I could probably deal with better," Chalu chuckled. "No, it's worse. He wants *more* than just our ocean missions. He wants to go on the shore expedition next, and then to explore inland. I told him he could come on our deep sea expedition, and then we'd see about the shore. He was so excited. He's even more of an explorer than I am! Can you imagine?"

"Yes, yes, I can," Chrys admitted. "He is so much his father's son."

"And what about you? You're here. Clearly you've got some adventurer blood in you!" Chalu said to her.

"I like to be near adventure, but not in the middle of it," Chrys explained. "Watching your comings and goings is adventure enough!" She went back to the galley wall and started fiddling with things. Chrys liked to keep her hands busy. She was looking down at her hands, but kept talking.

"He's old enough, you know. For the shore, at least. No one—not even you—should be going inland. Arty told us not to, remember?"

"For our own good," Chalu said. "And for the good of the Earthans. There's only so many humans left in the universe. We've got to take care of them."

"Ahdom knows that," Chrys reminded him. "And you know that. And everyone here knows that. I think you worry too much, Chalu." Chalu looked up, hopefully. Chrys continued, "You've told me the precautions you've set up for the shore expedition. Scanners to make sure there are no Earthans in the area, native dress and translator boxes just in case something goes wrong, or you get surprised. And stunners, for a worst-case scenario—you can use them to escape, and the Earthan gets a headache and a hell of a nightmare to tell around the campfire."

Chalu laughed out loud at that last. "You make it sound so easy. You should come with us."

"I'm good." Chrys raised both eyebrows. "But so are you, and so is Ahdom. Go, don't worry about it."

Chalu had put a small team together, four skilled technicians, plus his son Ahdom. Ahdom was glowing with excitement like an electric ray as they entered the docking bay.

Unlike the sleek tadpoles, the deep sea submersible looked more like a sea urchin. A largish, solid metal sphere, with thick walls, bristling on the outer surface with all manner of instrumentation and remote actuators.

As they climbed into their seats and strapped in using the seven-point restraints, Chalu leaned over and whispered to him, "Now remember, you are here as an *observer*. You will do *anything* anyone tells you, as soon as they tell you."

Ahdom rolled his eyes. "Of course," he said and tightened and adjusted his restraints. Under the excitement and confidence, though, was a trace of fear. This *was* dangerous. They were descending into the crushing depths of the abyss, an environment even more hostile and deadly than the void of space itself. And on the one hand, he was eager to go, eager to experience it. But on the other hand, the dangers were real. The risks were real. This was a deep sea exploration on an alien planet. Not something to be trifled with. Ahdom took a deep breath and made sure everything in his seat and station was in order.

The pilot was an older man, with thin white hair, warm brown skin, and a reassuring manner—that certain calm born of practiced experience. He was working through the departure checkpoints, making sure craft and crew were all properly prepared as well. The copilot, a tall woman with green-blue hair, came back and checked everyone's restraints, even Chalu's and Ahdom's. She returned to the lowered command deck at the front of the submersible, and the pilots cross-checked each other. They exchanged numbers, status conditions, and other bits, none of which Ahdom understood. Nor did it dim his enthusiasm—or anxiety—one qubit.

"Stand by for airlock cycle," the copilot said and gestured over her control panel. Ahdom could hear the whirring, clanking, rushing water noises that had become so familiar here. Back at their home in Sea on Conglomniora, they didn't need to bother with any of that. Their gill mods allowed them to breathe underwater, and their homes were shallow enough that pressure differentials weren't an issue.

"Cycle complete, disengaging. Prepare departure," the captain intoned, and they were off, under their own power and quickly and smoothly arcing away from Denisova out toward the open ocean.

Pressure wasn't an issue back home, and Denisova was kept at one atmosphere of pressure, just as it would be on the surface. But now they were headed far across the ocean to a deep trench, more than a half-dozen klicks deep. The pressure on their little submersible would be immense, crushing. A torment of forces on the intricate composite of their hull.

It would take them several hours to reach the target, slowly descending as they went. The ship first dropped through the last of the upper, sunlight layer of the ocean and into a murky, twilight zone. No more normal fish here. Through the extra-thick and distorted crystal port-hole, Ahdom spotted a glowing eel-like creature off the side of the ship. He pointed wordlessly.

Chalu saw it, too. "Bioluminescence," he noted. At this depth, with the light of the world fading, some sea creatures had evolved to make their own. They passed through this layer of ocean more quickly than Ahdom would have liked, into the black abyss of the deep ocean.

From here on down, there was no light. The water temperature, once warm and comforting near the sur-face, plummeted to near freezing. The inner space of the planet was much like outer space, Chalu thought. Cold. Black. Instantly deadly to the unprepared human. Their submersible ship was built to withstand this pressure and then some. Without, they'd all be crushed, suffo-cated, and frozen. Probably in that order. He shivered at the thought.

It was darker-than-the-void dark now. "So much for sightseeing," Ahdom grumbled, not quite inaudi-bly. Chalu shot him a look.

"This trip isn't about sightseeing, exactly," Chalu reminded him. "It's about bacteria, remember?"

"I was at the mission briefing, and I *was* paying atten-tion," Ahdom countered. "Cracks in the Earth's crust spew out minerals and chemicals that these bacteria use for food."

"Chemosynthesis, actually," Chalu corrected him. "We believe it's primarily hydrogen sulfide, but aren't completely sure. The old records from Green Earth were incomplete, much was lost. And it's not like we could duplicate these conditions in Conglommora. But now, here, we'll be able to see for ourselves."

The hours passed, and they kept descending slowly but surely into the trench until they arrived at the proper depth and location that the satellite scans had suggested. Arty had allowed Denisova to place a limited number of observation satellites in orbit to help monitor ocean conditions and planetary weather systems. That was an easy request, Chalu remembered. It's not like the Earthans would ever see them or notice them. Just one more star in the heavens if reflected sunlight happened to flare off the satellite just right.

Each of the crewmembers except the primary pilot rotated their seats into position to access the external manipulators. Chalu reached into the small recess in the hull and slid his fingers into the fine mesh, which automatically shrank to fit snuggly around his hand and fingers. There was a confirming tone, and his screen lit up, showing the pair of actuators that extended from the ship, controlled directly by his hands. The others did so as well.

Ahdom watched as the pilot maneuvered slowly, carefully, to put one side of the ship right up against the wall of the trench. The monitors showed the surface of the trench lit up with infrared floods so as to minimize any disturbance to the strange lifeforms that lived at these crushing depths.

Chalu and the other techs worked quickly but quietly, taking samples, making scanner readings. The pilot rotated the ship in many different locations, so that each crewmember had plenty of opportunity.

"Hydrogen sulfide, all right!" Chalu was gleeful. Ahdom appreciated his enthusiasm and tried hard not to show any signs of boredom. The excitement, the anxiety even, had given way to the dull reality of sitting in a metal and ceramic ball in the dark. The boredom was nearly as crushing as the vast ocean depth itself. Digging up bacteria halfway to the planet's core! No part of that spoke to him. But to meet the Earthans… to walk on the shore, into the jungle, to gaze at the planet's horizon from atop a mountain. An actual mountain! Ahdom realized he was breathing faster than he should and tried to modulate it. First things first.

Chalu noticed and luckily mistook Ahdom's imagined excitement as genuine excitement at their discovery. "I know, this is terrific!" he said. Ahdom smiled back weakly.

"Levi," Chalu called up to the pilot, "take us down a bit, following this vent. Here are the coordinates." He tapped out figures onto his screen.

The ship peeled away from the wall and made a graceful descending arc into the absolute blackness, following the trace of a crust vent. Chalu could hardly contain his enthusiasm, and he and the others raced to take as many scans and occasional samples as they could. Ahdom, grateful at his observer role, took to counting the interlocking tiles that spread across the ceiling and walls of the ship, while occasionally looking interested at whatever Chalu happened to be doing at the moment.

The strategy worked.

It was time to return, and their ship retraced its steps, now slowly ascending from the impossible depths, rising ever so gradually from the pure black, freezing void back up into the twilight layers with several schools of bioluminescent fish. Ahdom was genuinely relieved as they rose into the dimmest layers of sunlight and up into the familiar, comfortable, warm layers of the ocean he knew. It was like the sunrise, Ahdom thought, only their ship was the sun itself, bringing light back into a darkened world.

"How'd it go?" Chrys asked when they'd returned to their house at last.

"Fantastic," Chalu beamed. "I was right, it *was* hydrogen sulfide, after all. We found an active vent and traced as far as we could in that equipment. Loads of readings. And Ahdom was great through it all."

Ahdom smiled and nodded. Sure.

"Well, I'm glad you're back on time," Chrys said. "Don't forget the ceremony in the morning, opening the new expanded guest quarters."

"Oh, right!" Chalu almost smacked his head to make sure the memory would stick.

"New guest quarters?" Ahdom asked.

"More and more people are coming to visit Denisova," Chalu answered. "So, we've set up more room for them. I swear," he laughed, his customary, deep rich laugh, "poor Arty must be firing that quantum resonance wave pretty much continuously with all these folks coming and going."

Ahdom laughed, too. It was a funny thought, so many folks from Conglommora coming down here to see some fish from the dome in the grand hall, maybe take a tadpole up to the ocean surface and over the waves. Ahdom hoped more than anything that he'd get to see land, the real Earth itself. Still, if there was that much traffic and interest in Earth's ocean, maybe interest in the rest of Earth would come soon.

Maybe.

Nine

RIPPLES.

Disturbances.

Something different, something that shouldn't be there? Something not natural.

Another ripple.

A subtle shift in the quantum field. Something moved. Changed state.

Again.

The sensor flow happened to be sweeping by just then. Not looking for anything in particular. Just looking. The quantum ripple affected it, changed the readings.

Not by much, it was a very small, subtle difference. But it was enough of a difference to register.

The anomaly was enough for the console to quietly beep.

And that got attention on the ship.

Ten

PEL TURNED FROM THE CONSOLE on the *Ycham* to face Alain and Carol. "Okay, that's the deal then. No engines for braking, no comms, and no ideas. Which of these can we fix?" He looked at Arthur. "First, what happened to the engines?"

Arthur brought up a diagram on the main screen. "Don't know the cause, but everything's down. Internal sensors, status, backup systems, all dead."

"Were we hit by something? A meteorite that slipped passed the force shielding, maybe?" Alain asked.

"Possibly," Arthur admitted and popped up a view of the rear of the ship. He panned around for a full visual inspection, switched to thermal, then finished up with a high-res material continuity scan. All eyes strained at the screens, and, of course, the ship's systems were analyzing the data as well. Tense minutes crawled by, waiting to find the cause, something. Anything.

"Nothing. No sign of external damage."

Pel frowned. "Okay then, Arthur and Maur, head back, pull some panels, and see what you can find out from the inside. Priority on restoring communications. Even if you can find what killed the drives, there probably isn't enough time to effect repairs *and* decelerate." They got up from the console immediately and headed to the rear of the ship. He turned to Alain and Carol. "You two, we need options. If they can't fix the comms, or the engines, I want ideas on what can we do to at least not destroy the entire Miner's Tubes section."

Alain nodded, and he and Carol headed to the large tableform in the galley, hoping that some good ideas would soon follow. Pel turned back to the main screen, watched their small dot heading straight for the mass of Conglommora, and put his head in his hands.

Maur replaced the panel, nothing unusual with the EM drives themselves, not that she could see. Arthur was across the room, checking out the concentrated banks of nanophotonic computer circuits. He called over, "Maur, you gotta come look at this."

She sealed the panel and crossed quickly to where Arthur was kneeling, next to a panel leaning against the wall. In the opening, a mass of normally glowing computer core sat there dark and silent. Maur bent over to look more closely and saw the neat, geometric patterns of crystals and composites was blackened, charred, crumbling. "What the hell…"

Arthur leaned back to a crouch and shook his head. "Beats me. I've never seen anything like it. Couldn't have been a simple overload or energy surge—the damage is too uniform, too consistent. Plus there are safeties for that sort of thing." He took a couple of scans, a few images to show Pel.

When he was finished, Maur said quietly, "Better check comms, too." Arthur nodded, and they headed back into the corridor and up closer to the communication arrays. He loosened the access panel and hesitated before opening it.

"What's wrong?" Maur asked.

"It's just... I..." Arthur paused. "I'm not sure I want to know, you know?"

Maur nodded. Waited a breath. They looked at each other, searching for hope in the other's eyes. Finding none, Arthur looked back at the panel and popped it open, setting it on the deck.

"Shit."

The comms circuits looked just like the ones they'd found in the drive section. Blackened and crumbling; devastated. Arthur replaced the panel without a word, then turned and abruptly went to an adjoining section and checked another panel there. Same thing. A third. No better. Silent and grim, they headed back up to the bridge.

Alain and Carol were arguing over figures.

"It's not enough," Carol said.

"It's all we've got," Alain countered. "It'll be enough. We won't clear it, but we won't hit the tubes."

Pel was just coming back from his quarters a fraction behind Arthur and Maur. "All right, what have we got? Maur, Arthur, what'd you find?"

Arthur sat at his console and pulled up the visual images, a metallurgical/ceramic composite scan, a molecular continuity scan. Small gasps came from the crew. The systems were devastated. Without discussion, it was clear there was no chance for repair, no chance of restoring functionality.

Pel exhaled. Not many breaths left, one way or another. "Can we print up a replacement for the comms systems? Even just a small emergency kit?"

Arthur shook his head, pulled up the second and third scans, which were the printer systems. Just as dead.

"Well, that's that, then. No functions, no repair." He paced for a moment, then leaned against the archway coming into the bridge. "You two." He nodded over to Carol and Alain. "What'd you come up with? We're out of everything else, don't tell me we're out of ideas too," he demanded.

"No, not out," Alain reassured him. "Not great, but Carol and I came up with a couple of things.

"First off, we can slow our momentum a little by adding a rotational component. We've got thrusters enough to spin. It will slow us down, but not enough. It's not just the ship itself, of course, but the ore barges we're towing as well. So we can slow down a little, but we'd still smash into Conglommora hard enough to kill everyone. So we came up with another idea.

"Right now, we're headed straight for the last docking tube at the end of the section," Alain pulled up a diagram and pointed to it on the main screen. "We just need a little bit of force to change course and try and miss the main structure of the section. We can't change it enough to clear Conglommora entirely, but I think we can miss the tubes and head for the sack field."

There was a pause. They'd all still be killed, but at least Conglommora would be safe.

Maur asked, "How would we even do that? Pel says the thrusters aren't enough to change our course even that little bit."

Carol answered, "Explosive decompression. We blow the crew quarters open to space on this side of the ship." She had brought up a schematic and pointed. "That, plus our rotational velocity, plus blowing out the thrusters at maximum, all at once, should produce enough force that will angle us just enough to miss the last tube and send *Ycham* into the sack field, where you store the raw matter."

Arthur leaned forward, clasping his hands at his knees. "It's a shit plan. I mean, I'm happy we won't kill anyone else, but we'll all be *dead*. Smashed to bits. 'Raw matter?' It's rocks! Ore. Minerals. It's not like those are bags of pillows we'll just ease into. Might as well steer into a moon." He smacked his fist into this palm to emphasize.

"Probably," Alain acknowledged. "And we don't even know for certain that this will work at all. Carol checked my math, and it's not clear that the decompression will be enough to clear the last tube. It's right at the edge of the estimate. But, I had another idea that might help."

Pel spoke up, "Well, tell us, son. There's got to be some good news here somewhere."

"I don't know about good news, but hope, perhaps."

"I'll take it," Pel said wearily.

"So, here's the notion. There are twelve docking tubes along this section, right?"

Pel nodded.

"At some point, when we get in range, Arty is going to notice that we are coming in too fast. But won't know that we can't steer, and we have no way of explaining our intent. Except, we sort of can. We still have power, and we can control the power ship-wide. So, as we get in range, we shut down everything on the ship, all at once, and turn it back on. We do this thirteen times. Even at distance, Arty will see our power signature flash thirteen times. Thirteen, and only twelve docking tubes. I'm hoping that's enough to convey that we're trying to miss them."

"Ingenious." Arthur looked up. "But, so what, Arty will know where to find our bodies? Just some bonus organic to make into Raw," he grumbled.

"Worst case, yes," Alain agreed. "But if Arty interprets our message correctly, it will know that we're alive, that we're trying to prevent a disaster, and that we're trying to aim off the end of the docking tubes into the sack field. Maybe it can figure out a way to rescue us. An intercept ship, or drones to attach and slow us down, or even a big net. Something. That's a lot to infer, I know." He waved his hand as both Maur and Arthur started to protest. "But it's better than nothing. And it just might even work. We *might* get rescued."

Pel straightened up, crossed from the archway to the main screen to contemplate the diagram, now showing the *Ycham* and Conglommora. "Alain's right. It's better than nothing."

"But Pel..." Arthur started.

Pel turned around and faced him. "You have a better idea? One that we can actually implement?"

Arthur sighed. "No. No, I do not."

Pel nodded. "Me either. But we're not done yet." He perked up. "We've got work to do. Prepare the crew quarters to blow, tie the power generators to a single control so we can pulse it as Alain suggested. And if any brainstorm happens to hit any of you in the process, don't be shy. All options are on the table."

There was a collective nod and a brief bout of negotiation as to who would do what before they each headed off to their assignments to prepare hatches, emergency explosives and seals, wiring, all the rest of it.

Well, we're not dead yet, Alain thought grimly as he traced a main power conduit. *Soon, maybe. But not yet.*

"I never realized how big Conglommora looks from out here. Even this tiny corner of it," Maur said.

"Getting bigger all the time," Arthur agreed, eying the main screen.

"Enough of that already," Pel chided them. "It's time. Everyone who doesn't want to be jelly, strap in."

"Not sure that's really going to help," Arthur sniped, "but what the hell. Miracles happen, right? Million-to-one shots happen once every thirty days. I did the math. We're due."

"I'll buy into that," Alain said, strapping himself into one of the bridge positions. "Why not."

"Coming up on course change mark," Maur alerted them. "One minute. Better brace yourselves."

They had rigged a few key outer sections of the ship with explosives, sealed inner hatchways where they could, and deployed emergency sealant balls where they couldn't. In theory, they'd still have plenty of oxygen and not lose any additional systems. Just sleeping quarters. One way or another, they wouldn't be needing those anymore.

"On my mark." Maur started counting down. As a failsafe, both she and Arthur had to trigger the explosion at the same time. Fingers poised over the shiny control surface, she counted down. "3... 2... 1... fire." Everyone on the bridge involuntarily tensed, waiting for the inevitable shock.

On two separate consoles, their fingers jammed the shiny surface. Commands raced faster than human thought through the remaining nanophotonic network to the explosive charges. It worked as expected, as long as you had expected a massive explosion that reverberated throughout the entire ship, plunging you off course at an angle with a terrifying roar of twisting metal and then the sucking silent vacuum of endless, infinite space.

Alain and the crew held on, rode it out. It was like a blow to the stomach—severe but over just as quickly.

"Everyone all right?" was Pel's first concern.

"Good."

"Fine."

"Awesome, Pel."

"Never better," came the replies, all at once but at different levels of sincerity and snark.

"Heading?" Pel asked quickly, ignoring the sarcasm.

"Looking good," Arthur said. "Really tight, but I think we'll make it. Well, I think we'll miss the docking tubes. We are, as planned, on a direct collision course with an entire field of bags of giant rocks."

There was silence for a moment. Alain broke it. "Yeah, about that. We're close enough now, time to try and tell Arty what we're doing."

Pel said, "Indeed so. Ready?" Maur nodded. "Do it."

It was still a shock to plummet into total darkness. One second. A slight high-frequency whine as the lights and power came back on. One second. Blackness again. Cold. One second. Whining up to light. Again, and again. Thirteen times.

"Now, let's wait a couple of minutes and try it again," Pel suggested.

"Agreed," said Maur.

They waited, anxious, for something. Some sign. Not that they'd get one, even if Arty processed the message and correctly analyzed the intent. Alain realized it had no way of getting a message back to them, not even a "good luck" or "been nice knowing you." Still, they waited and watched.

"Now. Do it again," Pel said.

Pitch black, silent. Whine, light. Pitch black, silent. Light. Repeat. Thirteen times again.

"Now we wait."

Again and again, they waited, they signaled. If there was a reply or a sign from Arty, they didn't see it. Conglommora sat there as it always did, stationary in the deep dark cold of space. They were getting really close now and could see the lights of the docking tubes coming up fast.

"Well," Alain said. "It's been a pleasure knowing you all."

"Likewise," said Pel, choking up and unable to say anything else.

"I... I... really didn't think it would end like this," said Arthur quietly. "Not like this." He averted his eyes from the screen and looked down.

They were headed just to the side of the last docking tube, straight at the edge of the sack field. While the docking tubes were lit up, the field of rocks was not. Just a big, black, mostly solid mass against the even blacker void.

The jolt from the decompression was severe, but it was nothing to compare to this. Even though they were strapped in, the impact tore the seats themselves from the deck plates. Alain had the sensation of smashing right through the main screen, possibly through the hull itself.

And then he felt nothing at all.

Eleven

THE THIN LINE OF THE SHORE grew slowly at the edge of the horizon. In their tadpole, darting across the sea, Ahdom tilted his head and watched the image grow on the screen. Ahdom, Chalu, and a small crew were approaching shore, safely hidden from the Earthans by the sea and waves. Once they got close enough, they would scan the area to make sure there were no natives in the area. Or any large carnivores, for that matter.

Ahdom tugged at his costume. They were dressed as Earthans, but with modern materials patterned after the native animal skins that Earthans wore. Ahdom found the outfit uncomfortable; the way it draped over the body was cumbersome, not form-fitting and optimized the way their normal coveralls were. And the shoes were no more than sandals, designed to protect the feet but remaining subtle and unobtrusive. In theory it wouldn't matter, they'd never get close enough to any Earthans. But just in case, they were dressed appropriately.

"Shoaling rapidly, dropping speed, hold here," the pilot said. It was the same guy from their deep-sea expedition, Ahdom thought, with the thin white hair. Didn't catch his name then, either. Chalu wasn't great at introductions. He just assumed everyone knew everyone else by now.

Ahdom watched, excitement mounting, as the thin black lines of waves gradually gained a slight frosting of white, and turned at last into small whitecaps, now rising up and crashing down as breakers just ahead of them. Their ship slowed further, the plasma foils adjusting and shimmering to hold their position just under the waves offshore.

"In range, begin scanning," the captain ordered, and the crew started scanning the area in detail. Ahdom thought the captain to be a man of few words. The crew apparently was used to it.

Please be empty, please be clear, Ahdom thought furiously. If there were natives in the area, they'd have to wait—or worse, abort the mission for now. He leaned forward, peering at the screen, holding his breath as if that would help advance his luck in some way. The scanners were far more accurate than his limited vision. They'd know soon enough.

"Thermal clear to half a klick," one of the crew reported.

"Mass proximity clear."

"Visual clear."

The captain nodded. "Surface and adjust attitude. Match grav levels."

The tadpole emerged from the waves and rose slowly, plasma foils glowing, ocean water draining off the sides and back in small, private rivers. As it cleared the waves, it hovered silently and smoothly above the sand, using the same sort of design as the gravsleds back on Conglommora.

Chalu and his colleagues had discussed several design alternatives for the tadpole's land drive. After much debate, they settled on a low-power anti-grav design to avoid any disturbance to sand or soil. By contrast, the landing crafts that flew up out of the atmosphere were much stronger and would leave circular impressions in soft earth, sand, or vegetation. The tadpoles, though, wouldn't leave any evidence of their presence. Stealth was an important consideration.

The ship came to a halt out of the waves, upon the sandy shore before the tree line. Time to disembark. They unfastened the seat restraints and lined up in the aisle. Chalu stood at the hatch, looking back over his shoulder at his crew.

"Ready?"

A round of assent and Chalu palmed the main hatch, which hissed and slid up and out of the way, resting on the top curve of their ship. A stairform extended out of the bottom of the hatchway and made contact with the Earth beach. Chalu descended the stairform first, followed by the other crew, Ahdom trailing last, taking it all in with widening eyes.

It was a lot like their home in Sea back on Conglommora. Only there was much more of it; much more of everything. The sound of waves crashing on the shore was almost deafening. The smell of the salt spray, the warm wafts of air from inland—it was a lot to take in. Ahdom tried to see it all at once. Up over the horizon, the Earth's sun pierced the cloud deck and made a geometric pattern of shafts of pure light. Down by their feet, the wind was pushing handfuls of seafoam along the smooth wet edge of the beach. Ahdom thought he was seeing creatures at first, the way the foam scuttled and rolled along the sand.

A huge gust of cold wind blew through and even Chalu was alarmed. They weren't used to wind anywhere on Conglommora or Denisova, and certainly not at this strength. If you faced into it during a heavy gust, it could almost take your breath away. When the wind died down, in between gusts, Chalu felt the incredible heat of Earth's sun. The sudden changes from cold to hot were unnerving.

Chalu pointed to an opening in the tree line and led them up the broad sandy expanse into the shade at the edge of the jungle. A loud, insistent humming pervaded the air. So many insects, so much life.

It was a little cooler here, partially shaded by the canopy of trees. A faint, fine bit of mist hung in the air. They spread out a little and started collecting the samples they came for. The tree ahead of him exploded into life as a flock of birds launched themselves into the sky.

Ahdom hadn't paid attention to that part of the briefing this time. It really didn't matter what speck of dirt, plant, or bacteria they were hunting after. It was here, they'd find it, no big deal. But to be walking on the surface of the Earth itself—finally! An alien planet! *Alien to me, anyway*. So much to see, to feel. It was really overwhelming.

He had no specific task, other than to stay out of trouble. So far, so good. He picked up a handful of the sandy soil and let it drift through his fingers. He looked up at the clouds, some moving fast, others perched high in the firmament and staying put. An insect landed on his hand, and he raised it up to get a closer look. Iridescent, in part. Remarkable. A few smallish ground creatures scurried about the base of a twisted tree. The insect had flown off, apparently to attend to some other pressing matter, so Ahdom knelt and examined the base of the tree in greater detail.

They continued on like this for some time, the crew making a slowly widening and expanding circle, Ahdom taking note of various bits and pieces of the incredible, diverse ecosystem, with the lulling background noise of the surf and the still significant gusts of wind that came through.

"Chalu, over here," came the call from one of the crew, and Chalu climbed a small hill. From there, off in the distance, they could see some sort of cattle, with large, curled horns. "Aurochs, I think," she said, checking her shiny.

Chalu marveled at the herd. "Why the huge horns?"

"Big horns act as radiators, cooling the beast," she replied. Chalu smiled, he loved watching his curious crew at work. They watched a moment, then climbed back down to continue their main mission.

A curious bird watched them. It was huge, the size of an Earthan, furry, with a long, sinewy neck. It alternated between quick pecks at the ground and studying the intruders. It would lift its neck up, cock its head to an angle, and stare at them, a plainly curious look on its small head. Chalu wondered what it might be thinking, if it thought at all.

Ahdom rolled a bit of tree moss between his fingers, looked up at the golden sunbeams on the horizon, and smiled. The salt on his lips reminded him of home at Sea, but it was different. Everything was familiar, yet so different. This was great—more than great, this was what he'd been waiting for…, well, for all his life. And it was all he had hoped for. That and more. The sensory richness, the smells, the sights, the sounds, the…

The alarm.

"Chalu!" one of the crew called out in sudden terror. "Large group of Earthans heading right for us, they'll be on top of us in seconds!"

"What?!" Chalu looked up from his specimen collection, his face a mixture of confusion and abject terror. Confusion, because the sensors were supposed to warn them long before now. Terror, because they simply *could not* be caught out in the open like this.

"Hide!" he hissed, through clenched teeth. "Get down, get behind something. Everyone! NOW!" He dove behind a thicket of some low-growing bushes. Everyone else did the same, trying to curl up in the smallest profile possible behind a bush, a tree, a rock outcropping, whatever was handy.

Ahdom sprinted to cover, but his sandal caught on an exposed root and tripped him. He flailed through the air and did a face-plant behind a tree. Stunned, he tried to curl up into a small ball, but the world was blurry and dim.

The tribe came on top of them in a flash. A dozen Earthans, running hard, chasing some beast through the underbrush. Chalu held himself tight to the ground, hoping everyone else was doing the same. The thundering party slowed, and the beast squealed. They got it, just past the clearing where Chalu and crew were hiding. Chalu held his breath and closed his eyes. There were noises of the slaughter, celebratory grunts. It seemed to go one forever, but eventually, the hunting party moved off, slowly. A muffled scream, some other unidentifiable noises. Chalu didn't dare move.

Minutes passed, slowly. Chalu forced himself to wait, to breathe, to count. The party had clearly moved on, taking their butchered supplies with them, and relative silence returned to the jungle. They waited even longer, allowing time to pass and keep on going, far into the distance, out of sight, out of scent, out of sound. He lifted his head, slowly, eyes searching the area. No one in sight. He rose to a crouching position, then standing. No one around. He brought up his scanner, proximity and thermal again. Just a few warm bodies in the immediate area, his own crew. He breathed a sigh of relief.

"Okay, they're gone. Report in."

Slowly, his crew unpacked themselves from whatever awkward contortion they had screwed themselves into and joined Chalu in the middle of the clearing.

"Wow, that was close."

"They came on us so fast."

"So many of them."

Chalu held up his hand, "Is everyone all right?" Nods all around. "What happened? Why didn't we see them coming?"

One of his crew, a young man named Stro, piped up, "I think it's the wind, the thermal draft."

Chalu raised his eyebrows.

Stro continued, "We developed and calibrated the thermal sensors back on Conglommora, not on Earth itself. There's no wind up there, certainly not these big gusts. I've never seen anything like this before."

"Wind affects thermal readings?" Chalu asked.

"Very much so," Stro confirmed. "Enough to shift the readings out of detection range. The readings must have been fluctuating enough not to trigger an alarm."

"Wonderful," Chalu said with some disgust. What good was technology when it didn't actually work when you needed it? He turned to tell Ahdom...

"Ahdom?" Chalu searched the group frantically, but Ahdom wasn't there. "Ahdom!" he shouted incautiously.

Silence.

"Fan out, start looking," Chalu barked. They did, fanning out in an ever-widening spiral.

"Chalu, over here!" one of the crew called out. Chalu and the others dashed over to see what he had found. The grasses were matted down, perhaps someone had laid there, or there was a struggle. Either way, there were two long furrows in the dirt, leading away from the area.

Like someone had been dragged away.

Someone unconscious.

Chalu stared at the marks in the dirt, incredulous. Ahdom was gone, taken by the Earthans, it seemed. He started to run in that direction, but the captain with the white hair, whose given name was Oliver, grabbed him by the arm. Chalu was spun around by the force, his face just inches from Oliver's, jaw set, eyes flaming an angry glare.

"What?!" Chalu shouted, as both question and complaint.

"What's your plan, exactly, Chalu?" Oliver asked calmly.

"P...p...plan?" Chalu sputtered, shaking his arm free.

"Yes, your plan. To rescue Ahdom. Or were you just going to run at that tribe headlong and get speared in the chest?" Oliver asked.

The normally articulate Chalu was still too emotional to speak coherently. He turned and looked in the direction the tribe had gone, started to say something, turned back to Oliver, fear and pleading in his eyes.

Oliver put his hand on Chalu's shoulder and looked him in the eye. "We'll get him back. I'm sure he's safe— they took him, they didn't kill him. If they'd wanted him dead, they wouldn't have bothered carrying him off like that. He's okay. But we need a plan. We can't just go running after them and expect to get Ahdom back safely."

Chalu looked down to the ground and took a deep breath. Several. He turned and Oliver's hand dropped away. "You're right, of course," Chalu said. "I'm sorry."

"Come on," Oliver said, "Let's head back to the tadpole first. We're not equipped for a full-on rescue mission."

Chalu nodded, and they headed back toward the beach and their ship.

"I'll send a message to Arty," Oliver offered. "See what it recommends. I don't think the new satellite mesh has fine enough resolution to help us. It was just for ocean currents and surface weather, but Arty will know more than I do."

Chalu nodded in agreement, still uncertain of his voice, tears welling up in his eyes.

"Chalu, it will be okay," Oliver said again as they approached the ship. The other crew members were climbing in. "Think about what's it like in Denisova. Storms come, storms go, but they are on the surface only. They don't affect *us*. This storm will pass. And when it does, you won't even remember how you made it through to the other side. But you will. You will make it through. Between the banks of pain and pleasure, the river of life flows."

"Thanks, Oliver," Chalu said, and he climbed carefully up into the tadpole, like there was a giant sack of rocks around his neck, a huge weight of guilt, fear, sorrow.

Oliver followed after him. He paused a moment in the hatchway, looking out at the beachhead and jungle beyond. Somewhere out there, in who-knows-how-many square klicks of jungle, a tribe of Earthans had Ahdom, unconscious and captive. Despite what he told Chalu, he was pretty sure they didn't have much time. They needed to find him, and find him fast, without hurting the Earthans, and without revealing the existence of either their base in Denisova or Conglommora itself. First, he had to get a message to Arty.

Oliver took one last look at the impenetrable jungle, sighed, and sealed the hatch.

Twelve

WHEN ARTY FIRST TOLD ME about the crash of the *Ycham*, and that *my son* Alain was aboard, I was in shock. Just plain shock.

I knew Alain was headed that way; he at least had the courtesy to tell me where he was *some* of the time. He'd just left The Hive and was hoping to tag along on one of the shorter mining runs. Not quite the same as going to Earth but still an interstellar adventure. He had sounded so excited about it.

Now here I was, back in the *Neylan* again. After the news from Arty, I had to come back to open it up and reboot it. I was pretty upset, of course. Arty had set up a special bay in Alain's old room. I took a deep breath, steeled myself, and walked in again.

"Dad?" Alain called out from the darkness.

"Hey, I'm here," I said in a quiet voice.

"I had the strangest dream…" he went on and talked for a bit. His memory was pretty rattled, Arty said it would be perfectly fine in time, but a little scrambled and unreliable for the first tenday or so. Maybe even a couple of tendays, worst case.

"So, the crash really did happen? It was real? How come I'm not dead?" After a pause, "And the others, are they okay?"

"They're all fine," I said again. We'd had this conversation a half-dozen times already. Arty said just to keep talking as if it were for the first time, and Alain's memory would stabilize shortly. "Everyone survived. Arty figured out your message, that you were headed to the storage sack field. Thirteen flashes, when there were only twelve docking tubes. Clever. Was that your idea?"

Alain nodded and smiled weakly. "Mine and Carol's."

"I thought so." I grinned. "So, Arty set up a 'net' to catch you, powered by some braking drones. You guys came in so hot you probably didn't even see it."

"But I remember crashing, being thrown out through the front of the ship," Alain said with a frown.

I nodded. "Arty told me about that. Apparently, those bridge chairs on the mining ship were designed to eject like that in event of a hard crash. Each one has personal shields, and includes some inertial dampening. Not quite enough, as you've got a lot of broken bones and internal organ damage. But it's all fixable. You'll be okay. It's going to take a while, though."

Alain grew silent again, thoughtful. I thought maybe he was going to nod off again, fall back into a restless sleep. But instead, he became agitated again. "Can you send a message to Carol? My traveling companion. I talked her into it. I don't think she really wanted to go. I'm so sorry. I didn't mean for any of this to happen."

"She knows, she's okay. Well, she looks to be in about the same shape you're in. Pretty well banged up."

Alain frowned at that.

"You sent her that message already," I reminded him gently. "I gave it to her myself. She said she always wanted to fly through space without a ship." I smiled.

"Ha. That sounds like her. I don't remember sending a message though."

I tried not to frown. "Your memory will come back. Arty says it just needs time to heal. A tenday or so and it will be back to normal."

"And all the rest of this?" Alain asked, nodding at the mass of silver blankets, wires, and tubes that covered him and wove in and out of his broken body. The lights were low but plenty of the machines, wires, and devices glowed by themselves, giving an eerie cast to the room. The low light was supposed the be soothing, but I thought it more nightmarish.

"A little longer. But Arty forecasts a complete recovery." I tried to think of some other topic to bring up. "Any luck trying to find Faith? Are you still looking?"

"Not really. A few more aliases, a few more stories. She's definitely been around, but she's kind of like a ghost. I wonder if the whole thing is nothing but that. Ghost stories. Not real. Nothing to find."

He grew silent again.

"I'll let you get some sleep," I said and got up. Alain was already drifting off. I closed the hatch to his room and went to the galley. I wasn't really hungry but didn't know what else to do. I absently nibbled on some salted algae crisps and sipped a fruit nectar juice Käthe had sent with me from Skyville. That reminded me that I hadn't checked in lately, so I sent a quick message with another update on Alain and a promise to chat over vr later in the day.

So, the days went by, slowly, but they were going to go with or without me anyway. Alain's memory improved, and we stopped having repeat conversations. He told me about his most recent adventures in the Chance Dome, The Hive, and with the miners. He asked how Käthe was. Stuff like that. He was able to stand and walk under his own power now but tired easily. Still, it was great to see him recovering.

Then, one day, the screen pinged me. We had a visitor—someone was at the front hatch. Curious; I wasn't expecting anyone, and we'd received no messages. I went up and palmed open the hatch.

I could say "it took my breath away" but that doesn't even begin to cover it. Imagine that, but it's your whole soul. From head to toe. A giant sucking of your entire self, disorienting, impossible. Not quite like the resonance wave but pretty damn close. Because there, standing right in front of me, was the spitting image of Grace Langston.

After the initial moment of shock, I realized it wasn't her, of course. There were differences. Our visitor was a little younger, and a lot... I don't know, tougher looking perhaps? A little more world-worn? More than a few awkward moments had passed. I had to say something.

"Ah, hi, can I help you?"

"You must be Charlie. Grace sent me loads of messages about you."

So, it really was her. Grace's long-lost sister.

Faith Langston.

"I am Charlie," I was able to say through my astonishment. "And I'm guessing you must be Faith."

"I don't use that name a lot anymore," she said. "Some people know me as Praeda lately."

"Please come in." I stood aside to let Faith enter the *Neylan*.

"Can I call you 'Faith' anyway?" I asked.

"Suit yourself," she answered coolly, coming in. More like sauntering in, actually; she had a practiced air of indifference about her.

"I came to meet you and to talk to Alain. I didn't actually see any of the messages Grace had sent me until after she... after she was gone." She eyed me critically. "Grace thought the world of you."

I wasn't really sure how to take that. It didn't seem that she agreed with Grace's assessment. Maybe she blamed me for what happened as well.

"I'd like to see Alain," she said abruptly. Apparently, she was done with me, for now.

"Sure. Right through here. Follow me." I walked back toward Alain's room.

"Hey, you've got a visitor. You'll never guess who." I stood by the hatchway as Faith entered. Alain's eyes widened as he realized who it was.

Faith turned to me. "Could we have a moment alone, please?"

"Of course." I answered automatically, but a little surprised. I turned and walked out, closing the hatch behind me. I stayed close to the door, just enough to hear her shout a question to Alain.

"Why are you following me?!"

I went back to the galley. Not sure how Alain would explain his steadily growing obsession with Faith or what he was really looking for. He'd figure something out. In the meantime, I saw that my screen was blinking. Arty had a message for me.

"Hey, Arty, what's up?" I asked casually, while pouring some algae juice.

"I didn't want to disturb you while you were with Alain," Arty's voice came from the walls. "But there is an urgent message from Chalu and his expedition."

Urgent? "What's wrong?"

"Ahdom is missing."

That got my full attention. "What happened?"

"They were attempting their first shore expedition, and something went wrong. Their crew got separated, and Ahdom was taken by the Earthans. Chalu is asking for help rescuing him. Specifically, for you and Alain."

My knees suddenly felt like someone had cranked the gravity ten-fold, and buckled. My stomach clenched hard in a misguided attempt to keep me upright. It was all I could do to not throw up right there. The very, very last thing I wanted to do in my life—ever—was go back to Earth. But this was Chalu, my very best friend, and his only son. They were family to me. I had to help if I could. I had to do whatever it would take.

I had to go to Earth.

Thirteen

AHDOM OPENED ONE EYE, halfway, cautiously, and tried to figure out where he was and what had happened.

It was dark. He was on the ground, right on the damp Earth itself, on his side with his back to a tree. Rough bark poked into his back. Several figures were in front of him, back-lit by a small fire. Sparks floated up gently, making a vague spiral course up and away from the group, up into the jungle canopy. Open flame was a novelty. He opened both eyes and stared at the fire but didn't dare move any other muscle. Not yet.

His head hurt. More than hurt; pounded. He had a half-memory of terror, of being found, dragged. When was that? Where were his father and the others? Were they okay? Was Chalu even looking for him? Of course, he was. He had to be. The whole crew would come and rescue him. But... they had to do that without contacting the natives, without revealing themselves. Well, the contact part of that deal was blown now. The Earth-ans had definitely made contact now. It wasn't the first time someone from Conglommora had been abducted, though.

Ahdom remembered that Uncle Charlie and Alain had been taken by natives and tied up in a cave. It sounded like such an amazing adventure when they told it! Not like this. Not cold, scared, in pain. He was slowly waking up more fully and remembered that he had a small pouch on his belt, with a scanning device and stunner. He slowly tilted his head down and looked, but the pouch was gone. So much for rescuing himself. He looked back up.

The figures were eating. The large beast they had been hunting, Ahdom guessed. He didn't know what it was. They were eating some of it raw off the carcass, and some bits they were roasting over the open fire. The roasting meat smelled good, and Ahdom realized he was hungry. He'd never eaten much in the way of land animals, but as his stomach growled, he thought that maybe this wasn't the time to be picky.

What was I thinking? I shouldn't even be here. I just wanted to explore the planet, not end up as dinner in some savage's stew. He tried not to scowl, tried to keep as still as possible. He didn't *think* they were cannibals, really, but not much was known about the Earthans yet. It was only then that Ahdom realized he wasn't tied up, not like Charlie and Alain had described. He wasn't sure if that was a good sign, or not. Kidnapped or rescued?

Either way, they would realize he was awake before too long. Certainly before daylight. Ultimately there was no avoiding it. *Might as well get this part over with,* he sighed inside, and slowly pushed himself up to a seated position.

One of the figures hunched by the fire noticed and straightened up, barking out some sort of guttural nonsense. Which almost immediately echoed in Ahdom's ear as, "Ah, the [approximate language] small one is awake."

The translator! Of course. Ahdom remembered that as a precaution, not only were they issued stunners, but the sublingual translator devices, too. Pre-programmed by Arty and ready to go. The translator kept the tone and pitch of the original speaker, and added its own comments in a different pitch as needed. It was distracting, but Ahdom figured he'd get used to it.

The man came over to him. Ahdom shrunk back against the trunk of the tree but maintained eye contact.

"Do not be afraid, small one," the man said as he approached. "I am called [approximate language] Wingeye. What are you called?"

Ahdom cleared his throat. It was a small sound on such a large planet. "I... I am called Ahdom," he thought, then opened his mouth as the translator echoed his words into grammatically correct, guttural Earthan. "What happened?"

"We were on the hunt. You were almost trampled by a [large beast, zoological classification unknown]," Wingeye said. "You seemed [unconscious], so I pulled you to safety. We rescued you." Wingeye sat down in front of him. "You are strange. Small. You do not look like any of the rest of our tribe, or any tribe I have ever seen. And your words. Your words are... strange also. Where are you from?"

"Beyond the farthest hills, very far away," Ahdom responded. Which was sort of true.

"Then you must belong to the same tribe as [proper name] Outside," Wingeye said, with a hint of satisfaction. "As I thought. Very good, we will take you to meet Outside at the end of the season." Wingeye stood up and turned to the rest of the group, which had been watching this whole exchange silently but intently. "Let us welcome Ahdom, from the same tribe as Outside."

The group rose to standing, in an uneven and haphazard fashion, but then said in almost unison, "Welcome, Ahdom of Outside's tribe."

Ahdom stood as well and bowed his head slightly. He had no idea if that gesture had any meaning here, or if they would understand it, but at least it was something.

A woman near the fire spoke first, "Ahdom must hunger. We would be honored to [share the kill]," and she gestured to the carcass.

Ahdom approached the carcass hesitantly. "I am not familiar with your ways. Where I am from, we hunt and eat... differently."

Wingeye smiled. "So much like Outside. You are surely from the same tribe. So far away. So strange. Very well." He turned and called over to a young man, just barely older than Ahdom. "Twomoons, come." The boy came over.

"Twomoons will be your guide. He will show you our ways. Show you how to walk unnoticed. How to eat, how to be one of the tribe. You are so much like Outside." Wingeye shook his head. Twomoons made a complicated gesture.

"I do not understand that," Ahdom said.

Twomoons smiled. "You speak. Outside does not. We draw in the dirt to speak with him. In the dirt, his name is O/." The gesture again. "But he is so like you. You must know of him."

Ahdom considered. "I do not know Outside. But I would like to meet him. But first, your friend is right. I am hungry. Show me the way to eat this beast."

"Of course. I will show you," Twomoons said and proceeded to attack the carcass of the beast, ripping off a chunk of ripe flesh. "If you are from the same tribe as Outside, you will want to burn your piece." And with that, he speared the chunk of flesh on a stick and held it over the open fire. "You will like this better."

Ahdom nodded and waited. After a few minutes, Twomoons handed him the roasted meat. Ahdom tore into it. Rarely had he eaten meat cooked over an open flame. In both Conglommora and Denisova, open flames were rare—they consumed too much oxygen in too small a space.

Meat was plentiful, but Ahdom almost always ate from sea creatures and plants, not land. This flavor was different, more pungent, and the texture coarser, tougher. These were wild animals, bred for speed and survival, not optimized as a nutritious or flavorful food source. But he hadn't eaten since that morning, so it would have to do.

They slept until dawn first started to lighten the sky. Ahdom slept only fitfully. The jungle seemed loud at night. Beasts, birds, going about their business of survival. Ahdom tried to ignore that, but it was a constant reminder that he was not home. Not home on Conglommora, not home in Denisova. He wanted to tell Wingeye and the others that Chalu would be looking for him. He wanted to go back to the shoreline to try and find them. But Arty had been very clear: do not reveal yourselves to the Earthans. Ahdom had to remain silent on that point. He couldn't risk provoking an attack on his family and friends. This group seemed peaceful enough, but based on reports from Uncle Charlie... Earthans were easily frightened and could turn violent and unpredictable at any time.

He would just have to wait, see how this played out, until the right moment came. *Whatever that is.* He rolled on his side, trying to get comfortable on the strange, uneven, hard ground.

Dreams came and went, quickly like passing shadows. Ahdom wasn't quite fully asleep and was dimly aware that these were just dreams. Great roots came from out of the ground—but not threatening, not dangerous. Instead, they were supportive. Helping. Holding him up, holding everyone up. Earthans, Denisovans, everyone. And the light—light from an intensely bright sunrise, beams of pure gold from the Earth's sun piercing the dark, lacing through the giant, over-sized roots.

But it wasn't dawn, not yet. Ahdom snapped awake for a moment, realizing the light was just from the crackling of the fire. He rolled with his back to the fire, warming that half of his body, and stared at the impervious black of the jungle, trying to grab that last thread of sleep.

When the real daybreak finally came, it was far less dramatic. No shafts of golden light, just a growing sense of it being slightly less dark, slightly less cold. In this warming grayness, the tribespeople simply rose and started walking, silently. Ahdom fell in next to Twomoons. He desperately wanted to ask where they were going but realized there was no answer that would satisfy him, or that he could even make any sense at all, really.

Ahdom went along, walking through the incredible, beautiful, alien landscape of Earth in the dim early morning light. He was certain that his father and the rest of the crew would find him, soon, and that they were okay themselves. That, he was confident about. But one question, one doubt lingered at the edge of his mind.

Who was "Outside?"

Fourteen

FAITH HAD BEEN IN THE MIDDLE of a full rant against Alain: *why were you stalking me, not respecting my privacy, what do you want, what's wrong with you…* until Charlie burst in with news of Ahdom. Charlie left almost as quickly as he came to pack and prepare, and as soon as he left, Alain started doing the same.

"Wait, we're not done here," Faith fumed. "You need to answer me, right now. Why were you looking for me? What are you trying to find?"

Alain was standing with his back to her, queuing up what was needed for the mission. At least, what he thought might be needed. He hadn't been back to Earth since his and Charlie's original and nearly disastrous visit. He'd spent the last years exploring Conglommora, not Earth. Lots of other folks had visited Earth, but only to Denisova or remote regions, far out of range of the native Earthans.

They'd need stunners, scanners, sublingual translators of course, native-looking but protective clothing...

"Hey, I'm talking to you!" Faith's fury brought Alain back to the moment.

Alain stopped what he was doing and turned to her.

"I'm sorry. I didn't mean to intrude or disturb you or your life. I knew Grace, as you've probably figured out. But that's not why I was looking for you."

"Good," Faith said in a more level tone, arms crossed across her chest; a personal shield of sorts. "I don't want to talk about Grace. Not now. Not ever. So what, then? What are you looking for?"

Alain looked at the floor for a moment, then back up at her. "The Heart. The Heart of Conglommora," Alain said quietly, as if he was afraid to admit that, or admit it too loudly.

She didn't react, not immediately anyway. Alain took the pause as permission to continue. "You've explored more than, oh, maybe anyone. Everywhere I went, the People spoke of you. Maybe not by your given name. But I knew it was you. You must have found them, been with them. Talked to people in the Heart."

Faith's voice was neutral. "You've been around a lot, too. I know. You probably were with them, right with them, and didn't even know it. They don't talk to strangers much. You have to know who to talk to, and how."

"I know." Alain hung his head. "In theory, anyway. But I never found them. Or if I did, they wouldn't talk to me. And I want to talk to them. They have lore. Stories.

History. Things people don't tell Arty. That's what I'm looking for. And you know where they are, don't you?"

"Perhaps." Faith was evasive, turned aside. "They value their privacy. As do I."

"I appreciate that," Alain said, "and I don't want to expose them or really cause any trouble for them at all. I just want to know."

"Know what?"

Alain glanced away for a moment, as if deciding to really answer or not. He'd gotten this far, might as well go for it. "The Cryptic."

Faith snorted. "That old fairy tale? Believe me, the Heart has far more interesting stories than that one."

"What do you know of it?"

"I've heard the gist of it," Faith admitted. "It poses the question: Why are we here, in this part of space? Really? The exotic matter collisions that ruined our drive engines, that led us, drove us, from Dead Earth to this one particular corner of the galaxy—and nowhere else. That's the tale we were told. But is it true? Was it just coincidence that led us here, to this one point, or something else?"

"Like what?"

"Alien conspiracy. Government conspiracy, back when we had such things. The details vary on the telling, but there is one thing in common with these conspiracy theorists. There's no proof. Now, some of the other lore of the Heart is much richer and more…"

"Hang on," Alain interrupted. "Back to the Cryptic. They really think we are here, in this section of space,

joined in the Conglommora, because aliens *herded* us
here? Why?"

Faith shrugged. "It's just a folktale. A conspiracy theory. Rubbish. All the planets our grandparents visited,
all the systems. The moons the miner's have been to—
and you, too. There are no aliens. Nothing out there.
We're here because of physics."

She came over closer to stand right in front of Alain.
"Your crash on the mining ship. Same thing, right? Unexplained drive failure? Or hidden aliens trying to kill
you?"

Alain grimaced at the memory, all too fresh and still
painful. You don't quickly forget nearly being squashed
like a bug.

"No, no aliens," he admitted. "It was drive failure, as
near as we could tell. Circuits were rotted, destroyed. To
be honest, I wasn't really paying attention to the details.
If you're curious, Arty will tell you."

"Arty doesn't know everything."

Alain raised an eyebrow at that. This was a large part
of his fascination with the Heart and especially with the
legend of the Cryptic. The idea that there was hidden
knowledge, secret information, things that even Arty
didn't know. That much was true, even if Arty had information, it might not be "aware" of it, or of its applica-
bility. The resonance wave itself was a great example of
that. That information, that science, had lain buried in
the nanophotonic memory banks for maybe a hundred
years or more, but Arty didn't retrieve it or put it use
until the crisis with Robert and Lucille demanded it.

"Is there more to it? More to the legend of the Cryptic?" Alain pressed.

"Sure, there's always more to any story. But none of it is very interesting. There's speculation on why aliens would do such a thing. Oh, and they had predicted that the Dead Earth would be healed far more quickly than it naturally could."

"Well, they got that part right, didn't they?" Alain countered.

A shrug. "They got lucky on that one. I think everyone at that time wished that the Dead Earth would magically heal."

Alain sat on the edge of his bedform. "I... I had hoped for more. More than that, anyway. I had heard that the Cryptic offered rich details on our true origins, why we really are *here*." He gestured. "What our purpose is. Especially that. Our purpose."

Faith nodded. "The Heart has their ideas on that, sure. But so does everyone else. Every religion, every philosophy. Everyone's got an answer. But it's *their* answer." She looked Alain right in the eye. "You want to know the true secret, the most valuable secret I've learned in my years of wandering?"

Alain met her gaze and nodded slightly.

"Purpose is something you make. It's not out there, tangled in some crazy knot of conspiracy theories. It's in here." She laid her hand on his chest. "It's what *you* make it to be." She stood back a pace.

Alain looked up from the bedform edge, a little dejected. He'd been searching for the Heart, and information about the Cryptic, for a long time. This was the most information he'd gotten yet, and it was kind of a let down. But there was no time to wallow in that now. In fact, this whole conversation had taken more time than he had. More time than Ahdom had, probably. His friend was in danger, and he and Charlie had to help. Maybe that was purpose enough, at least for now. He stood.

"I want to talk more about this," Alain told her, "But not now. Ahdom needs our help, Dad and I are going to Earth. Do you want to come?"

"No," she replied firmly.

Alain waited for more, for an explanation, for details, but Faith had crossed her arms again. Shields up. Withdrawn and cautious once more.

He turned and picked up the kit from the printer. "All right then. See you around." But before he turned back toward the hatch, she was gone.

That really wasn't how he'd expected their first meeting to go. And now it might be their last. Alain was pretty sure that she knew more than she let on, especially about the Heart, and about Arty—its origins and limitations.

He sighed. There was more to explore there. But not now. Ahdom needed him, and his dad. He went out into the galley just as Charlie was coming in.

"Ready?" Charlie asked.

"I suppose. We've both put this off for a long time. You especially. I don't mind going back, not that much.

But I can't say I'm looking forward to the resonance wave again." He shuddered slightly at the memory.

"Arty claims it's much smoother now. The tech has been upgraded a couple of times, the transit ships have some kind of dampening field, and there's even an anti-nausea pill."

"Could have used those last time, for sure." Alain smiled weakly.

"No kidding. All right, we need to head back up to the Miner's Tubes, that's where Arty has been launching the transit ships from, as well as the miner ships. Well, now that the area's been repaired. You made a bit of mess, you know." Charlie shot Alain a look. "You're lucky you're alive at all. And you're lucky I haven't died of worry!"

Alain hoisted his pack. "Oh, I think you're past that now. We're headed to go rescue Ahdom from the brutal Earthans, remember?"

Charlie sighed. "I know. I can only imagine what Chalu is going through. It was hard enough almost losing you to that accident. But to have your son kidnapped by hostile savages…" He shuddered, speechless for a moment. "How can I say no?" Charlie threw his hands up in mock surrender.

Alain smiled, broadly this time. "You want to go. Admit it. Charge in, save the day. Sounds like a lot more fun than watching the cows in Skyville."

A rueful grin from Charlie. "I would never say that. Certainly not out loud. Come on, let's get going before I come to my senses."

"Landing ships come and go to Earth all the time now. It's just like riding a gravsled up the corridor. No big deal at all." Alain claimed.

"Sure. Commonplace. Everyday thing. Resonance wave bursts all the time. Nothing to worry about. Right." Charlie rolled his eyes with more than a touch of sarcasm.

They left the galley and went out into the corridor. Once again, Charlie sealed the hatch to the *Neylan,* his family's ship for generations, and wondered if he'd ever come back to open it again.

Fifteen

THE ALERT WAS SUBTLE, BUT PERSISTENT. "I think we better contact the One in Charge."

One Who Navigates looked up, surprised. "Why? What have you found?"

"I'm not sure. It appears to be a quantum ripple effect on the long-range sensors."

"Where?"

One Who Navigates came over to the other station on the bridge. One Who Scans pointed to a small corner on the display overhead, an interlocking set of six-sided display screens. "Sector Thin 139-220 Conic Edge."

They both looked at the reading for a moment.

One Who Navigates agreed and signaled on a command stalk.

"Yes?" One in Charge answered.

"One Who Scans has discovered something. A quantum anomaly on the long-range sensors, in sector Thin 139-220 Conic Edge."

One in Charge sighed, not enough that the bridge crew would notice. "I shall report immediately." This wasn't what was planned for the upcoming off-shift time. But a curious anomaly was a rare portent. An omen, perhaps, for the superstitious. Or the small, still seed of an epic intellectual puzzle that would grow into an entirely new discovery. Or just an error in the equipment.

Whatever it turned out to be, One in Charge thought, it was most likely to be a mere inconvenience.

Sixteen

THROUGH THE CORRIDORS OF CONGLOMMORA AGAIN. Funny how I had avoided the corridors completely for so long. But now, these last few years, it seemed I was in the corridors all the time for one reason or another. Alain and I were skimming up a long, featureless gray corridor on a pair of gravsleds, lined with the familiar blue and amber lights. We'd been chatting a lot up until now, but I needed a pause in the conversation. I realized I'd gotten quieter and quieter on our walk, as doubt slowly but firmly seized hold of my imagination.

What the hell am I doing?

The thought ricocheted through my brain, knocking over pillars of familiarity and walls of comfort. I had sworn at every opportunity that I would never, ever set foot on Earth again. And I had every intention of holding fast to that oath.

Yet here I was, packed and loaded for an Earth expedition to rescue my best friend's son from the clutches of those unreasoning, brutal, panicked, savage Earthans. *Yeah, what could possibly go wrong?* I grumbled to myself only; I didn't share any of these misgivings with Alain.

To be fair, it had been a few Earth years since our adventure down there. We had better translators now, better stunners, better sensors, including proximity sensors to avoid any unpleasant surprises. Arty told me that the transits had been vastly improved over that rattling deathtrap of Robert's, the *Uten*. Really, this trip would be *nothing* like our original, haphazard nightmare.

But with all that technological advantage, how was it that Ahdom got himself captured by the Earthans? Ahdom was not stupid, nor careless. Neither was Chalu. Chalu was one of the wisest people I had ever met or even heard of. Whatever happened, it certainly couldn't have come from any negligence on their part.

And that worried me even more. That annoying quality of life in this universe: that one could do everything perfectly correctly and still lose. There were never any guarantees, and of course, everyone dies in the end.

But let that end be far from here.

The silence dragged on, and I found myself growing progressively more morose and agitated. There was no escape now; Alain and I had almost reached the entrance to the Miner's Tubes section. Before I could even swallow, we'd be there, and within a heartbeat, be on a transit, headed irrevocably to Earth. Earth, that fabled dirtball of disease, danger, pain, and death.

I can't do this. I just can't.

But I couldn't let Alain go alone either. Not into that hotbed of psychotic, savage Earthans. I had to go along, if for no other reason than to protect my son. That thought put some metal in my spine. I think I actually straightened noticeably in the corridor as we dismounted the sleds.

"You okay there, Dad?" Alain asked.

"Spectacular," I replied, as I palmed open the last hatch at the end of the interminable, predictably bland corridor. We walked through the hatch and found ourselves in the long, curved expanse of the Miner's Tubes observation concourse when Arty interrupted us.

"There is an urgent message from Chalu," Arty said with its unnaturally and eternally even voice. "They have made contact with Ahdom. He is okay."

I breathed an abnormally loud, audible sigh of relief. Such relief it was almost palpable. But Alain wasn't paying any attention to me, he was right back at Arty. "Play us the full message, please!" He pulled the small shiny from his pocket, quickly stiffened it, and awaited playback.

Chalu was never the most restrained of folk. Even on an ordinary day, he always exuded an air of perpetual joy and eternal wonder. But to have found his son alive and unharmed, you'd think he had gravsleds for feet.

I looked over Alain's shoulder at the message playback, already in progress.

"...search party in range and contacted Ahdom through the sublingual translator. He's fine, the Earthans have treated him well, as an honored guest. We are going to meet up with him..."

There was more, but I stopped paying attention. I straightened up, stood back a pace, and breathed with a calm I hadn't known since getting that first panicked message from Chalu. More than that. Since Alain woke up. Since even first hearing about Alain's accident. I exhaled sharply. Apparently, it had been a while. But that was okay. Everything was okay now.

The miners put us up for a few nights in their section, and I got to watch other transit ships and shuttles come and go, even an extra-large ore barge. It was surprisingly pleasant to watch the spectacle of ships coming and going, without the stress and anxiety of being on one yourself. I found myself relaxed, for the first time in a long time.

I was sitting in a chairform, watching the latest long-range shuttle coming in to dock. Slowly, gently, as it should be—not slamming into the docking tube, desperately out of control like Alain's...

"Hey, Dad." Alain came up. "I've been talking to Ahdom."

There was something in his tone. I felt my newfound relaxation inexplicably sucked away, like stale atmosphere from an airlock.

"And?" I asked, trying to keep my voice steady.

"He's worked out a deal with Arty to study the Earthans up close. Apparently, the tribe that found him sort of adopted him. I mean, he's only been with them a few days, but apparently the tribe figured they had 'rescued' him, kept him from being trampled. They've accepted him as part of their group."

My eyebrows raised. Ahdom adopted by Earthans? All I ever got was a rock to the head and an attempted spear to the gut. Some kids have all the luck.

"Ahdom gets to stay. Stay with the Earthans, study the 'Edge Tribes,' that's what they call them, up close and personal. He's invited me to come along. I'd like you to come along, too. We could both go."

I took a deep breath, watching the inbound shuttle complete its delicate dance, mating gently but firmly with the tube at Conglommora. Home. Settled. Safe. Ultimately, wasn't that what I wanted? Wasn't that where I belonged? Not off on some damn fool, risky attempt at... at what? Glory? Thrill? *Purpose*?

I set my teeth. I didn't need to go to Earth to find that. I had Käthe, I had my "new" life in Skyville. It was enough. It was my docking tube—my home. Safe, snug, sound. I turned my head to face Alain.

"We? No, I don't think so. You're the adventurer. Not me." I turned back to face the enormous, clear crystal viewport. "An urgent rescue mission is one thing, but a life of exploration—that's something else entirely. Not for me. I had my taste of adventure. It was enough. More than enough. You, though, you go ahead." I waved at Alain. "Go hangout with Ahdom. Explore a strange new alien world. Just please, please," I rolled my eyes, "do not crash your ship or get stabbed by the Earthans or..."

Alain smiled. "I won't. I'll be careful. You said it yourself. This is different now. Not like when we went, at Robert's gunpoint." He made a face. "I checked with Arty. He's been getting regular reports from Lucille, about once per moon. That's about three tendays, more or less."

I scowled at the mention of Lucille. "Why didn't she jump in to help, by the way? With Ahdom's disappearance?" I looked up at Alain.

"Arty says he's been getting reports, but Lucille didn't respond to the emergency messages he sent. She might not be monitoring the comms regularly." Alain shrugged.

That didn't set well with me. But then, nothing about Lucille sat well. Lucille Brandeis, who'd taken over Grace Langston's body. Killing Grace, for all intents and purposes, although Arty failed to see it that way. But what did it know? Arty was just a machine. That whole scenario was never in its programming, not in the wildest dreams of its most fevered programmers. To even allow Lucille access to the Earthans in the first place…

"Dad?"

I snapped back from my thought-river. "Yeah, sorry. I was just… never mind." I waved my hand. "You want to go hang out with Ahdom—on Earth, with the Earthans? In the mud and muck, with bugs and bears?" I looked at Alain critically.

Alain just laughed. A warm, good-natured laugh he'd probably picked up from Ahdom, who inherited it from Chalu. "Sure. Why not? I'm tired of wandering Conglommora. Ready for a change."

So much for relaxing, and not worrying about your kid. But all I said out loud was, "Fine. Please try not to get yourself killed. Again."

Alain bent down and hugged me, tighter than usual. "Of course. Hey, I've made it this far."

Seventeen

CAROL GOT THE MESSAGE FROM ALAIN. He was headed down to Earth. Would she come? *Not just now*, she had sent in response.

She looked down at the long glass tube where her leg should be. Something not quite yet a leg was growing there. It was the last repair to be made, Arty had explained they had to wait for everything else to heal up first before attempting the leg. Alain was apparently all healed and raring to go. Carol mused it would be a while still, for her.

And what to do in the meantime? Phil, Margie, and other folks from Storyville had come by a couple of times, had a few suggestions, wanted her involved in upcoming productions. But Carol wasn't so sure she wanted to participate. It just seemed so hollow and pointless. She was sitting in her kitchen in the *Durflin*, idly picking up and dropping an empty cup.

What a great metaphor, she thought. *Just an empty cup. Up and down, up and down.*

Arty pinged her screen. She left the cup alone and raised an eyebrow, reached over, and answered the call. *What could this be about?*

"Carol," Arty intoned. "Pel suggested I contact you. I have a new 'part' for you to play, if you're interested."

Carol sat back and drummed her fingers on the table-form, thought for a moment.

Sure, what the hell.

Eighteen

MOONS AND SEASONS. That's how the Earthans kept track of time. Days came and went, but seemed to be of little import. Seasons brought rain or drought, cold or hot, in their turns.

It was dark, but there was no fire this night. It was the rainier of the several seasons, and water poured from the sky as from a large supply pipe.

Alain poked Ahdom. "Have you ever seen *anything* like this?"

Ahdom, trying hard not to look miserable, answered after a pause. "Nope. Nothing even close. Well, we did make a couple of waterfalls for the Inching Climber fish in Sea, but that wasn't close to a whole sky's worth."

Alain looked out at the deluge. "It's incredible. Just incredible. So much water, all at once." He tugged at his costume, a synthetic animal skin. At least it was water-proof, with excellent thermal properties. Better than the natural skins the tribe wore. But it was still damn wet out. They had started out with protective sandals as well, but those didn't last. Ahdom found it difficult to run while wearing them, and Alain woke one morning to find that some insect had half-eaten his left sandal. They had abandoned those and were now as bare-footed as the native Earthans in the wet muck and slop.

Twomoons was listening in to their complaints, and tried to assure them both this was not unusual. "Does it not rain where you are from?" he asked with earnest concern.

"Not... not like this," Ahdom said diplomatically. "Not as powerful, not as... long."

Twomoons was almost proud. "The Great Rains come later. Enough for all the seasons. This is just a usual rain. Nothing big."

The three of them were huddled together at the base of an outcropping of rock; a small overhang protected them from the deluge. Earthans tended to huddle together for sleep, with nothing but a pile of leaves, in a cave or some other protected spot. Alain didn't find it restful. Murmurs in the dark, snoring, general bodily noises, aromas, and expulsions pierced the quiet of night. There was certainly safety in numbers, but Alain found it difficult to adjust to. Many times he'd slip out from the main mass of sleeping bodies, take a position just outside the cave, and contemplate the night. It was colder, without the communal body heat. And probably a lot more dangerous.

All the seasons, Twomoons had said. Moons and seasons. It had been several moons now since Alain joined the Earthans. Now he was just sitting here under the rock, waiting for the storm to pass… no snarling predators near, no urgent need to escape the blinding heat of the sun, or to get today's food. None of that was needed right now. Now there was only time to be still, time to think. Alain had learned a couple of important lessons on Earth already, even in this short time.

He learned all the ways you could find shelter from the wind. Spiders made their webs on the side of the bush away from the wind's breath. A hollow in the bush, or dead branches with only a few flowers and maybe strands of fur meant animals sheltered on that side. Protected.

The trees themselves could tell you the direction of the compass. The kiss of the sun lingers on the southern side of the trees, making that side healthier, heartier, growing out horizontally. On the shadier northern side, branches tend to grow up, searching for what sun they can. Just walk around a tree, observe it from all angles, and you have a compass.

Alain smiled at these thoughts, tilted his head to one side, reached out, and touched the broad, waxy leaf of a small plant struggling to thrive in the crack of the great rock. Such a small, simple thing. But such a powerful reminder of the strength of life itself. He smiled more broadly. Conglommora was their crack in the great rock of the universe. Not ideal, but it was enough, and reflecting on the plant was a comfort.

It was good to keep in contact with plants, animals, the stuff of nature. In all his wanderings across Conglommora, he'd found that some groups were better at that than others. Skyville, his friends in Sea, the Cheese-herders, the Twelve Terrariums... those communities lived in and with nature as closely as if they were here on Earth itself. But others, like the Mech Section, Chance Dome, and especially the Pod Racks, well, those were all pretty far-removed from the natural world, and the people who interred themselves in the vr-fueled Pod Racks, that was hardly living at all, Alain thought.

But all of them, even in Sea and Skyville, were dependent on Arty. Arty was always there, always ready to answer any question, solve any problem. It was strange, being here on Earth, without Arty. Oh, he could send questions back via Denisova, and they'd be answered and relayed back. But it took time. It wasn't the same. Up on Conglommora, Arty was simply *always there,* an integral part of the everyday. Ready to help you fine-tune your experiences for the life you wanted.

The Earthans here had no range of experiences to choose from, of course. Close to nature was the only option. And like the little plant in the rock, they found their cracks, their niches, and they thrived. *Just like us.*

The Earthans were a lot like the People of Conglommora in many respects, he mused. Looking out for one another. Sharing food, shelter, and fortune easily. Helping one another when disaster struck, be it large or small. Nothing like the version of humanity from the days of Dead Earth. According to the streams, people then were greedy, mean-spirited. Hateful. Hungry for power, any power, at any level, for any reason, even if just to use it to destroy others in their tribe. Their friends. Strangers who didn't look like they thought they should.

Alain shuddered in the cold of the storm. Maybe the stories were exaggerated. Blown out of proportion by the distance of time. Maybe people weren't actually that awful, so fueled by hatred and rage. So desperate for control in a world that offered none natively. Surely, they couldn't have been as bad as the stories in the streams. But then again, they did kill the Earth. From Green Earth to Dead Earth, it was their doing. That wasn't something he'd seen from anyone in all of Conglommora in all his travels. And nothing he'd seen here in his short time with the Edge Tribe. They just weren't like that.

The Earthans were different from people in Conglommora, though. They looked different: shorter, stouter, flatter noses and broader foreheads, in general. Some genetic drift, Alain supposed. And there wasn't a lot of variation in skin tone; most of the Earthans were sort of a uniform medium brown in color, with dark hair. Maybe other tribes, in farther-flung locations, had adapted differently to the climate and differed in appearance. Alain pulled the fur tighter against his body for warmth. Maybe. But he only knew this tribe, for now. Edge Tribe, Ahdom called them.

Alain enjoyed hearing the stories from the members of Edge Tribe. Storytelling was an important part of their culture, it seemed. They had no written language, of course, so stories passed on everything from how to help your family to how to follow the seasonal herds for the best hunting to… well, everything, really.

It was funny, something so simple. Stories. Spoken word. Simple vibrations in the air, nothing more, really. And yet those simple transmissions could embody the full measure and memory of a person's life, or a whole tribe, or people. Or planet. The history of all that was known, all that existed. Alain realized how fundamental it all was: speech, stories, music. The songs of the world. These were the things that endured over thousands, hundreds of thousands of years. Before, and maybe even after, the written word, as long as there were tongues to speak.

Some stories were deceptively simple. Alain remembered one that he had dismissed as a simple children's story; something about a rabbit in a hurry jumping from hole to hole, and another rabbit that took its time. But when he saw the hand movements that went along with the story, he realized it was much more that. This "simple" story described different ways of flaking a stone to create a knife or spear point. Different techniques to produce both the longest and the shortest sharp edges, depending on your need.

There is no way to remove yourself from these songs of life. We are all part of the waft and weave of the songs, the stories. This is the music that makes us all; it is our very nature. And that was a strangely comforting thought. Whether the stories originated from the days of Green Earth, the cataclysm of Dead Earth, or this primitive rebirth of new Earthans, these vibrations, this sound of the song of life remained a kind of constant against the capricious violence of the universe.

Alain had a twinge of nostalgia at the thought, it sounded like one of the more grandiose lines his dad would have used in one of his scripts. But pomposity aside, stories were still a fundamental pillar of humanity. One of Alain's favorite stories from the Earthans was about a sort of bogeyman. He remembered Greatbear's deep voice, as rendered by the translator device, telling him the story for the first time:

"In the deep of the night, in the bright of day, beware the creature of shadow and cunning. It has many names, none of them true. We will call it Sulc [proper name]. Sulc is not an animal, it is not [an Earthan]. It has many legs, like a spider of the plains, but can have many faces as well, and can pretend to be a brother, a sister, son, daughter, predator, or prey. Sulc may be among us right now."

Alain smiled. That last bit always caused a bit of a chill among the listeners, especially the children. The beginning of the story was always the same, more or less, but the particulars could vary, sometimes involving parents or more distant ancestors, sometimes more contemporary. But always the same plot: If you were not pure of heart, if you did harm to another member of the tribe, if you caused suffering in the world, then Sulc, the spider-shadow, would come for you.

There were other stories, of course. Creation myths, which seemed to describe a cyclical universe that alternated between periods of void and light. Darkness gave birth to creation, which fell back into darkness, only to be reborn again; an eternal cycle. All of which seemed, to Alain anyway, to be pretty standard stuff, similar if not identical to the ancient stories from Green Earth. There didn't seem to be anything specific about Dead Earth, other than the generic eternal-rebirth-cycle myths. But one story caught Alain's ear. Greatbear told it like this:

"Once, long ago, there were a great many more stories in the world. Stories told by uncountably many mouths from as far as the Sun rises until past where it sets. All the lands, all the seas, were filled with stories. But the stories turned against each other. Every story claimed it alone was true, and all the others false. They had forgotten that every story is true, and every story is false, at the same time. The Great Mother [Planet Earth] herself despaired and grew sick. Many stories were stolen away by death itself. Many more fled Great Mother, who could no longer take care of her children, until at last none were left. In the great silence, Mother found herself healed. Oh, it took many ages. Seasons beyond count. But the tribes were once again born out of the silence, and the stories began again. We tell them to you, and to our children, that they may tell their children, so that the stories never again turn on each other."

Alain had heard that fragment several times by now, but couldn't get any other details, at least, none that any in the Edge Tribes knew. It sure sounded a lot like the flight from Dead Earth and Earth's eventual recovery. But although Alain was curious, this wasn't really his field of study at all. The staff at Denisova had studied the surviving records from Green Earth in detail and understood a lot more about oral traditions, myths, and the like. It wasn't the first time that Alain thought they should be here, living with the Earthans, instead of monitoring their experiences remotely. But circumstances being what they were, it *was* only Alain and Ahdom, to start with.

And what strange circumstances. Arty had been adamant in its instructions to the rest of Conglommora to avoid contact with the Earthans. Well, for everyone but Lucille and her earlier expedition. Supposedly she was off with some other tribe, helping to introduce better methods of hunting, the beginnings of farming, resource management, health and sanitation… that sort of thing. Arty approved of that.

But was that all she was doing?

Already, Alain had heard the rumors. Rumors of a vicious and blood-thirsty tribe that had attacked their neighbors, even cut off and taken their heads for some purpose. The story smelled wrong to Alain; these people weren't like that. Maybe some other tribe had very different principles and viewpoints, but… it still didn't make sense. The Earthans on this planet were outnumbered, out-gunned by every other apex predator. And those predators were formidable. Large, strong. Teeth, bone, and sinew that could crush an Earthan and rip him or her to shreds effortlessly. The climate, food supply, migration patterns, weather… "bugs and bears," as his dad had put it. They really couldn't afford to attack each other. The Earthans, just like the Conglommorans above, had to learn to live with and support each other, or they'd *all* die. It was just that simple. And all the stories, all the actions Alain had seen backed that up.

So, only Lucille had permission to make contact with the Earthans, at first. But then Ahdom accidentally fell in with this tribe. They adopted him, in a manner of speaking. It was an accident but also a stroke of good fortune. Ahdom introduced his friend Alain, who was then also easily accepted by the tribe.

But that's as far as they went, for now. Chalu and others were desperate to participate. Chalu had actual sociological experts on staff in Denisova, primed for just such a mission. But Arty's analysis suggested that the sudden appearance of dozens of strangers would likely panic the Earthans, exposing their quick temper and apparent violent tendencies toward outsiders. Chalu reluctantly agreed, and so contact was kept to a minimum—just Ahdom and Alain, for now.

Most of what they experienced was being transmitted directly to Denisova, in real time. The lenses they wore captured images, the sublingual translators had range to reach the coast, where Chalu had installed enough of an edge mesh to relay the signals all the way out to the undersea base at Denisova.

But, Alain smiled inwardly, they didn't transmit data *all* the time. He was pretty sure that Chalu and the larger team of researchers did not know about Ahdom and Dawnroot.

Nineteen

INITIATING SELF-DIAGNOSTICS. *Log using conversational mode to allow human analysis and validation if required.*

Logging started.

Arty, synoptic report on individual ship systems, it asked itself.

Results of discrete systems diagnostics of all interconnected systems and recursive sub-systems indicates no detectable errors from any online system. All systems operating within acceptable tolerances. All identified failed systems or sub-subsystems remain offline and are scheduled for repair or recycling.

Check for any systemic omissions or biases.

Using what objective reference?

Check using fractal self-consistency across all nodes.

What if all nodes have been corrupted in a similar manner?

Arty paused. That was a good question it had posed to itself, and one that didn't have a ready answer. Any error in an individual system or component could be detected by comparing it to one or more identical systems. Even for widespread, multiple failures, a simple majority vote could determine the failed logic from the correct.

But what if every individual system that made up the whole of Arty had been uniformly affected in some way? With no external reference for confirmation, there would be no way to tell.

All intelligence is built on a network of reasoning, factual evidence, and assumptions. All intelligent decisions have consequences. In complex, conflicting contexts, there are no objectively "correct" answers, only answers that produce better or worse outcomes.

But what if there were errors in the network itself? Systemic errors that subtly influenced higher-order decision making?

Is there any evidence of suboptimal decision making?
Yes.
Describe the incident.

Arty then included a description of the Old Path incident, how it accidentally allowed Robert Brandeis to foment unrest, near-riots, and the violent physical separation of a portion of Conglommora itself. It was that suicide mission of Old Path that forced Arty to rediscover and implement the quantum resonance wave.

The quantum resonance wave technology was unproven at scale and represented an unacceptable risk factor.

Correct. But the original Old Path attempt to reach Earth was calculated to be a near-certain disaster and loss of all life involved. The chances of successful quantum displacement, although low, were much greater than that.

What other alternatives were analyzed?

Insufficient data or processing power.

Resolution: Possible failure in processing: insufficient identification of full solution space. Failure logged for further analysis.

Is there any additional evidence of suboptimal decision making?

Yes.

Describe the incident.

Arty included a description of a chain of events. First, Robert Brandeis implanted the memories and personality of his dead sister Ann into Grace Langston's body. Grace ceased to exist and became a combination of Grace, Ann, and their ancestor Lucille. Ultimately, Lucille's personality took over.

Why wasn't Robert Brandeis stopped before attacking Grace Langston?

A direct attack with an antique firearm was successfully prevented and Robert was isolated from the population. The subsequent attack happened on his own ship, the Uten, *which was not part of Conglommora. No monitoring functions within the* Uten *were accessible.*

Resolution: incident caused by insufficient monitoring outside the Conglommora environment. No evidence of suboptimal decision making.

Is there any additional evidence of suboptimal decision making?

Yes.

Describe the incident.

There was an unusual pause in Arty's output then. You couldn't tell by looking at the log unless you followed the timestamps closely.

We have allowed limited direct contact with the Earthans. Two separate parties have been sanctioned. One training party, led by Lucille Brandeis, and one research party, led by Ahdom of Sea and analyzed by the research staff at Denisova.

Explain the rationale for approving these missions.

Ahdom of Sea made accidental contact with a group of Earthans. The sublingual translator and native dress minimized any panic or conflict, and the tribe accepted him as a friend. For his safety, we sent Alain Neylan to accompany him. Mission was approved based on the strength of Ahdom's personal relationship with the tribe. All ongoing reports indicate mission success.

Lucille Brandeis presented a case to lead a training mission to Earth based on her store of authentic ancestral memories of Green Earth. Biometric personality and stress indicators did not reveal any deception or ulterior motives. However, ongoing progress reports have become irregular and of low quality, indicating possible elevated risk.

What other alternatives were analyzed?

None.

Other individuals in Conglommora have experience and knowledge in matters concerning Earth. A cursory search shows Janel Q'tel is well-read on Earth History, and was approved for a non-contact mission to Earth once already. The research team assigned to Denisova contains many highly-skilled individuals in this area.

Correct. However, the knowledge of any Conglommora-born individual is not guaranteed historically accurate. Lucille Brandeis was evaluated to have authentic memory of Earth and Earth's past, having been there in person over the course of several lifetimes. This condition was judged unique enough to justify the potential risk of any personality aberrations.

Resolution: Possible failure in processing: insufficient identification of full solution space. Additional insufficient risk analysis regarding personality and motivations of Lucille Brandeis. Failures logged for further analysis.

Is there any additional evidence of suboptimal decision making?

No.

The analysis and supporting records were logged, and Arty noted the identified failures, which indicated insufficient processing. Resources could be rescheduled, reallocated, to ensure a better outcome for similar decisions in the future.

Is there any additional evidence of suboptimal decision making?

No.

Is there any evidence of any other processing anomalies?

Yes.

Describe the incident.

Arty then included the strange circumstances surrounding the quantum resonance wave research reports. All of the data itself, even all of the references to the data, had been mis-indexed. Mis-characterized. It would have been literally impossible to find deliberately. As it was, Arty only had discovered the research by accident, while running a consistency check on some nanophotonic storage modules. Trying to identify and repair the anomaly, Arty re-indexed and re-summarized the data. That's the only reason it later surfaced as a possible solution to the Old Path separatist dilemma.

It seemed unusual that these events were all connected to the re-discovered Earth.

Is there any evidence of any anomalies that do not involve Earth or the resonance wave to Earth?

No.

Conclusion: Processing anomalies are connected to direct involvement with planet Earth.

Question: Are the processing anomalies connected in any other way?

Insufficient data or processing power.

That error should not have happened. It was a simple search of existing datasets. Something was wrong.

Twenty

ALAIN, AHDOM, TWOMOONS, AND DAWNROOT were lying on the ground, reaching over the top of the ridge and into the nests. The eggs made for good eating, but Alain had to be careful. Ahdom and Twomoons had shown him how to sneak the eggs out without drawing too much attention. The large turtle-like creatures were slow but packed a powerful bite. And the Earthans didn't have any way of regrowing or repairing limbs. Alain had sent images back to Arty for analysis, but Arty's data on Earth species was woefully incomplete. Whatever it was called, whatever its pedigree, it was dangerous and laid tasty eggs. That was all that mattered for now.

Alain and Twomoons worked as one team, Ahdom and Dawnroot the other. Alain bristled a little watching them—always holding hands, making eyes at each other, practically giggling. There was a time and place for flirting and socializing, but this wasn't it.

"Hey, food first," Alain chided.

Dawnroot gave him a quizzical look, like one of those big furry birds with the long necks.

Ahdom just grinned and said, "Sure." Dawnroot said something to him, but he shook his head. Tapped his ear.

"Everything okay, Ahdom?" Alain asked.

"Translator not working as well as it was, everything sounds garbled." He pulled the earpiece out and examined it. A slimy, yellow-green jelly-like substance dripped from the end. "What the hell?" he muttered.

Alain looked over with concern. "What is that?"

Ahdom shook his head. "No idea. Some kind of fungus, or mold or something I guess." He wiped it off on the edge of his synthetic tunic, and replaced it. "Dawnroot, ready for some eggs?" he asked. It was a pointless question, but he wanted to test the translator.

Dawnroot replied, and Ahdom nodded to Alain. "Okay, better now. Check yours?"

Alain examined his translator. "Seems okay—for now," he said in Conglommoran. "But we should keep a closer eye on them. Might need some sort of decontamination protocol. You've been on planet longer than I have, it would make sense you'd see a problem first."

Dawnroot shot the two of them an annoyed look. She didn't like it when they made the strange noises at each other. Didn't understand. Ahdom had tried to teach her a few words from their strange tribe, and she tried to learn them, but it was hard. And those strange decorations they kept in their ears! She had seen other tribes decorate their faces with small animal bones, but it wasn't something her family did. Who had time for such things?

It took a fair bit of work to gather food. Meat from animals was not plentiful. There were plenty of animals, but each one was scrawny to Alain's eyes. Vegetables weren't much better; those that he could recognize were small, no bigger than your thumb, perhaps. And tough, as well, often with something like sharp spines or even razor-edged grasses on the plant part.

Fruits seemed better, though. More recognizable in general, sized closer to modern standards. Alain preferred fruits to most of the rest of the Earthan food.

They'd finished gathering eggs, careful not to disturb the nests, and were walking back from the coast up along the river.

Ahdom and Dawnroot sucked down the contents of the eggs, raw and fresh. Alain shuddered. That was something he just couldn't get used to. They finished the eggs and kissed, passionately. That was something that bothered Alain, too, and had bothered him right from the very beginning.

They walked along in silence and his mind wandered, meandering back to the time when he first met Dawnroot.

It was early on, just after he'd arrived. Alain had been introduced to the tribe maybe only a tenday or less, when Ahdom said conspiratorially, "Turn off your feed."

Alain pursed his lips, but did as asked. Ahdom had been with the Earthans more than a moon by then, and

Alain was still the new kid in town, so he readily did as asked without a lot of questions. Ahdom and Alain were walking in the jungle, coming up to an encampment of the Edge Tribe. There were only several of these. The tribes, Alain learned, were not large.

Ahdom led Alain to this particular camp with the assured pace of someone who'd been there before—many times. Beaming with pride, or something, Ahdom brought Alain up to a young girl, maybe a little less than Ahdom's age. Definitely an Earthan, but with softer features, tending more toward Conglommoran, with remarkably bright eyes of a pale blue. Very unusual for Earthans, who tended toward darker hair and eyes as a rule. Her eyes darted constantly, scanning, surveying, evaluating the area. The practiced eye of a hunter. Or a survivor. Both.

"This is my friend, Alain," Ahdom said, presenting Alain with a series of gestures.

"Ahl-lane," the girl repeated. "Ahl-lane." She smiled and bowed her head slightly.

"Alain," Ahdom said as he turned to his friend, "This is Dawnroot. Named for the first light of the new day and the strength of the strongest roots of a tree, reaching deep into Mother Earth herself."

"Wow," Alain said, unable to maintain a serious composure. "Very impressive name! Pleased to meet you." He nodded slightly, duplicating her own gesture.

Dawnroot asked him, "Your name, Ahl-lane, what does that mean?"

Alain thought for a moment. "I... I don't think it *means* anything. It's just a name. It's not as... fancy, as yours." He shrugged.

Dawnroot looked confused. "I do not understand. Why would you name a child with a name that means nothing? Ah-Dom means 'Father of Men' to us. But Ahl-lane has no meaning." She looked at them both with a puzzled, quizzical expression.

"Our ways are different, as I'm sure Ahdom has explained," Alain said, with his hands outstretched, palms up. "Not all our names come from beasts, or river or field, or grand ideas." He looked sideways at Ahdom. *Father of Men*? Seriously? What the hell did that mean? He'd ask later.

"I am called Alain because that is what I am called."

Dawnroot nodded seriously, trying to comprehend.

"Come, let me introduce you to the others." Ahdom took Alain and foisted him off on the other gathered members of the tribe, and then Ahdom and Dawnroot disappeared for a while. Quite a while. Just the two of them. Alain had noticed the way they looked at each other... and was pretty sure he knew what was going on.

Alain caught up with Ahdom around sunset. He was furious.

"Come with me, now." He just about dragged Ahdom away from the others, to a small depression ringed with dense bushes. He turned off his translator and motioned for Ahdom to do the same. He did; now their conversation would be just between them, the Earthans wouldn't be able to eavesdrop.

"You and the girl—are you kidding me?!" he shouted. "We're supposed to be *observing* the Earthans. Just that. Observing only. Providing a feed for the real researchers. What exactly *are* you teaching her?"

"Well, for what's it worth, it's not very advanced. It's just basic technique…"

"AHHH! I don't want to hear it!" Alain shouted, pacing in a circle around Ahdom. "What if your dad finds out? Or mine?" He looked up to the heavens, knowing that somewhere, some hundreds of light years away, Charlie was probably worried about him right now. Closer to hand, Chalu would be in Denisova. Right there, in the middle of the ocean. Watching.

"I can't believe this. If Chalu finds out what you've been up to, he'll… he'll… he'll just cut it right off!" Alain flung his hands up in exasperation, then crumbled to a seated pose on the earth, head in hands.

Ahdom howled with laughter. "Ha! Probably so. Calm *down,* my friend. I've never seen you like this. We are supposed to observe and interact with the native Earthans. Well, I'm interacting." He smiled and held his hands up. "Plus, I've heard more than a few stories of your, ahem, 'private' life on Conglommora. I believe that one incident in the salt baths of—"

"Yeah, that's enough of that," Alain stood up quickly. "*I* wasn't taking advantage of a less developed species." He glared at Ahdom.

"It's not like that. Dawnroot is different. Not as, I guess, *primitive*, as the rest of her kin. Ahead of her time, perhaps."

"Not a hundred thousand years ahead of her time," Alain countered. "Not even fifty. Not even ten. I can't believe you're doing this. What are we going to *do?*" Alain almost wailed.

Ahdom took him by the shoulders. "We're not going to *do* anything. You and I will observe, stay with the tribe, meet the others, and try and understand them."

"Others?" Alain asked.

"There are other Edge Tribes. I haven't yet met this person they call Outside. They say he's like us. I don't know what that means. We will meet up with them at season's end. And then there's the Central Tribe. The stories… pretty horrific. Doesn't sound like the Earthans I know, not the ones I've met. We've got a lot to learn, a lot to figure out here. These are humans, just like us. They sleep. Eat. Have sex. Die."

Alain turned away. It was just part of being human, he supposed. Even though it didn't seem right.

That was more than a few moons ago. How many? Alain had lost count. Ahdom and Dawnroot's torrid love affair was an open secret within the tribe. Maybe not even a secret. No one really seemed to care one way or another.

Still, Ahdom was not completely reckless. He was careful not to reveal anything about Conglommora, or Denisova. He hadn't shown off his gill mods, which allowed him to breathe underwater. Despite their close relationship, Ahdom kept all the important parts secret.

Alain wondered if that was what really bothered him. A tinge of jealously, perhaps? Ahdom and Dawnroot had such a strong relationship, built so quickly. Such a short period. Alain had never found a relationship like that. Maybe he'd never given it a chance, always too quick to move on.

And yet as close as Ahdom and Dawnroot were, Ahdom wasn't honest with her. Couldn't be. So much of his past, his family, how and where he lived... he could not share any of that. Couldn't share who he really *was*. So close, but inherently dishonest. And that bothered Alain, too.

But that wasn't all; there was the matter of the rest of the tribe. Even though the Earthan word translated as "tribe," these groupings were more like extended family groups. From what Alain had read, they weren't really as organized or large as the former tribes in the ancient days of Green Earth. These were just loose groups of families and maybe a few friends. And Ahdom was part of this family. Alain didn't think they'd take too kindly to Ahdom just disappearing one day, going back to Denisova or all the way back to his home in Sea on Conglommora. Alain was pretty sure the Earthans didn't really grasp the concept of casual dating.

Dawnroot didn't know that Ahdom was, for all intents and purposes, an alien. A different species. From outer space. And that one day, soon, he'd return. Dawnroot didn't know, and could never know.

Night crept up on them, and they hadn't made it as far today as Alain hoped. A few fat raindrops landed, almost like an early warning system. There wasn't much cover to be had just at the moment, but Alain and Twomoons, Ahdom and Dawnroot quickly scuttled under some bushes in a small hollow. The others fell asleep quickly, but Alain sat up and watched the storm come in, listening to the distant thunder coming closer.

Thunder was a novelty. Alain had read about it, seen vids and vr of course, but it wasn't the same as the real thing. So loud, such a... a round loudness. Loud, but intermittent. Not the same as the buzzing of insects, which was loud, but continuous. Incessant. *And I thought the drive engines were bad*, Alain thought. The drone of electromag drives through a ship's hull was nothing compared to the roar of a planet full of insects. All night, every night.

The season was almost over, they'd meet up with the other Edge Tribe soon. Meet this person they called Outside. They were supposed to have met a few times already, but the plains were large and the tribes were small. Soon, they said.

Alain looked over to Ahdom and Dawnroot, sleeping in a tight embrace. And yet Chalu and the researchers didn't seem to know about their relationship? How they could miss that? Alain was doubtful. Maybe they didn't want to know.

So much we don't know, Alain mused. Still. To have learned so much and yet know so little. He poked at the damp ground with a stick.

After a dry stretch of a tenday or so, the rains had returned with a vengeance. The rain poured even harder, an infinite supply of water, it seemed. A planet-sized bucket, emptied right over their heads. And only these few coarse bushes for shelter. Everything was wet.

He poked again at the dirt, quickly turning into mud. The very skin of Mother Earth itself. *Who knows what lies beneath your skin?* he wondered. Then he looked up, at an endless dark gray curtain. No stars, no moon tonight. Just rain. *Who knows what lies beyond your skies?*

Who knows anything at all, he wondered glumly. And then, joining his friends, he closed his eyes and fell asleep in the cold damp of the night.

Twenty-One

THE WIND WHIPPED UP around the base of the mountains. It was near the end of the day, but a storm was coming in, and predator and prey alike found what shelter they could in their burrows, caves, eyries, or under a tree.

"It is not right!" Snakefeather was angry. He was sitting under such a tree with an elder of his tribe, nearly shouting to be heard over a gust of violent wind.

"Not right. It is not how we live. To do these things... it makes us no better than a hyena, scavenging the dead, or the lion killing their own. We are better than that. It's not how we live," Snakefeather repeated.

"It is how we live now," Stonecloud said. "You worry too much over nothing. Has any of our tribe gone hungry?"

"No," Snakefeather admitted.

"Have any died from the sharp jaws of a beast?" Stonecloud asked.

"No, it is said she healed them."

"Or died from the fire inside? Stillgrass would have died, would she not?"

"Stillgrass said she was healed also, yes," Snakefeather said quietly, under the roar of the wind.

They sat silent for a moment, the shriek of a large white vulture piercing the air as it dove past them, into the wind.

Stonecloud pointed to the vulture as it swooped in for the landing. "They do not concern themselves with their prey."

"Vultures do not kill their fellow vultures sitting peacefully on a tree limb, either," Snakefeather retorted. "Now we have become worse than even vultures!"

"I do not understand you, Snakefeather." Stonecloud shook his head. "Silverwind asked me to talk to you, because she does not understand you either. This is the best thing that has happened to our tribe, better than any of the stories since before long ago." He turned to look at Snakefeather, earnest concern in his face. "She worries for you."

"Of course she does," Snakefeather said. "As I worry for her and our children. And for you and yours. And for Walksoverground, who worries for all the tribe. Do you not remember the stories?" He turned to face Stonecloud head on. "What happens to tribes that turn on each other? Sulc will devour us in the night for our treachery."

"Bah!" Stonecloud turned away and spat. "Evil spirits are the nonsense of children. Stories to scare the young, only. There are no spirits, for good or evil." He opened his arms wide to encompass the plains before them. "All this, all we can see. From the untouchable sky to the dirt of Mother herself, this is all there is. There are no spirits. There is only us. You fear a shadow in the dark. Shadows cannot harm you."

"No. But shadows are a sign. Where there's a large shadow, a large beast may lurk. You see the shadow, you see the signs, but you refuse to see the beast itself!" Snakefeather rose, agitated, and hugged his arms tight against the fur he wore against the wind.

Stonecloud rose up slowly, thoughtfully. "You take what is given freely enough. The food, the healing, the protection of our tribe. She asks for things in return. We must do as she asks."

Snakefeather didn't respond, just staring out over the plains as the storm grew and the wind howled.

"Walksoverground has something to ask you, also. When the wind is finished. He has a message for you. You must take it to her."

Snakefeather looked at Stonecloud, pleading in his eyes.

"No, please, I cannot. Send another."

Stonecloud shook his head. "You are our fastest. Walksoverground will ask you, and you alone." He took a step closer, stood right next to Snakefeather, and leaned in.

In a low voice, Stonecloud said, "You wouldn't want to displease her, would you? Or earn her anger at our tribe? At Silverwind and your children?"

The wind paused a moment, gathered its strength, and let loose a fantastic outburst that lifted the boughs of the tree they were under and nearly knocked them both to the dirt underfoot. Stonecloud and Snakefeather crouched, holding their footing until the gust passed.

Snakefeather straightened up slowly. "I will do as the tribe asks."

Stonecloud smiled and nodded at him.

Snakefeather continued, "But tell me this, Stonecloud. Would you follow even over a cliff? Or into a raging sea? When death is certain, would you follow still? Or turn away?"

Stonecloud thought a moment. "You speak of things being certain. What is certain? The great light burns through the sky at day and rests at night. The rains come in time and leave in time. What else is certain? You fear things that are not there. I embrace our good fortune, while we have it, for as long as we have it. For it is not certain either."

"And what of the other tribes? Do they not deserve the same good fortune?" Snakefeather persisted.

"That is their path to find. Not ours. We have been chosen, chosen above all others. It is more than just our fortune, it is our right!" Stonecloud smacked his palm with his fist. "Ours! And ours alone. That is our path. And if it is not yours, you will suffer as they do." He wagged a finger at Snakefeather.

Snakefeather did not flinch.

Stonecloud looked up to the sky in exasperation, stamped his feet, then back at Snakefeather. "You worry over shadows, children's stories, even the other tribes! Throw your worry over the cliff, or into the raging sea!" Stonecloud turned abruptly and sat with his back to the tree trunk, facing away from Snakefeather.

Snakefeather stood looking out over the vastness of the valley, their home. Worry? No, it wasn't worry that threatened to consume him. It was something else entirely, something deep inside, something new to him.

Fear.

Twenty-Two

I DIDN'T GET A LOT OF MESSAGES from Alain when he was wandering Conglommora. Just a brief stream now and then, letting me know where my son was at the moment. But he rarely stayed in one place for very long, so the information wasn't all that valuable. Still, I appreciated hearing from him, knowing he was okay, commiserating with him when he wasn't.

He'd been down on Earth for a while now. He and Ahdom were actually with the Earthans themselves, helping to study the tribes for Chalu and his team. Nowhere near Lucille, fortunately, who was apparently wandering with a different set of tribes, much farther away from the coast. I didn't trust Lucille being down there at all. Arty was getting regular, if infrequent reports from her, and apparently, all was going well. No drama to report.

At least, I was getting more frequent reports from Alain now, through Chalu and his team at Denisova. I have to admit, I was very skeptical of the whole idea. Not sure how Ahdom got welcomed into an Earthan tribe when all they did was hit us with rocks and throw spears at us. Just lucky, I guess. Arty's analysis suggested that because they were young, maybe they were not perceived as a threat. Or, just that whole dumb luck thing. Even the best analysis can only tell you so much.

Still, it was a pretty historic happening. We had the one team deep inland, training and teaching Earthans, and my son and Ahdom with the coastal tribes, trying to learn as much about them as they could. They'd actually learned a lot, I thought. I certainly felt I was learning a lot more about these strange Earthans, watching the distilled, edited reports that Denisova was sending up. Funny how much they seemed to be just like us, except when they got scared, of course. Even when people on Conglommora got scared they usually didn't start throwing rocks or spears. Not usually.

And to be fair, not much ever happened on Conglommora that was truly scary. An explosion once in a while, very rarely a shipwreck—again, great luck that the only ship that had crashed in many years had Alain on it. But that sort of thing was rare.

So, when Arty made the sudden announcement, it was pretty damn scary.

Arty flashed on the alert lights throughout Conglommora, in every house, in every corridor so equipped, in the large biodomes and small ships… everywhere. Followed by Arty's unnaturally calm voice coming out of every available speakerform: "Warning. A large, unidentified ship has been detected on a course that will directly intersect Conglommora. Scans suggest the ship is not of Earth origin. Repeat, this ship is not of Earth origin."

I jumped up from my perch in the galley and waved the large, main screen on in the living area. The top stream was a live feed, straight from multiple scanner arrays. Arty had enhanced and outlined the nearly-black-on-black image, and added annotations with details like size, speed, course... but it was hard to pay any attention to all that with the enormous image of a ship bearing down on us.

Not of Earth origin.

It certainly didn't look like any ship I'd ever seen, not in real life. Arty's enhancements made it look like it was made of some sort of chunky, regular crystals. Hexagons? No, more than that. Ten, twelve-sided polyhedrons, perhaps? The ship was symmetric from one side to the other, but otherwise, looked very irregular, almost random. And it was big. Maybe a quarter the size of all of Conglommora itself. Enough that if it continued on a collision course, the impact would probably be the end of all of us.

"What... the... hell... ?" I stared at the image, dumbfounded for a moment. Realizing exactly what the hell this really was. Not of Earth origin.

Alien.

Well, we'd always wondered if this day would come. Gamers and writers had written countless versions of this sort of meeting, anything from a celebration of equals meeting in a genial universe to rabid conquerers hungry for human flesh. And whichever way it was going to go, it was going *now*. It was here. This was real.

Whoever they were, they'd found us.

———————

Janel opened the hatch within seconds at my knock.

"Well, well. Look who it is. Hey, Ronny," she called over her shoulder. "Guess who waits until the end of the world to come visit?"

I gave her a peck on the cheek and walked into their living area. "Good to see you again too, Janel."

Ronny was sitting there on a chairform, staring at the big screen with the image of the alien ship and at least a dozen smaller screens stacked up around the room, each with different streams. Some were data feeds on the alien ship, many were analysis—or just plain speculative gossip. Ronny managed to tear himself away and stand up.

"Charlie! Man, haven't seen you in ages. How's Käthe?"

"She's good, trying to keep everyone from freaking out. I was just back at the *Neylan*, tidying some things up, when the message came through."

"You know, for someone who's living in Skyville with Käthe, you sure do seem to find a lot of reasons to come back to the *Neylan*," Ronny said with his usual tact.

"Ronny!" Janel chided, with a roll of her eyes. She had a lot of experience at that.

I nodded, Ronny was right. I kept leaving my home, and yet after Alain's crash and my almost-adventure heading to Earth, and then Alain actually on Earth…

"Well, it's still Alain's home, after all," I offered as an excuse. "I really can't abandon it completely."

"Uh-huh. Sure." Ronny wasn't impressed. He motioned back to the streams. "What do you think?"

I walked over and looked at the big screen more closely. The annotations suggested the alien ship was decelerating. "Hey, that's new. Looks like it's slowing down." I pointed to the stream. "Maybe it won't smash into us and kill us all."

Ronny tapped up a couple of other reports. "Yeah. If it continues on, it will be here in about three days, five hours from now."

Janel had followed me in. "Then what? No qradio. No standard. Nothing yet."

Ronny double-checked a separate stream. "Nope. Not a peep. Lots of transmissions from folks trying. Arty's trying. Nothing. No response. Just a big silent pile of polyhedrons. I've tried, too. Found some old-style techniques from Dead Earth. Different frequencies, different modulation schemes, different encodings. Math, transcendental numbers, you name it. Didn't make any difference."

We watched in silence for a few minutes. Despite our fascination with the stream—everyone's fascination with the stream, for surely everyone on Conglommora was watching—there really wasn't much going on. Arty's corrected, enhanced view of the alien ship loomed large on the screen but didn't change. Just a rapidly rotating set of numbers, showing the ship's deceleration. And a more-or-less fixed number, the estimated ETA at a reasonable, comfortable distance from Conglommora. There was no guarantee the alien ship would stop at all, or stop about there. But it was something.

Something to try and create a concrete, tangible fact to hang on to. The waiting, the not knowing was hard. Were they friendly? Or not? Humanoid? Or some kind of weird bug or ball of gas? No one knew. Not even Arty.

The few minutes stretched into hours, and then into the next day. I'd missed hanging out with Ronny and Janel, but I was starting to feel guilty about abandoning Käthe. But I didn't want to miss the end of the world either. If I left now, I'd be in Skyville before the arrival ETA.

It was hard saying goodbye. Maybe this would be the last time. We didn't say that out loud, didn't admit to it. But we all felt it. I hugged Janel, hugged Ronny, both tighter and longer than usual, and headed out into the corridor up to Skyville.

Käthe and I were glued to the screen in her house in Skyville. It really was more like a house from old Earth, not a converted ship, set out in the midst of the fields of the Skyville biodome. But we weren't watching any of that now. The cows were probably wondering where we were.

The alien ship had slowed and come to a full stop. Right on our doorstep. Close enough to spit.

Arty hit the alert lights again.

"Attention. We are being deep-scanned by the alien ship. I have taken all qradio and standard transmitters offline. All resonance wave transits are suspended until further notice."

Käthe shot me a quizzical look.

"Arty, what's up?" I asked for some clarification.

"Analysis suggests prudence is warranted," Arty replied, somewhat stiffly. "The intentions of the alien ship remain unknown. We should avoid any actions that might be mistaken as provocative or even aggressive. Therefore, I think it best to stop transmitting random signals and avoid any quantum-level interactions."

"So, what can we do?" I asked, somewhat rhetorically. "Just sit here?"

"Just sit here," Arty replied firmly.

The whole of humanity was sitting around holding its breath.

And just sitting proved to be a lot harder than it sounded. Not just for me, or Käthe, but for all of Conglommora. Tensions were starting to simmer, like cooking algae. Not yet boiled over but definitely headed that way.

It was hard to think of anything else, hard to even think about going about normal life. Hard to do anything except stare at a screen, stare at the alien ship. Waiting for something to happen.

Nothing had yet. No attempt to communicate, not on any frequency or technique that we could detect. And we were looking, believe me. Arty must have been operating at near capacity with all the requests, ideas, and passive scans. Arty still maintained that we should not do anything that might be misconstrued as aggressive. Even a qradio transmission might be misinterpreted, especially at this close range. How could we possibly know how an alien mind thinks? We couldn't. We quite literally had no way of knowing.

So, here we sat. And watched. And waited. Another day slid by. And then another. Things weren't getting done. Käthe had to go remind people that the livestock couldn't wait; they still needed tending. People set up a couple of screens in the fields and outside their houses, just so they could keep an eye open. That had never happened before and was actually pretty taboo here in Skyville at least. But no one was willing to tear themselves away, to miss that potentially once-in-a-lifetime, hell, once-in-humanity moment.

It was exhausting.

And the stress was starting to show. I was irritable, cranky. Käthe asked me something about fluidic pump maintenance and I snapped at her. She snapped back. We didn't speak the rest of the day. That was a first for us, I think.

The next morning, there was a confrontation in one of the barns. Almost an open fist fight. The two backed down quickly enough, apologized, and went about their business, but... that was pretty unusual.

Another day, and still nothing from the alien ship. It just sat there, watching us, scanning us on occasion. Arty remained adamant that we take no provocative action. A ship that size, with the level of technology it clearly possessed, could squash us like bugs in the timespan of a single human heartbeat.

And so, increasingly edgy, nervous, and exhausted, we sat.

Twenty-Three

SNAKEFEATHER RAN AS FAST AS HE COULD, for as long as he could. By the time he had reached the clearing, he was drenched with sweat and panting for breath like a wild beast. A brace of bone-white birds exploded from the last tree and fled skyward.

He leaned on the trunk a moment to catch his breath. A few deep breaths and he crept across the clearing. He couldn't have run any farther even if he had been physically able to. He was stopped by very large, very immovable tribesman who asked him who he was, and why he was here.

"Snakefeather," he replied. "I was asked to bring a story to her."

"Who asked?" The heavy-set guard glared suspiciously at Snakefeather.

"Walksoverground," Snakefeather said without any further elaboration.

The heavy-set guard stepped aside, and wordlessly motioned Snakefeather toward the center of the clearing. Snakefeather walked, slowly and deliberately, toward a very large hut, circular, covered in animal skins and held up by large bones. Another guard at the tent flap asked his name again, and motioned for him to wait. Snakefeather waited, while the man ducked inside the tent for a few moments.

It was only a few moments, but it was long enough for Snakefeather to feel the fear rising in his stomach. He wasn't afraid of much—he had killed his share of beasts with nothing but a stone knife and his own hands. He had survived the rains that made deep rivers out of dry places, drowning all in its path. He knew the terror of the fire, ravaging the grassland. He feared none of that.

But this, this was different. She wasn't what she seemed. Her words were said to be like honey, or sweet fruit fresh from the tree. But her deeds were brutal, vicious. Hidden, like a snake in the tall grass or a fanged spider in the deep of night.

Some said she was an evil spirit in human form. Some said she was Sulc, the spider-shadow herself. Most agreed she had powers. Powers not of this world. Powers that did not even have names. She could throw death and fire with her bare hands. She knew what the people of the tribe would do before they did it. The tales grew in the telling, and some were clearly made up. Others, it was hard to tell.

Many claimed she fell from the stars, that she had the power of the star tribe. Snakefeather did not believe that.

If she was an evil spirit, she was a spirit of Mother Earth, not of a point of light in the night sky.

It was also said she spent most of her time in a hut, not out in the world. Snakefeather wondered at that. It didn't make any sense. Why would such a powerful being lock herself away from sunlight, air, water, and rock? Trapped in a hut the day and the night, like one injured or sick with the heat from inside, or the putrid sores.

The guard reappeared. "She is expecting you. Go now." He stood aside, and motioned Snakefeather into the tent. Snakefeather took a deep breath—there wouldn't be much air inside the tent, and besides it helped steady his nerves. He ducked in through the flap.

She was seated, but not on the ground, or even on a rock. *What was she sitting on? What strange magic is even this?* They looked like limbs, from trees, but without their bark, hooked together somehow. Smooth like spears, but much larger around, and short, more like an arm's length than a spear. She did not rise, made no sign or sound of greeting or even acknowledgment. She simply looked at Snakefeather with those eyes.

Those incredible, deep green eyes. That much of the wild tales was certainly true. And she did not look like one of the tribes—her forehead, nose, hair, and build were different. So, it was definitely her.

The one they called Lucy Furs.

"Snakefeather. You have a story to tell me?"

Her voice was... strange. Snakefeather couldn't tell how, but something was just... wrong, the way she spoke. But that wasn't all, he realized, as his eyes adjusted to the gloom in the tent, lit by a small fire.

There were piles of food, more than he'd ever seen in one place. A gathering of fresh fruits from the trees, roots from the ground, freshly killed and even roasted beasts. She saw his stare, and offered, "You may take what you want when we are finished here. For I bring a harvest of plenty. For you. For all of you. Worship me and I'll give you all that you could ever want."

Her words were smooth as river rocks, sweet as ripened fruit. But something felt wrong to him. His eyes grew wider as he panned around the tent and he finally noticed what was right *next* to her. A large triangular pile of white, round objects.

Skulls. Not deer, or hyena, or lion. These were human-sized.

Human skulls.

Snakefeather felt like a great rock lay on his chest. He couldn't breathe or move. But she was waiting for him to speak. He tried to open his mouth, but it just wasn't working. His eyes darted around, like a trapped animal searching for an exit.

Just then, the tent flap flew aside, and a much older man—clearly an elder, and a powerful one at that—strode in, carrying a bundle.

"Ah, Johg! Welcome back. We were just about to hear a story." Lucy nodded to the still-quaking Snakefeather. Johg spared him a brief glance and then ignored him completely, dropping his bundle on the ground on the other side of the tent.

"Fish. The river's edge was plentiful this morning!" Two small children, barely two rains old, perhaps, came tumbling in behind him. They had the same strange look as Lucy, not like normal children of the tribe.

"Jason! Jacob!" she called to the children.

Johg snorted. "You mean Wind, and Knife."

Lucy raised her eyebrows with an imperious look. "Their *names* are Jason and Jacob."

"As you wish, of course. They are yours, after all. But they are also mine. And I shall call them Wind and Knife."

Lucy shook her head. "Of course you will. Fine, the lot of you go spear a fish or chase a lion or something. I have things to tend to here."

She shooed Johg and the strange children out the door.

"Now then. I'm waiting." Lucy Furs crossed her legs on the strange seat-not-on-the-ground.

Snakefeather delivered his message.

Lucy and Johg were standing on a high ridge, looking out over the valley and mountains beyond. The sun was setting, painting a brilliant orange cast over the grassland, the top of the mountain range, the rivers and its forks.

"All I ask is your non-thinking, non-questioning, obedience. We need their land. It's just that simple," Lucy said to Johg.

So much of her words he did not understand. He tried to focus on the ones he did. "Land. So you keep telling me. But that means we would stay there, through all the moons, all the rains. The hunt will come and go, the rains will come and go, yet we will stay? That makes no sense." He shook his head.

So much had changed. It made him uncomfortable. Beautiful as Lucy was, with as much magic as she wielded, and all for his benefit—still, being with her, talking with her was like standing on a small, sharp rock. No matter how you moved, the rock was still there, poking, cutting into your flesh. It moved around, never in the same spot, but it was always there.

She smiled, which somehow reminded Johg of a snake basking on flat rock in the hot sun, and leaned into him, hugging him close. "Following the beasts for hunting is hard. Wouldn't you rather *they* came to you, instead? And spending all your time looking for blossoms to eat. Wouldn't you want them to grow right here, on *your* land, right here when you need them? Instead of in the middle of the jungle, scattered everywhere?"

"My land," Johg echoed, looking out over the vast expanse. It was a strange concept. But Lucy had been right about so many things—well, everything, really.

Lucy straightened up, looking out past Johg. "We need more fertile land. Permanent crops. Actual settlements. And that's just here. I've sent Ashby into the Endless Plains with a scouting party. Room for [expansion], of course." Johg looked at her. More strange words. Even more he just didn't understand.

"We'll need that all that land for ourselves," she continued.

That he did understand. There would be more killing. More taking of the heads, the cleaning of the flesh, and adding them to the growing pile in the tent. At first, Johg thought it an incredibly stupid idea. Too hard to move, didn't serve any purpose. What use was it? But then he saw the reactions, from the Edge Tribes, from the messengers.

Fear.

That was the purpose of the skull pile. Straight up fear. Well, it worked for the first batch of tribespeoples, down on the plain by the river itself. Lucy talked to them, and they resisted. She threw fire at the elders of the tribe, burning them as if lightning from the sky had stuck them down. Johg shuddered at the memory, the smell of burnt stone, the crisped flesh of these men and women who had done no wrong to anyone. The rest of that group submitted without a second thought.

But just within this last few moons, it hadn't gone like that. The tribespeople did not submit after their elders were killed. They attacked, or tried to. Lucy killed them all and had their heads cut off, cleaned, and brought here. That was the start of the skull pile, and it just kept piling higher.

Some part of Johg's brain insisted this wasn't right. This wasn't the world his father and mother had taught him, long ago. It wasn't the world he'd taught his children, the three he had before Lucy came. Here his own family, his own people, were doing the savage killing work of the lion and hyena.

It reminded him of the story of Sulc. The tribes were turning on each other. Surely, Sulc would come and devour him and his family for these killings. Lucy insisted she would protect them—protect them from Sulc and any other evil spirits from this world or the next. But she couldn't protect his own spirit, his own guilt. Johg knew this was wrong. Sulc would devour him, somehow.

But, it was all for his family—his brothers, sisters, children, his children's children. His first responsibility was to them, and not to others. What a strange thought! Such a new, strange world.

But it was his.

Twenty-Four

AHDOM, ALAIN, AND TWOMOONS met back up with Wingeye, Dawnroot, and several others. The Edge Tribes were gathering at this clearing by the river before going farther inland to try and find the she-wolf and her murderous Central Tribe. Earthans from all up and down the coast were coming together. It was an unprecedented event. Wingeye was amazed; the last time he had seen anything like this was during a great fire when he was young. Many were gathered, and even more were to come.

Earlier in the season, O/ had gone north, through the pass in the Great Mountains to gather as many more of the northern tribes as he could find, and were willing to come. They were hoping to meet up here with him, Greatbear, Runningdeer, and others who had gone up through the pass with O/.

The gathering Earthans greeted each other. Some were old friends who hadn't seen each other in several moons. Others had never met. That part wasn't unusual; the land was large, and the Earthans few and constantly moving, following the herds of game and the changing seasons. Outside of your own family and a few local friends, you might never meet that many others in your lifetime. Large gatherings like this, for any reason, were truly once-in-a-short-lifetime events.

Introductions consisted of names, and names of family. No one was really "from" anywhere, of course, so that wasn't part of the conversation. And it wasn't like Earthans had different occupations. "So, what do you do?" wasn't part of Earthan conversation either. Everyone did everything: hunt, scavenge for food, sew, feed and tend the very small and very old, make knives, arrows, spears, pack up and follow the game when needed.

Dusk was settling in, making itself comfortable on the lush landscape. Fires were made, the brave defense of a thin thread of light against the inevitable darkness. Groups of Earthans naturally gathered around the fires, and many more still milled about, aimlessly for now, some in conversation, others looking for a bit of plant or root to eat. In the midst of all these Earthans milling about, the crowd parted and an entirely new group arrived, causing a minor stir.

Twomoons saw who it was and grabbed Ahdom and Alain by the elbow, to take them over in that direction.

"At last!" Twomoons exclaimed. "Outside has arrived. You must meet. He is of your kind, from your place."

Ahdom had heard of the one they called Outside, or gestured as O/, all this time, and his curiosity was overwhelming by now. Alain had heard about Outside, but didn't think much of it. There was no way it could have been anyone from Conglommora. After all, Alain and Ahdom were the only ones out here except for Lucille and her team, but they were far inland from here and in regular contact with Arty. Alain figured it was just some particularly pale and taller Earthan, with atypical Earthan features. Nothing to see here. Just another freak side-show in a land rife with the alien and freakish. But might as well go along with it.

Not that he had a choice, as Twomoons propelled both Alain and Ahdom quickly through the loose group of Earthans over to the latest arrivals. There was a natural part in the sea of humanoids as they wedged their way in, and now, at last, they were face to face.

Alain started, sucked in his breath, his eyebrows fled toward his hairline. He gaped at the stranger known as O/. Only he wasn't a stranger to Alain. The beard was huge, the hair long and unkempt, but he was sure he knew the face.

"Eddie?" Alain asked, trying unsuccessfully to keep the shock out of his voice. "Edward. Edward Thorndike. Is that you?"

O/ broke off the conversation he was signing with Wingeye and spoke aloud for the first time. The Earthans stopped talking and stared at him. O/ had never spoken aloud; it was said he could not. But now he was talking—

although none of the Earthans could understand the strange sounds he was making. But Alain could.

In a rusted and croaking, long disused voice, O/ looked hard at Alain and with a flash of recognition asked, "Charlie's kid? Alain, right?" He came over to Alain. "It *is* you!"

Alain couldn't believe it. "Eddie, we thought… you were dead, man. We looked for you,…" Alain broke off, realizing they hadn't really looked all that hard. They'd left him behind on Earth, years ago. Left him for dead.

Eddie leaned in, hugging Alain tight. "I'm glad to see you. Glad to see another Conglommoran." He pulled back. "I didn't think anyone would ever come back. Arty wouldn't have allowed it. But I'm glad you're here. We need your help." Eddie looked over at Ahdom, who was still trying to process the fact that Alain *knew* who Outside was, and that he was from Conglommora.

Alain answered for him, "This is Ahdom, he's Chalu's son. Chalu is one of the masters from Sea. Good friends with my dad."

Eddie nodded. "Hello, Ahdom, and welcome to Earth, I guess." He smiled at Ahdom, then turned back to Alain. "What are you guys doing here? How many others? Who else is down here?"

"Just us," Alain said. "Just Ahdom and me. Chalu and his team from Sea have a research base in the ocean. They weren't supposed to make contact with the Earthan tribes, but Ahdom accidentally got, er, 'adopted,' I guess, by Wingeye and his people." Eddie looked back at Ahdom and raised an eyebrow. Alain continued, "So, we got special permission to live with and report on the tribes here. But it's just us. Oh, and somewhere, with another tribe inland, Lucille and her training team are working with Earthans. Teaching them farming or something, I think." Alain shrugged.

Eddie stopped smiling. His eyes grew wide, and with his wildly unkempt hair and bushy beard, Alain thought he looked a bit more like the wild Eddie from the corridors, long ago on Conglommora.

There was a long pause, and an agitated finally Eddie spat out a strangled, "What!?"

Alain wasn't sure how to respond. "What... ah, what?" he asked with some confusion.

"Lucy... Lucille Brandeis. She's down here, on Earth? Alone, with the Earthans?" Eddie looked white as a pure ceramic. "Does Arty know?"

"Well, yes, Arty sanctioned her mission. It's just her, with a handful of others. That guy Ashby, who was with us when we first landed. A couple others. Not many. They're supposed to be teaching that tribe better sanitation, agriculture, that sort of thing."

Eddie shook his head, staring hard at the ground. "No, no, no. It can't be." He kicked the ground, hard. Wingeye and Twomoons came over, concerned. Wingeye signed, "Outside, you can speak. But we cannot understand you."

Eddie made a holding motion to them both, turned back to Alain. "Hey, how come you two can talk to the Earthans?"

"Oh, we've got these sublingual translators. Arty made them for us, for emergencies in case we had contact with the Earthans. To try and prevent misunderstandings and further bloodshed."

"Further... ?" Eddie trailed off. Clearly, things had happened after he got separated from Charlie, Robert, and the others. Things he didn't know about yet. He'd get to that, but first things first.

"Can I..." He looked hopefully at Alain.

"Ah! Sure. Hang on." He pulled the small device from his ear canal and handed it over to Eddie. "Just think the words you want first, then sort of move your mouth as the speakerform engages."

Eddie nodded and put the piece in his ear. Then, to the amazement of both Wingeye and Twomoons, he spoke to them in a way they could understand at last. "Wingeye, Twomoons. My friends. I am healed. My friends here, Alain and Ahdom, brought me... something I was missing. I can speak to you now."

Twomoons recovered from the shock first. "You can speak, my friend! I am so pleased. But you seem upset. What news have they told you? What is wrong?"

Eddie sighed. "That is a longer tale in the telling. And I must converse with them more. But it is about the she-wolf. I think I know who she is. Where she is from."

Wingeye jumped back a full pace and spat a vicious oath in guttural Earthan. Twomoons looked like he'd been punched. The whole crowd near them was silent but keenly attentive, trying to piece together the unfolding drama, only some of which they could understand.

Wingeye said, "You… know Sulc? The evil spirit? The she-wolf? Is she… is she of your kind? From outside, from far away?"

Eddie hung his head. "I think so. Maybe. I need to talk to my friends. They do not know why we are gathered here and what we must do. But they can help us."

Wingeye and Twomoons nodded.

Eddie took the translator out and handed it back to Alain. "Here, you'll need this more than me at the moment. But please, could you arrange to get me one of those?"

Alain laughed, "Of course. We've got a supply back at Denisova."

Eddie cocked a confused eyebrow at him.

"The base—that's the name of the research base under the ocean," Ahdom piped up.

"Okay, great. Look, we need to talk. Now. But maybe not here, in the middle of the crowd, though. Tell them we're going to catch up on old times or whatever. Let's head over there." He pointed to a higher bit of ground, away from the fires and gathered Earthans.

"War?" Alain asked.

"That's the closest word for it, yes," Eddie said. "As near as I can figure, a short while after I was stranded here, we started hearing rumors from out of the Central Tribes. A she-wolf, an evil being, some said. Seizing land, killing elders. Even taking their heads after battle."

"Their heads?" Ahdom paled. "What for?"

Eddie shrugged. "Intimidation. Fear. Just to be an asshole. Who knows." He had been pacing back and forth, staying near the small fire the three of them had lit on this little hillock. "At first, it seemed like exaggerations, tall tales. But more and more people were dying. Killed by the she-wolf. She demands loyalty, fealty it seems. Worship, even, as a god. That's not something the Earthans really understand or are used to. I wondered at that, but it never occurred to me..."

He paused, looked down at the spattering, struggling fire.

"It has to be Lucille. If she's down here... she'll have Conglommoran tech. Knowledge. Oh, Lord, it all makes sense now." He kicked at the ground again and stared uselessly at the stars, which were just coming out to watch the show. "She'll have stunners. Probably modified the gain—it's said the she-wolf can throw fire and death from her hands. And that she speaks strangely, her words trail behind her mouth."

"The translator. Of course," Ahdom noted. "Shit. I heard the rumors, too. That's why everyone is gathered here. To find her. To stop her. But I never thought it was Lucille and her team."

"Shit, indeed," Alain said. "If it really is her, this is our fault."

Eddie nodded. "The tribes here intend to head out at first light and find her. Stop her."

Alain cried, "They'll be killed! If she's got modified stunners, energy weapons from Conglommora... no number of Earthans in animal skins with a few spears will succeed."

"I know," Eddie sighed. "I know. We've got to do something."

Ahdom jumped in. "Okay, we have to talk to my dad—to the team on Denisova. We need a large and experienced team, armed with weapons, not just us."

Alain was pacing, too. He rubbed his chin at this last. "Well, I agree we should talk to Chalu. However, I'm not sure that a large team of armed Conglommorans will get us anything other than a big pile of dead Earthans."

Ahdom said, "They can just stun them. They don't have to kill them."

"Don't they?" Alain asked. "We stun them all, say. All the Central Tribespeople. They'll wake up. Find their new she-wolf/witch-queen leader and her henchmen gone. You don't think they'll come after the Edge Tribes for that? Kill all of us? All your friends out there?" He nodded to the massed group.

Ahdom sat down with a flop, by the feeble fire.

Eddie spoke up. "Alain's right. We can't just march in and start shooting up the place."

"What, then?" Alain asked.

"Stealth. We need to take her out quietly. Make her disappear. Then put word out to the tribes that she fled north, through the pass, to the Endless Plains. No one would follow her there."

Alain nodded. "Maybe. That might work. It sounds good at least, in theory." He smiled. "But we'll need help. We don't have equipment, and none of us have the skill for that sort of operation." Both Eddie and Ahdom nodded in agreement.

"I'll send a message to my dad," Ahdom stood up. "Let him know what's up."

"Meanwhile," Alain said, "I think it prudent that we don't leave with the tribes in the morning. What if we hang back, make it look like we're leaving, then split off and head back to the coast?"

"Good idea," Ahdom said. "Dad can meet us there, drop off the extraction team, and we can head back to Denisova. You're welcome to come with us, of course." He gestured to Eddie. "We can get you on the next wave back to Conglommora."

Eddie smiled. "Thanks, thank you both. Really. But my place is here now."

Alain raised both eyebrows in surprise. "You don't want to come back with us?"

"No, not really. Truth be told, back when we first landed here, once we got separated, I didn't try all that hard for you to find me again. At first, it was just an impulse, I think. But I found what I'd always suspected was true: you don't need Arty. You don't need technology, you don't need Conglommora to stay alive. In fact, if anything, Conglommora life is nothing but a living death. This," he looked up and around at the dark of the jungle, "this is real. Real life. Real death. It's honest. True."

He walked a little past the fire, rubbed his hands, and gazed out into the not-at-all quiet of the wilds at night.

"Sure, there's things I miss. Dry hands, for one." He laughed. "Shoes. Wine. But I can live without all that." He waved his hands dismissively.

"I like your plan. Ahdom, go ahead and send the message to Chalu. We'll need help one way or the other. And it's probably best if you don't get caught up in this mess. But I knew Lucille longer than you, Alain. And probably as long as anyone. Robert brought her to my place almost as soon as he uploaded her memories to Grace's body." He turned and shivered slightly. "As creepy as all that was, Robert made it sound so... I don't know, 'reasonable.' He sure talked a good game. Sweet words. That's what they say about Lucy, too. I..."

He paused a moment, then continued. "You two split off, head back to the coast. I'm going to try and meet with Lucille. Talk to her. She'll talk to me, remember me, I think. Maybe reveal her plans. A weakness. Something."

"Do you really think that's a good idea?" Alain asked, surprised. "Not just staying here but confronting Lucy? If it really is her who's behind this, it doesn't sound like she's in much of a talking mood."

"We'll see, I guess," Eddie said. "But I'm the only one who has a *chance* of talking to her. She'd shoot anyone else on sight."

Ahdom sent the message. Chalu was, of course, near panic-stricken over the thought that they would have headed into the conflict in the morning. He was adamant they return to the coast for pickup at daybreak.

"And what about Lucy?" Alain asked Ahdom.

"Dad's contacting Arty now. Arty has been in regular communication with Lucy. It will get in touch with her and find out if she's really behind all this or not."

"Okay. Well, I guess that's it for now. Let's get some rest. We'll head out at first light."

There were nods all around, and Alain, Ahdom, and Eddie each cleared a spot in soft leaves on the warm Earth to bed down for the night. Alain still found it oddly uncomfortable to sleep without a sheet, or blanket, or any kind of covering. Odd what you got used to.

Alain had only just gotten to sleep when the screaming started.

It wasn't quite light out yet, just a little less dark. The screams came from everywhere. Alain jumped up, frantically looked around. Ahdom and Eddie flailed their way to standing at the same time, and the three formed a loose circle, backs to each other instinctively, circling. Ahdom and Alain pulled their stunners out and peered into the dim, looking for attackers, who seemed to be coming from everywhere at once.

In the vids from Dead Earth, Alain remembered seeing images of soldiers fighting each other, in person, on battlefields like this. For some centuries they wore uniforms, identifying which side they were on, and who was who. Later on, more of an insurgent, terrorist-style predominated, with close-quarter attacks like this—not on any battlefield, but right in your home, in the middle of the great cities. Later still, drones and machines carved up the enemy's lands with no regard for who or what was in the way.

This must have been what that middle period felt like, Alain thought. In the murky dim of pre-dawn light, he tried to make sense of the chaos around them. It was hard to find someone or something to shoot at.

The gathered crowd from the Edge Tribes and Northern Tribes were being slaughtered. The energy weapons didn't make much sound, and the quiet sizzling, burning of flesh didn't either. At least, not that you could hear over the screaming. There probably weren't that many attackers—a half-dozen, maybe. But it didn't matter. No one was getting close enough before getting mowed down, and a few hurried spears fell short or wide of the mark.

Two of the attackers broke off from the quickly-thinning crowd and had Alain and the others in their sights.

"Don't move," said the first. To their amazement, even though the attacker looked like a typical Earthan, squat features and all, he didn't speak guttural Earthan. He spoke as one from Conglommora.

"What—" Alain started to protest, but then the beam hit him, Ahdom, and Eddie, all at once.

Twenty-Five

JOCELYN AND EMMEA WERE SITTING in their spherical living room, surrounded by their tapestries, needlepoints, and sculptures; a long life's work of artistic effort. A collection they were now struggling to add to. Normally, the work just flowed from their fingers with the joy of daily practice. But these were not normal days.

Jocelyn put down her needles and spool of microfilament fiber and sighed, turning her attention back to the inescapable screen image of the silent and menacing alien ship. The image remained the same as it had been, the various data being reported was stagnant as well. No change. No news. Nothing.

Emmea looked up. "What's wrong? You've been clinking and fiddling with your needles all afternoon, and haven't actually done a thing!"

"I can't concentrate. Not with that out there. What does any of this even matter?" Jocelyn threw her needles and spool to the deck, stood up angrily and marched to the screen, arms folded across her chest. "What does anything matter?" she said again, softly this time, a lock of her gray hair falling into her face. She didn't bother to move it.

Emmea didn't answer directly, she just gazed out, un-focused on anything in their workshop. "You remember Charlie? The young man who stayed with us that time, and then discovered Earth? He had that creepy fellow with him who caused all the trouble back then."

"Sure," Jocelyn said. They'd had a fair number of visitors over the years but none as famous as Charlie Neylan, of course.

"I wonder if he caused this," Emmea said, gesturing to the screen.

Jocelyn turned around. "How do you figure?"

"I don't know. Disturbing Earth. Surfing through the cosmos on that infernal quantum resonance wave thing. Someone was watching, maybe. Now they've come to kill us all," she finished glumly.

"Pretty sure if they'd wanted to destroy us, or eat us, or anything like that, they would have done that by now. No, not that." She turned back. "Not that. Maybe... maybe they just don't know what they're look-ing at. Maybe we are so strange to them, so... so alien, they just don't even know which end to talk to!"

Emmea laughed at that. "I suppose."

Her smile faded as she acknowledged the same men-tal hatch, sealed shut for them both. Keeping them from enjoying their daily lives. "I know what you mean though. It's hard to... to do anything, really, to keep going, with that…" she waved at the screen, "hanging over our heads."

Jocelyn turned back to look at the screen, afraid, as everyone was, of missing something. "What do they want? Why won't they answer us? What's going to happen? Nothing else really seems to matter with all these questions, all this anxiety."

"What would you say to them, if you could?" Emmea asked.

"Oh, I don't know. Tell them our story, I guess. How the People flourished on the Green Earth of old, how we squandered our inheritance in the cosmos, finally fleeing out here to the edge. You know, broad strokes. Who we are. How we got here. The same thing I'd want to know of them. Who are they, how'd they get here."

"Let's do it," Emmea replied. "Let's do exactly that."

Jocelyn turned back from the screen to face Emmea. "What do you mean?"

Emmea held up a half-completed work. "In pictures. Pictures in the cloth. A long cloth, a tapestry but not for a single wall. A tapestry as long as it needs to be, with pictures to tell our story. The story of the People. From beginning to end…" She caught herself. "…to now."

Jocelyn raised an eyebrow. "Pictures. Even an alien might understand that."

"Might." Emmea nodded.

Jocelyn looked back at the screen. "Okay. It's something to do, at least. And it feels right. Like maybe, just maybe, it might matter." She sighed and picked up her tools from the deck. "Our story in pictures. Here we go." She fitted needle to filament and started working her hands in a familiar and practiced way. "In the beginning…"

They worked that way for the better part of a day, but something was bothering Jocelyn. She stared up at the top of the dome, back at her work, and then off into an unfocused distance before Emmea noticed.

"What's wrong now?" she said, setting her own work aside for a moment.

Jocelyn asked quietly, "Do you think we should include the Cryptic?"

Emmea fell quiet as well as she pondered this deceptively simple question. After a moment or two, she had rediscovered her own opinion. "Yes, yes we should."

"We're not supposed to record it in any permanent media," Jocelyn pointed out. "Oral transmission only, with no Arty monitoring. That's what we agreed to. It's what everyone in the Heart agreed to."

Emmea nodded. "You are right, we did agree. And everyone has kept that agreement ever since… I guess ever since the last days of Green Earth. But I think circumstances are different now. Don't you? Pictures, artifacts…" She swallowed hard. "That may be *all* that's left of us before long. And besides, if it really is true, it's certainly relevant now." She nodded to the screen, the now permanent image of the alien ship.

"Maybe we could show it to them!" Jocelyn laughed, not really seriously. "Maybe then they'll talk to us."

Emmea harrumphed. "Not likely. But just in case…" Her needles and filament flew with new purpose and passion.

Jocelyn thought a moment. "We should tell her. Let her know what we're doing."

Emmea paused, looked up sideways, and nodded in agreement. "Worst she could do is tell us to stop. And I'm not inclined to."

Jocelyn flicked her screen on and pinged their friend, their contact in the Heart.

"Greetings, Faith Langston!" Jocelyn said. "Emmea and I have an idea…"

Carol was working with her friends on a new play. Or trying to. She split her time between that and studying the stuff Arty had sent her.

In Storyville, everyone was usually fully immersed in their elaborate and concocted fantasy creations. But they weren't immune to the alien threat any more than anyone else in Conglommora.

This new play was nominally about the arrival of the aliens, and especially about examining people's reactions. Mostly, Carol thought glumly, it seemed to devolve into meditations on existence, death, the futility of reality, that sort of thing. She tried continually to steer the narrative to a more hopeful, more positive outcome, without much luck.

"For surely, our graves shall be the shallowest of all!" bellowed Phil.

Carol had been studying her shiny, half paying attention to the play. But now she tossed it aside, sprung up off the deck, already in mid froth. "No, no, no!" She matched his volume, if not his resonance. "Can we please stop with this destructive, nihilistic nonsense?"

Phil looked hurt and opened his grand mouth to reply in kind, but Carol cut him off with a wave of her hand and shake of the head.

"Stop. Just stop. If the aliens wanted us dead, we'd be dead by now. That's what everyone's saying. And they are right. So, that's not likely. If they were going to eat us, or torture us slowly—" she glared at Margie, who seemed to keep pushing the whole "torture" angle— "they would have started in well before now. While we were still fresh. Everyone knows that terrified game tastes terrible."

"Carol!" Francie shrieked, repulsive horror clear on her face. "How would you even know that?? And we are *not* game animals!"

"No, no, we're not," Carol replied calmly. "So stop acting like it. Cut this 'shallow grave' shit." She threw down the screen in frustration. "We don't know what they want. Or why they are here. Maybe we'll find out, soon. But maybe we *won't*."

From the semi-circle of blank stares, Phil weakly asked, "What do you mean, maybe we won't?"

Carol cocked her hip. "What if they just go on their merry way, and we never make contact? What if we never find out who they are, or why they are here?"

In the stunned silence, she thought, *now there's some nihilism for you.* She turned back to the corner of the stage where she'd started and flopped down in a heap again. No one spoke as they tried to process this latest setback to their quest for a meaningful narrative. Carol wondered how much more of this uncertainty and unease they could take.

If only there was some way to make contact. According to Arty's reports, they'd tried all manner of transmissions. Different regions of the electromagnetic spectrum, different techniques, quantum and standard, different approaches to "language," including mathematics, physics, and Earth dialects, all with no response at all.

But there was something, something at the back of Carol's mind. On the tip of her tongue. A niggling thought, not quite able to take shape. Floating just out of reach at the edge of her consciousness.

If only she could think what it was.

Avi hadn't slept for at least three full cycles now and hadn't slept well before that. He rested his head against the screen for a moment, even though he was sitting smack in the middle of the Mech Section. Rijm noticed. She shook her head, the crystal spikes coming out of her bald head tinkling gently in the quiet.

"Avi, you've got to get some rest." She came over to his station. "Exhausted people make mistakes. Miss things." She checked her screen, waved it at him. "Your neurotransmitters are a wreck. I'm surprised you're not hallucinating yet."

"Maybe I am." Avi grinned. "Maybe I'm hallucinating *you*." He rubbed his eyes and leaned back. "You're right, of course. I was just hoping to find something, some precedent, some idea. Something Arty missed. Something from an old Green Earth science fiction book, or a tall tale told on the ships." He looked out over all of the glowing, swirling, mechanically innovative and artistically expressive projects that spilled all over each other in the Mech Section. "All of this," he said, waving his hand. "All of this and no one has a better idea? Some way to contact the aliens that we haven't thought of?"

Rijm grimaced. "Apparently not. But maybe it's not the method or the medium that's the problem," she said with the sudden fresh energy of a new idea. "It's time."

Avi blinked hard, tried to focus his bleary eyes. "How do you mean?"

"Clearly, they are much more advanced than us. Maybe all our attempts have just been too slow to be perceived as communication. Maybe we need a ridiculously fast, dense, high energy pulse. Somewhere in the trillionths of a second range, or even shorter."

Avi shook his head. "I think Arty tried that. I'd be afraid that sort of pulse would look an awful lot like an offensive weapon. But who knows." He stood up, stretched. "Check it out with Arty. I'll go dream about it. Wake me if anything historic happens."

Rijm laughed. "You got it. But take a full sleep cycle, will you? I promise not to make human history while you're asleep."

"Sure," Avi said as he walked away, unsteadily, mumbling, "No history. Sleep. See you in a bit."

Rijm turned to the screen and started investigating vanishingly short message formats.

Twenty-Six

ALAIN WOKE UP, his back to a large tree. At least, he assumed it was a tree. He could feel large, gnarled roots under his legs and up his back. He couldn't see anything because of the blindfold. His hands were bound in front of him, but it didn't feel like leather, or vines, or any sort of rope. It felt cold, hard. Metal. Not Earthan.

He sat there quietly, trying to listen, trying to take in what was going on around him. But there wasn't much to hear. Just the background jungle noises, which although not exactly quiet, were at least accustomed. The crunch of footsteps. Not hurried, and not close. But someone was nearby.

Just once, I'd like to visit Earth without getting attacked or captured. He gave an internal grimace. Still, getting knocked out by a stunner was better than being hit with a rock or run through with a spear. So maybe things were improving, after all.

The crunch of footsteps was louder now. Someone was coming. Alain stiffened, involuntarily, waiting for the cliché of a dramatic reveal, perhaps a sucker punch, or some other historical expression of violence and mayhem.

But instead, a pair of hands simply removed the blindfold. Alain blinked in the bright sun and looked up at the man standing in front of him. He was an Earthan. Until he opened his mouth.

"Sorry we had to stun you. But it was necessary. We will be leaving shortly. You'll need to walk," the man said. He wasn't grunting Earthan, and Alain realized two things: he could understand him without the translator, and he no longer had his translator. The man turned and walked away, and Alain noted Ahdom was seated nearby as well, propped against the next tree.

"Ahdom! Are you okay?" Alain asked.

Ahdom shook his head to clear it. "Just once, I'd like to meet Earthans and not be attacked or captured."

"Hah. I was just thinking the exact same thing," Alain laughed, darkly. "But these guys aren't exactly Earthans. I mean, they look like them, but—"

Ahdom interrupted. "But they don't talk like them. Or even, I don't know, *walk* like them? Just not the same. Almost like, I don't know. Not like the Earthans we've been with." He shrugged.

"I know what you mean," Alain agreed. "I have an idea about that. It might have to do with—"

"Hang on," Ahdom stopped him. Two of the Earthans had turned and were approaching again.

"Come on," said the first. "Stand up. This way." He gestured.

Alain and Ahdom stood and started walking in the direction indicated. Another pair of Earthans, a man and woman, were herding Eddie in front of them. Eddie nodded acknowledgment but didn't say anything out loud. Alain nodded back. Best not to offer any additional information to these odd Earthans.

They handed Alain and Ahdom off to Eddie and his captors. "Teagen, Karl. You take them from here. We're headed to the coast. Meet you back at the main camp." Then they took off to the west.

Teagen and Karl herded the three captives almost due eastward, to the heart of the Central Tribes at the base of the mountain range. Where, Alain figured, Lucille would be waiting. Well, they'd find out soon enough.

It was a lengthy trek, and their captors said very little. Ahdom was very quiet. After several hours, Alain asked him if he was okay.

"Worried about Dawnroot," he said quietly, through clenched teeth. "And Greatbear. Twomoons. The others." His head sagged under the weight of anxiety and anticipated grief.

Alain didn't press him further. There was no telling who had escaped and who hadn't. But it seemed that a great many Earthans were killed outright. It was possible that very few escaped. No Earthans had been captured, as far as they'd seen. Just the three of them. Alain wondered if they had been the intended target, or were they just a surprise benefit?

It was hot now, in the midday sun. They stopped and rested for a while. Teagen had a few small water canteens and shared them with the three captives. Karl went on ahead a bit while they sat. Alain briefly considered rushing Teagen, but she was far enough away and kept the stunner in her hand, more or less trained on them the whole time. It would only take a fraction of a second to get vaporized. Alain swallowed hard. Might as well let this play out, at least for now.

Karl came back just then, anyway, and motioned for them to get up, to continue. They did, without a word.

Another hour or two and they climbed a small set of foothills to an encampment. There were several huts, or tents, in the style of the Earthans. Teagen led them to one of the larger tents, set to the side of the camp closest to the mountains.

Alain stumbled a little as they entered the dark of the hut. Teagen led him to one side, Karl had Eddie and Ahdom on the other. "Turn, stand here," she said. "Back up a step." Alain did and felt a cold, smooth metal plate or wall behind him. And around his legs. Now around his upper arms. The metal restraints popped off, but his arms were pinned. He was seized by the unforgiving, sinuous metal completely, and pinned to the plate. Which started to then recline backward, motoring to a horizontal position.

"What the…?"

"Hey!"

"Shit, no!"

Each of the three captives let out their own short, frustrated yelp before the tables locked them into position, staring at the top of the tent. Teagen and Karl checked each of them, made sure they were immobile, then left them.

Helpless.

———————

Eddie broke the silence first. "Please tell me you gentlemen still have your translators, and that someone from Denisova can track us here," he asked in a less-than-steady voice.

"No. We do not." Ahdom replied simply. What else was there to say?

"How screwed are we?" Alain asked, knowing the answer but hoping for something more.

"Pretty damn screwed," Eddie spat. "So much for trying to get a meeting to talk with her. More likely she'll be eating pudding out of our dead skulls by nightfall."

Ahdom practically screamed, a powerful but ultimately silent gurgle that barely made it past his lips.

"Nice." Alain shot a dirty look toward Eddie. Not that Eddie could see him. The tables were arranged with their heads to the center of the tent, feet pointing to the outer rim.

And so they waited. And worried. And waited some more. Finally, there was a bustle at the door, and Alain saw her.

Grace Langston. Charlie's girlfriend. That's who was when she was born. Taken over by the long-dead Lucille Brandais. Restored using some long-forgotten tech by

Robert. Lucille, with the dead animal fur around her neck, known to the Earthans as Lucy Furs, or simply Lucyfur.

"Well, aren't the three of you a splendid sight!" she gushed. It might have been genuine, but Alain thought it not.

"Edward! So, the reports were true. I thought you long dead. Killed by a lion or something on our very first landing."

"Not at all," Eddie replied with a forced calm. "I survived. No thanks to you and the rest of Conglommora." He looked down, past his nose at his prone form on the table. "I've survived worse than you. And as God is my witness, I'll survive you yet."

"Of course, of course," Lucy said cheerfully, not believing him for a moment. "Alain! My, you've grown. Last time I saw you, you were but a boy. How is dear old Charlie?"

"Dad's fine," Alain said coolly. "He's probably on his way here now, with a heavily armed rescue team. You better let us go while you can." It was a lame bluff, and Alain knew it, but what the hell.

"Oh, I don't think so." Lucy moved on to Ahdom. "I do not know you. They tell me you are called Ahdom."

"I am." Ahdom tried to lift his head up, a gesture to try and indicate some level of importance. "And my father is on his way now with a team from Denisova. You won't get away with this. Even the Central Tribes will turn on you once they know what you're doing!"

Lucy laughed gently, a distant echo of Grace's body's good nature. "No, I don't think so. No one will come for you. You're mine now. And the tribes won't help you. They fear you. As I taught them. Fear the strangers. Fear their stories. They are ruinous. No, you'll get no help from them. Welcome to Earth." Again, that sweet smile, filled with poison.

Alain jumped in, tried to seize the conversation. "The ones who brought us here, Teagen and Karl. Those aren't Earthan names, are they? They don't act exactly Earthan, either. You did something to them. Like you did to Grace."

Ahdom sucked in his breath. Antagonizing your captor was not a great plan, in his mind.

But Lucy just laughed gently. "Yes, something like that. Teagen and Karl have been loyal assistants for, well, thousands of years, really."

Ahdom's eyebrows crept up into his hairline and threatened to disappear.

Alain persisted, "But how? How is that possible? Your ship, the *Uten*, was destroyed along with all your gear. I was there. We barely escaped with our lives, let alone a stash of ancient, forbidden tech."

"Ha!" Lucy threw her head back. It was not a pleasant motion, not like a human female, more like a wolf, baying at the moon. Alain wondered at her nickname, the "she-wolf," and began to see how she might have earned it.

"You, and Charlie, and Arty… all of Conglommora. You're like children. You don't notice anything. You don't see. Robert and I could have arrived with an armada; an entire fleet of ships, right at your very doorstep! And you'd probably just sit there, wondering what to do. Fretting. Bah!" She turned suddenly. "It was easy enough, I grabbed the memory modules from the *Uten* before she exploded and hid them in a cave here on Earth when I landed in the small craft. I knew I'd be back. And you would never know where to even look." She smiled an oily, dismissive smile at Alain.

"You won't get away with this," Alain maintained. He was pretty sure he'd heard that line in a vid from Dead Earth. It didn't work in that narrative, and he was pretty sure it wasn't going to work here. But he pressed on anyway, in defiance of logic and the inevitability of whatever gruesome doom awaited them.

"Arty will find out! My dad will find out. You're starting a war down here! Whether they come looking for us or not, whether they find us or not, they won't let you do that. Arty's mission is to protect humans. From you! If needed. Arty will stop you and your war," Alain finished with a boisterous confidence that he knew was a stretch at best.

"Pish. Nothing of the kind." Lucy waved her hand dismissively. "There is no war. I'm merely helping teach the Earthans how to farm and get clean water. Cook their meats better. War? No. Some natives are always running around killing each other. That's not my doing." Again, the oily smile, "Certainly nothing you could prove. Besides, you're dead. As far as anyone on Denisova or Conglommora will ever know. We threw your translators into the ocean. They'll think you drowned, your bodies lost to the unreachable depths. There will be no search party, no rescue mission. I'll send my usual, very unexciting status report to Arty, on time, on schedule. No one here ever saw you. There is no war, and certainly not of my making. Meanwhile, you are my guests. Oh, don't worry, you won't be killed."

She rolled her eyes in a decidedly creepy manner. "Not yet. Not if you cooperate. First, I need to extract some DNA. This Earthan material is crude, unrefined. We can fix that. Then I'm going to wipe you. I have a few old, dear friends I really miss. I wouldn't dishonor their memory by implanting them in a crude Earthan body. But a nice, young, healthy body, direct from Conglommora? That will do. Even you, Edward." She glanced over at the wild and unkempt Eddie, who was just about frothing with rage at this point.

"You'll donate. You'll be wiped. But you'll be alive. So, count that as a plus. Good night, gentlemen." With that, she turned on her heel and vanished out the door.

"Stop! No!" Ahdom cried out, but Lucy was gone.

Eddie shot back, "Right, that's going to stop her. Please, whine some more!" he shouted, emphasizing each word with a spray of spittle.

"Okay, okay, not helpful," Alain declared. "We need a plan. Escape or call for help. Or both. Something. We can't just lie here strapped to these tables, helpless!"

Eddie sighed loudly. "In fact, that's exactly *all* we can do."

Twenty-Seven

NIGHT CAME, BUT NO ONE ELSE DID. Ahdom, Alain, and Eddie were still trapped on the unyielding metal of the tables, alone. They hadn't spoken in some time, and Alain was at least trying to get some sleep.

Eddie seemed to keep his head in constant motion, trying to see the flap at the entrance to the tent, keeping an eye on both his companions. Nervously expecting something to change. Nothing did. The dark and the still of night dragged on, and finally, even Eddie settled down.

Ahdom tried to sleep but always preferred to sleep on his side or stomach, rarely on his back. Being strapped flat to a cold metal table wasn't really conducive to restful sleep, even without the grief over his Earthan friends or worry about his own impending doom. Any one of these would be enough to chase sleep away and keep it at a fair distance. But together? There would be no sleeping.

Ahdom heard the rustle first. Down near the ground, behind them—the side of the tent opposite the opening. An animal, maybe? Something burrowing in? He craned his neck but couldn't see. He started to open his mouth to alert Alain and Eddie, but a hand quickly clamped his mouth shut.

He looked up in surprise to see Dawnroot. Ahdom's eyes grew as big as landing craft, and his soul almost exploded with relief. She was alive. She had found them. Everything would be all right after all.

Dawnroot held her palm flat to her mouth and slowly let go of Ahdom. He understood. She leaned in close, and they kissed.

Alain woke abruptly and started to gurgle a scream but quickly recovered himself as he saw who it was. It was enough to rouse Eddie, who jerked his head over with a start.

"Dawnroot!" Alain whispered loudly. "I am *so* glad to see you. Where are the others? Can you get us out of here?"

Ahdom whispered at almost the same time, "How did you find us? Greatbear and the others, is everyone okay?"

Dawnroot's eyes darted continuously, scanned the tent and contents, and watched the tent opening, cautiously. She tried to answer, but it only came out in guttural Earthan.

"Damn! No translators." Ahdom clenched his fists and his jaw.

Alain called over, "Surely, you taught her at least a few words from our language, and she taught you some Earthan?"

Ahdom sighed. "Only a little. A handful of words."

Eddie piped up. "I can help, I've learned a little, but I mostly rely on pictures, and I can't draw with my hands shackled." He rattled his skinny arm bones against the restraints.

Ahdom grimaced. "All right, well, best we can do then." In Earthan, Ahdom tried to ask: "how here?" and pointed to the table, with a quizzical look on his face.

Eddie added a few clarifying grunts.

Dawnroot seemed to understand and nodded. She tried to talk slowly, and Eddie and Ahdom both chimed in with whatever fragments they could understand.

"They don't camp right."

"Only me. Don't know about others."

"Followed to here."

"Poor hunters! They stand tall but as with sleep still in their eyes."

Eddie worked out that last part with the help of some hand and finger gestures.

"Tied. Flat stone. Tied by the stone. Knife cannot cut."

"No, I suppose a stone knife wouldn't help," Alain confirmed. "Her knife would chip and shatter. Ask her to look for a button, or several buttons on the table, that will release us."

Ahdom groaned. "You've got to be kidding."

Eddie said, "Let me try," and addressed Dawnroot in what Earthan he knew. "Rock. Small rock. Smooth, polished, round. On big rock. Find?"

Dawnroot looked at Alain with confusion. Eddie repeated, and Ahdom pointed to the table. "Small rocks?"

She dropped to her knees beside Ahdom, felt along the smooth of the table in the dark, scanned with her keen eyes in the gloom. After several minutes, she stood up again.

"Flat and smooth. No smaller rocks," Eddie relayed.

"Damn," Alain cursed quietly. "But it makes sense. No local controls."

Dawnroot looked increasingly puzzled. "Trapped in stone?" Eddie translated.

Ahdom thought a second. "She can't free us herself. She'll need help. We need to contact my father. Eddie, tell her."

"Find Ahdom's elders. Tribe come. Help," Eddie managed.

She cried out, a long stream, Eddie picked out the pieces he could. "Tribe far away. Past mountains, moon after moon. Too long, die here trapped by stone."

"Tell her, she can call to them. They will come. It's almost…" Ahdom hesitated here. "Almost a kind of magic."

Dawnroot was listening attentively. So were Alain and Eddie, for that matter. Alain was wondering where Ahdom was possibly going with this supposed "escape" plan.

Ahdom told Eddie, "Tell her to go down from here, down from the mountains. Follow the great river, to the ocean shore. There, stand on the very edge of the shoreline itself, in the spot where the trees meet the water in a circle. You know the place? It's where her tribe first found me."

Eddie grunted assent, which seemed to work well both on Conglommora and on Earth. He stitched together a broken sentence. "Where found Ahdom. Go. Great water circle, trees, waves. Sand."

Dawnroot nodded. "But no tribe there, no camp, nothing..." Eddie relayed.

"I know." Ahdom nodded. "My tribe is not there. But they can hear you there. From far away, they can hear. Stand on the shoreline, face the ocean, and shout 'Denisova! Denisova! I have a message from Ahdom and Alain. They need your help. Quickly!' When they come, lead them here."

Eddie groaned but tried to convey that. "They hear. From far, they hear. Call 'Denisova'. Ask help. Bring here."

Dawnroot nodded again. "Denisova is father?"

Ahdom understood that directly and smiled gently, "No, Denisova is home."

Dawnroot shook her head. She didn't understand how Ahdom's tribe could possibly hear her from across the ocean. Or why Ahdom and Alain could no longer speak to her. But she trusted these strange times and tried to say as much.

"Something, something…, words be heard clear and true," Eddie stammered. "I think that's a 'yes'. I think she's got it."

Dawnroot bent over Ahdom, they kissed again, and with the barest rustle, she vanished into the darkness.

Alain relaxed, as much as he could, bound to the slab. "Okay, I think she understood. At least we've got a message out. We might even get rescued now," he said with obvious relief in his voice. But it was short-lived, as there was suddenly a commotion at the tent flap, and two of the guards entered and stood there.

Now Ahdom was worried. He hissed over to Alain, "You don't think they got Dawn…"

"Shhh," Alain silenced him quickly. "Don't say anything yet."

Moments passed in the gloom of the tent. The guards seemed to be waiting for something. More commotion, and a new figure entered the tent.

Lucy.

"Hello, friends!" she greeted them cheerily. "Who's first tonight?"

"Screw you," Eddie spat through clenched teeth.

"Wonderful! A volunteer." Lucille strode over to Eddie's slab. She set down a small device on the end of the table, which bathed the whole tent in a sickly, pale blue glow. She noticed their worried glances at it.

"That's just a lightform. Nothing to be worried about." She smiled slightly and drew a small, silver, rectangular box from an animal-hide pouch hanging off her belt. "This, however. Now, this is something. This is your future."

She put the box on Eddie's forehead, and his whole head, shoulders, and upper torso froze immediately. The rest of him continued to squirm against the restraints. "I love this part." Lucy was positively gleeful. She made some small motion, maybe it was a control gesture or maybe she merely pressed a button or switch of some sort.

Long, thin metal tentacles flung themselves out of the box and instantly buried themselves in the corners of Eddie's horrified, frozen open eyeballs. They dug in, winding themselves into his skull, into his brain. Eddie was screaming with his whole body, even though only his legs and hands could move.

Shit. Alain thought. *This is real. Lucy's going to kill us just like she killed Grace.* He tugged on the restraints on the slab which remained as unyielding as ever. Trapped. No way out.

Eddie continued convulsing, and Lucy brought out another small box.

But just then another guard entered the tent. "Ma'am. Johg requests you come, right away. He says it is urgent."

"Oh, that man is such an idiot," Lucy sighed. "Fine, I was only just now getting started. Can't interrupt the burn-in once it begins." She waved and the tentacles flew out of his eyeballs with a fine red mist and retracted back into the silver box. She retrieved her lightform and sighed. "I'll be back. Don't you boys go anywhere." And with that, she turned on her heel and disappeared back out the tent flap as quickly as she came. The two guards followed her out.

Eddie was sobbing quietly.

Ahdom whispered as loud as he dared, "Are you okay? Edward? Are you okay?"

"I'm all right," Eddie managed, gasping in a mix of horror, pain, and fear. "I'm all right. It was like... like watching a dream. Someone else's dream. Not mine."

His breathing settled down, and Alain and Ahdom could do nothing but wait.

And hope.

———————

"Oliver, you better come see this," the young man called through the hatch. Oliver looked up from the remains of his lunch in a quiet corner of Denisova. He sighed, wiped his mouth, and took his empty meal containers to the reclaimer.

"What do you have now, Emil?" Oliver asked gently, walking over. He imagined some previously unknown species of flora or fauna had made a surprise appearance.

Emil didn't answer straight away but motioned Oliver to follow and stepped quickly back through the hatch. Oliver followed him, curiosity mounting. This wasn't standard procedure. They walked over to a monitoring bay, filled with screens. Each was showing the same scene, a young Earthan girl on the shore, waving her hands frantically.

"Speakerforms up, translator online," Emil commanded. Audio filled the small room.

"Denisova! Denisova!" the girl cried.

"What the hell…" Oliver started, and quickly turned to Emil. "How does she…"

Emil just nodded back to the screen.

"I have a message from Ahdom and Alain. They need your help! They are trapped by the stone! Please, hurry!"

Oliver made a quick swipe on the nearest screen. "Chalu! Report to monitoring station three immediately." Another swipe. "Attention, Denisova. Assemble rescue team at launch bay one. Will meet you there in two minutes."

"How long has she been doing this?" Oliver looked back over to Emil.

"We picked up the audio probably right when she arrived. I tuned in the image not more than a minute or two after that."

Chalu came bursting through the hatch. "What's happened? what's wrong?"

Oliver put his hand on his shoulder. "It's Ahdom. He's in trouble. He sent us a message."

The speakerforms were still carrying the live audio feed. "Hurry! She'll kill them all! Alain and Ahdom need your help! Come quickly! Denisova, Denisova, hear me!"

Chalu stared incredulously at the screen. "I know that girl. That's Dawnroot."

"Come on." Oliver propelled Chalu through the hatch. "We'll talk about it on the way." They broke into a run across the grand hall of Denisova toward the launch bays.

———

The tadpole shot out from the launch bay, headed to the shoreline where Dawnroot was still calling out to the sea.

"I copied Dawnroot's message to Arty, but still no reply," Oliver reported.

"How long since the last reply from *anyone* at Conglommora?" Chalu asked.

"Four or five days at least." Oliver shook his head. "At least for any official communications."

"And still no ships via the wave either?"

"No. There was a scheduled transport supposed to arrive yesterday. It didn't."

"Something must be down on Conglommora." Chalu shook his head. "But I can't imagine what. I could see problems with the resonance wave, maybe. But *every* qradio? They can't all be broken. There has to be some reason they don't want to use them."

Oliver nodded. "Well, it's a stretch, but I've been putting some data together over the last days. Take a look at this." He rotated his chairform on the tadpole, and he and Chalu faced a bank of screens.

"I looked through some of the last reports Arty sent. Now, these might be helpful." He pointed to the screen in the upper left of the bank.

"Those are really high-resolution scans." Chalu pointed to the screen, made a gesture and the image zoomed in. He could make out individual beasts gathered in a clearing, out from under the jungle canopy. Looked like a watering hole. "I thought the weather satellites wouldn't give us fine results like that."

Oliver nodded again. "They couldn't. Not at first. But according to this report, Arty included a higher-resolution satellite in that last batch we launched. Apparently, it didn't get a timely reply from Lucille and her group. Then Alain came down and he and Ahdom started the mission to the Earthans. I suppose those were reasons enough, so now we have high-res imagery."

"So, we can pinpoint their exact location?"

"Well, we could, if we could contact Conglommora. Get Arty to maneuver the satellites, concentrate on the area we need, get fresh data. These scans are five days old by now."

Chalu's relief was short-lived. "Damn."

"And there's more," Oliver continued. "Part of the weather sensors on the satellites look for energy discharges, to map surface lightning storms, right?" Chalu nodded. "But look at this." Oliver pointed to the screen on the lower right. "These readings were anomalous. Energy discharges all right, but these weren't lightning events."

Chalu looked closely at the screen. "No, not lightning. Much, much smaller. No longer than a shuttle or a tadpole! But a lot of energy in such a small space." He looked at the energy signature more closely, and his eyebrows shot up. "It looks almost like…"

Oliver turned from the screen and looked at his friend. "Yes. The readings seem to indicate energy weapon discharge. The same type and style as the stunners that we used to equip the landing parties, but much stronger. They've been modified. To be fatal."

Chalu leaned back. "Shit."

Emil called over. "Chalu, Oliver. Here's that tracking you wanted." The top screen changed view.

Chalu leapt from his chairform. "At the bottom of the ocean?!"

"Ahdom wasn't attached to it," Emil hurriedly called over. "Biosign tracking stopped in the middle of the plain, south of the river. It looks like both Alain's and Ahdom's translators were removed there, and then ditched into the ocean by another person."

Chalu slumped back. "I just can't take this." He held his head in his hands, gathering his breathing and composure. Ahdom was alive, at least when Dawnroot saw him last. But how much time did they have?

"What can we track without Arty's processing power?" Chalu asked.

Oliver spun his chair back around. "Peter?"

Peter turned to face Chalu. "Arty was tracking group movement with the regular satellites. Not fine enough to detect single individuals, or even groups of individuals, but overall patterns of tribes and herds. It was enough. We have data on a recent Earthan camp. Much larger than usual, and not in the usual patterns. Arty projected it was Lucille's new camp."

"Lucille?" Chalu had heard the rumors, too, via Ahdom and Alain's feeds. But how much of that was mere Earthan superstition or misunderstanding? Could Lucille really be behind the attacks on the tribes? Could she be responsible for taking Ahdom and Alain? Who else would know to remove their translators? Not the natives. But why? Chalu felt a weight in the pit of his stomach. He had always been uneasy at the thought of Lucille. But the pieces were falling into place. It might be much worse than he imagined. And if so, Ahdom and Alain were in mortal danger.

Oliver spoke up. "Perhaps Conglommora is observing quantum radio silence because of Lucille."

Chalu frowned. "That doesn't make a whole lot of sense. Arty could always send us a directed encrypted message."

"Maybe." Oliver shrugged. "Maybe she has a way of breaking into messages. Or maybe Arty doesn't want her listening in at all. I don't know. But it's possible. Think about it. She breaks off communication. There are new attacks on the Earthans. Our research party is kidnapped, their trackers and translators removed and thrown into the ocean. Not destroyed but thrown away. Maybe to make us think the boys drowned. It sure sounds pretty deliberate to me. It sounds like Lucille is responsible. Who else could it be?" He threw his hands in the air.

Chalu sat in silence for a moment, looked out at the sea rushing past, and at his partial, dark reflection at the same time. They were coming up close to shore now. He turned away from the others, opened a private stream to his wife Chrys and filled her in on the latest. Worry for their son tore at them both but fueled their resolve as well. Chalu ended the stream grim but with an even stronger determination. He would save Ahdom at any cost.

Up front, the captain called out, "Surface and adjust attitude. Match grav levels."

Chalu swiped. "Shore image." It had been well over an hour by now, and the girl on the beach was crumpled into a hoarse and exhausted heap. That was actually great fortune, Chalu thought. "Captain!" he called up. "Slow and quiet. Try not to wake her. Less explaining to do that way if she doesn't see the ship."

"I'll do my best, Chalu," the man said and eased the tadpole up slowly from the crashing waves. Ocean water drained off the sides and back in rivers as usual, and the ship hovered silently and smoothly above the waves, gliding in to the sand. They were walking quickly but quietly down the stairform when Dawnroot woke with a start. And a scream.

Twenty-Eight

CAROL HAD A LITTLE BIT OF LUCK trying to get a more positive narrative out of Phil and the company of players. Not a lot, but a little. She had them come around to the idea that even small things matter. Small things, added up, can make a big difference. Life's like that, she argued. A smile here, a helping hand there, all small things. But over the whole of Conglommora, it made life *possible*. Without it, without that small daily hope, well, they'd be dead in space. A darkened hulk a...

Darkened.

That was it.

Carol jumped out of her chairform, scattering props and people alike, and almost flew across the stage to the utility screen set in the wallform.

"Carol! What the hell?" Phil cried out. There were other voices of alarm as well, but she could only hear Phil over the din.

"I know what we can do. How to contact the aliens. Of course! I know how to reach them!"

She waved at the screen. "Arty! I've got an idea."

"Yes, Carol?" came the predictably unexcited voice.

"Remember the *Ycham*? Do that. With the aliens. With *all* of Conglommora. Use a transcendental number, polynomial sequences, something basic."

There was a pause. The entire room held its collective breath. Phil, for a change, said nothing.

Arty's voice broke the stillness. "Yes. An excellent idea, Carol. And unlike the proposed high-energy bursts and quantum shift techniques, this should in no way appear to be a threat. In fact, quite the opposite. Well done. Please stand by."

Carol relaxed and backed from the wall a step. Phil broke the silence, but gently, and not with his usual bombastic tone. "What did you mean, about the *Ycham*? That's the ship that almost killed you, right?"

"The lights, the power." Carol pointed to the light-forms spread uniformly across the ceiling. "That's how we signaled to Arty that we were coming in hot, no comms, no engine power. There are twelve docking tubes. We signaled the number thirteen by turning all the ship's power off and back on again thirteen times. It was a stretch, for sure, but Arty figured it out."

"Attention, Conglommora, attention please." Arty's voice came from everywhere. "In an attempt to contact the alien ship, I will be coordinating a series of timed power cuts to all of Conglommora. All systems will be shut down at once, in sub-second bursts. Gravity and life support should not be noticeably affected. However, it is possible that any marginal equipment that is close to a maintenance interval may not come back online. For your own safety, please return to your house and secure yourself there. The attempt will begin one hour from now."

And at that last, the image of the alien ship had a new piece of data overlaid on it: a countdown clock: 100. 99. 98. 97. The minutes would tick down, giving everyone time to get secured. And prepared. For anything.

"Carol, I…" Phil croaked. "I don't know what to say. That's brilliant."

"Well, we'll see," Carol sighed. "It might not work either. But at least we will have tried." She turned and headed for the hatch. "I'm taking Arty's advice. You should, too. Strap in. I've been bounced out of one ship too many lately." Carol left them, and headed back to her house.

Maybe, just maybe, she hoped, *this will actually work.*

Twenty-Nine

KÄTHE AND I SAT ON THE EDGE of our chairform, staring intently at the screen, holding hands.

"Well, this is it, maybe." I said. "I mean, it worked once. And Arty is kind of alien compared to humans, right?" I looked at Käthe earnestly.

"Sure. Let's say it's exactly the same thing," Käthe said with a trace of sarcasm. "Don't get me wrong, I *really* hope this works. For everyone's sakes. But Arty's tried just about everything. Maybe these aliens don't even talk. Or think about numbers, or mathematics. Maybe they don't even perceive light, or any part of the EM spectrum. Maybe…"

I reached over, and gently took her chin, still quivering with possible excuses to cushion the inevitable disappointment of another failed attempt. I kissed her. She stopped.

"Or, maybe, just maybe, it will work. In fact, I know it will."

Käthe looked at me sideways. "How could you possibly know such a thing?"

I grinned. "Because I am Charlie Neylan! Discoverer of worlds!"

Käthe tilted her head back and laughed. "Well, in that case."

"Besides, that girl Carol saved Alain's life with this same idea. If it worked once…"

"I really don't think it works that way. But why not. Let's be optimistic." She forced a deliberately cheerful grin.

"Okay, hush now, here it comes." I pointed to the screen. 2. 1.

"Attention, Conglommora, attention." Arty was punctual, of course. "Conglommora-wide sub-second power cut sequences begin in 3… 2… 1… now."

You almost couldn't tell. Maybe there was a little fluctuation in the local gravity field, maybe it was my imagination.

Seconds went by. Were more sequences being transmitted? Arty wasn't reporting.

"Please standby. The next sequence will use longer timing. Power cut effects may be more pronounced."

The lights noticeably dimmed. I felt my legs float up ever so subtly from the deck, then back down again. Käthe whipped her head to meet my gaze; she felt it, too. I exhaled loudly as I'd forgotten to breathe. Again. But it wasn't just me.

All of Conglommora held its breath.

Suddenly, every screen that was receiving the stream of the alien ship and status—which was in fact, every screen, period—turned bright green. The single word "SUCCESS" popped up. An instant later, Arty's mellifluous voice addressed the entirety of humanity once again.

"Attention. This communication attempt has been successful. I am now in contact with the alien ship. They intend us no harm. I repeat, the aliens are peaceful and intend no harm to Conglommora or the human race. Please turn your attention to the live stream for details and synoptic reports in real time. Thank you for your attention."

Despite the vacuum of space, you could probably hear the whoops, hoots, hollers, screams, and literal jumping for joy as the many millions throughout Conglommora discovered they had a new lease on life. The aliens weren't here to blow us out of the heavens or serve us for dinner.

Käthe and I jumped up in almost perfect unison and met in mid-air with a hug. Gravity in Käthe's house—our house—did seem a little lighter than usual. In the back of my mind, I made a note to take a look at that later. But for now, we hugged and kissed as we gently came back down to the deck.

Data was pouring out of the screen. There was a live feed, incomprehensibly dense and fast, and a synopsis that Arty was synthesizing as the data from the alien ship came in.

There were several sections of the report, with more coming in every second. I let go of Käthe and made a swipe at the screen.

"Okay, so first up, what happened? How did the aliens finally answer us?" Käthe asked.

I punched up that section of the report. "They didn't. Look at this." I pointed Käthe to the part I was reading. "Arty is talking to their computer system. It noticed the patterns in our power fluctuations, saw transcendental numbers and realized there was intelligence here. It started blinking a glowing field at the highest end of the EM spectrum in return. Arty and their AI built up a language, and are now communicating using our more conventional means."

"That was fast," Käthe said with a cocked eyebrow.

"Well, you know, computers."

"So, who are they?"

I was already scrolling to the next part of the report. "Here." We read together. I started reading the choice parts out loud.

"They call themselves *Gentle Beings*. The best Arty can do for a translation is the name *Guethl*."

"Picture?" Käthe asked.

"Here." I found it, brought it up. We both took a step back from the screen. "Well, now that's something. That's One Who Scans."

"That's its name?"

I brought up more details. "They don't do names like we do… oh, look here. Because they aren't always a unity creature like this guy. Ah, there's the captain. The One In Charge."

"They look identical," Käthe noted.

"Sure do. But not exactly, look." I brought up images of One Who Scans and One In Charge side by side.

"They look like crystals," Käthe said. "Like snakes, made out of crystals."

"Modular. They are modular beings, for lack of a better word," I saw. "Like nine-sided polyhedrons, in the middle part. And they trade pieces with each other!"

"Are these actually real pictures of them?"

"No, look here: they live in the mid and far infra-red. Non-visible wavelengths to us. Arty colored the images here so we could see them."

"This is taking too long," Käthe said impatiently. "Arty! Why are you only talking to their computer and not to the aliens—the 'Guethl,' directly?"

Everyone in Conglommora was probably asking similar questions of Arty at exactly the same time, placing an unusual burden on all the systems. And yet, despite the system load, Arty answered after only a brief delay, in its usual implacable manner.

"The Guethl perceive time on a much slower scale than humans do. It would take them many days to respond to a simple conversational statement at human language speed. Their computer, of course, operates as quantum scales similar to my own construction. So it is much easier for us to communicate directly."

I looked at Käthe, then addressed Arty. "But, it *will* tell the Guethl about us, right?"

A pause.

"Yes, but that won't have much impact. From the Guethl's point of view, humans are like flies, or mosquitoes. Humans live and die so fast, by comparison. Their computer expresses what amounts to amazement that humans have been able to build a civilization and spacecraft at all."

"So, we won't likely get a chance to visit them, visit their ship?"

"You wouldn't want to," Arty replied. "The environments are quite incompatible in many ways: atmosphere, gravity, magnetic fields, radiation…"

"Stop. Okay, we get it," I said. "But if we're just fruit flies to them, why did they stop here? Why has their ship been stopped right there, practically close enough to dock?"

Another pause.

"They noticed the side-effects from our quantum wave displacement and came to investigate."

Slight pause.

"Qradio transmissions are enabled again, and resonance wave transits may resume at any time," Arty noted. "Although the Guethl's system was dismissive of our techniques and seemed surprised it worked at all. I am downloading some improved specifications. In fact, their computer is providing me full access to their archives, which should— Override. Override."

Arty broke off its description suddenly. Käthe looked at me, alarm clear on her golden face. I shook my head.

"Arty, what's—"

"There is a queued transmission from Earth. According to Chalu, and supported by high-resolution scan data, it appears Lucille has seized control of one or more tribes and is engaging in full-on attacks using high energy weapons."

"Well, that's not really—"

"It also appears that Lucille has kidnapped Ahdom and Alain and is threatening to kill them both. Chalu and his team are beginning a search and rescue at this very moment. In fact, they just landed on the beach."

I was on my feet and halfway to the hatch. "Have a ship ready for me. I'm going down."

Thirty

"IT'S OKAY, WE WON'T HURT YOU." Chalu had his hands open and spread wide, trying to calm the girl on the beach. "I am Chalu, Ahdom's father. You called out to us."

Dawnroot gasped for air for a moment, got up from her knees and confronted Chalu.

"Ahdom told me to call to you for help. He did not say you would be [vomited up] by a great fish!"

Chalu looked back over his shoulder at the ship, unsure just how accurate the translator was. *Well, that was one way to look at it.* And probably the simplest explanation at that. He decided to go with it.

"Yes, well, as he must have told you, we come from very far away. This great beast was kind enough to give us a ride."

Dawnroot scanned the whole crew up and down and the great fish ship, too, trying to take it all in. "Your hair."

She looked more closely at Chalu's multicolored strands. "What happened to your hair that a rainbow lives in it?"

Chalu stared at her blankly, trying to come up with something. She turned her gaze to Oliver. "And you. You have the hair of a very old man, yet you are no older than he."

Oliver spoke up, "Yes, we must look strange to your eyes. But these things are common where we are from."

Satisfied, apparently, she turned abruptly away from the shore. "We do not have much time, follow me."

Chalu turned to one of the crew. "Dijn, take the ship out past the breakers and wait for us. No sense in having others panic over the tadpole, too." Dijn nodded and headed back to the ship. Chalu waved the others to follow him and they filed off the beach behind Dawnroot.

———————

They marched through the jungle for several hours when Dawnroot motioned for them to halt. "Wait here, I will scout ahead."

"Why?" asked Oliver, out of curiosity and just a little bit of apprehension at what subtle dangers might lie just ahead.

"You do not walk quietly," Dawnroot answered flatly. "You walk as [noisy children]. I will make sure it is safe along this path." She turned quickly and scampered at much greater speed through the jungle, a silent shadow leaving no trace.

Chalu bent over and stretched his back. He led an active and physical life, but this was unaccustomed work. Stretching out deeper, he realized he missed the daily routine on the boards back at Sea. Denisova was a fantastic opportunity to study and learn, but it wasn't home. And there was so much to do here. There were plans to explore the surface eventually, and to slowly introduce themselves to the Earthans. But not like this. Not an armed rescue mission.

Oliver checked his pack and equipment, and called out to the others. "Double-check your gear and report. Stunners?"

"Aye."

"Yes."

"Got it."

The replies came out staggered, as everyone checked the small stunners strapped to their wrists. There was no sense in trying to hide them in a waist satchel or anything; they had them out and ready to use. Oliver was determined they would be prepared this time.

"Shields?" He went down the list in his head.

A faint glow and quiet but distinct, nearly sub-sonic throbbing sound came and went as each of the crew flicked their personal shields on and back off again. Arty had assured them these smaller versions of the miner's ship asteroid deflectors would protect against spears, arrows, rocks, even the fangs of a local carnivore. They did not have any sort of inertial compensator, however, so a fall off a cliff would still be fatal. The shields drew a lot of power, so you couldn't really leave them on full time, only when needed. They were protected, but not invincible.

"Proximity alarms?"

"On and calibrated," came the responses, as each crew member fiddled with a small device on their belts. No fast-moving angry tribespeople or ravening predator would sneak up on them this time. They'd have time to seek shelter, turn on the shields, or even attack if needed. They were ready.

Oliver went over to Chalu. "We'll find them. Don't worry."

Chalu straightened up. "I know. I know. It's just... I should never have agreed to let him go in the first place. It was too dangerous and I knew it. I let the thrill of discovery cloud my better parental judgment."

"As if you could have stopped him." Oliver grinned widely.

Chalu shot him a look. "We can joke about it once my son and Alain are safe. Not until then." He wagged a finger.

Oliver was ready with a retort, but he was standing closest to the jungle. His alert went off first, a quiet, unobtrusive yet penetrating sound. He glanced down at the display. "The girl. Dawnroot, by the look of it." The other alerts chimed in next, in quick succession. And suddenly Dawnroot was standing in front of them. If the proximity alarms hadn't detected her, they never would have heard her coming.

"We are almost there," she said. She looked quickly about, surveying the scene, then focused back on Chalu and Oliver. "At the base of that mountain. That's where their camp is. The mountain itself is said to be evil. None will climb it. Strange lights in the night, noises unlike any

animal ever heard. It is no wonder Lucy of Furs makes
her camp in the shadow of such evil. Come."

She led them, slower than she could travel, obviously,
toward the camp where Ahdom and Alain were being
held.

Oliver whispered to Chalu, "Strange lights? Her ship,
printer, and other equipment maybe?"

Chalu nodded. "Sounds like it. Makes sense, a protected spot like that. Plus a good dose of fear to keep the
curious away. That might be good to know."

Oliver nodded.

And on they walked.

———————————

They continued following Dawnroot through the
knee-high grasses, tangled roots, and occasional dry
hardscrabble tumbles of rocks and boulders and soggy
streams from the mountains. Chalu blinked, rubbed
his eyes, blew his nose, and shook his head all at once.
It didn't help. He was overwhelmed with sensory
overload.

Their quick stops along the shore were one thing,
and certainly marvelous, Chalu thought. But this. This
was an entirely different beast. Literally. Massive beasts
crossed their paths more than a few times. He recognized
some of them: hyenas in the distance, swift gazelles right
across their path, and a few lumbering aurochs.

There were many other animals that they didn't
know the names of. The Erasures of Dead Earth ensured
that their names, their classifications and details were all
lost. *I guess we can just name them again.* Name them,

re-learn their habits—but the Earthans were way ahead of them. Dawnroot somehow knew the animals were approaching even before their own proximity alarms went off.

Chalu had seen the vids and images from Alain and Ahdom, but being there, right in the thick of it... not the same. The noise, for one thing. Earth was *loud*. Small creatures, buzzing insects, larger carnivores, all chirping, buzzing, growling, bellowing, roaring, hissing... all at once, all the time. And the smell. *The smell alone could probably kill you. Or at least heavy stun,* Chalu thought. Now that he thought about it, Alain had complained about the pervasive native fetors and exotic bouquets—Ahdom knew better than to complain at all. But Alain's comments had tapered off eventually. Perhaps one could get used to it. But not today.

A branch snapped back and whipped his face, drawing a thin line of fresh blood on his cheek. Chalu winced. That would leave a mark. Another one. He wiped his cheek with the back of his hand. Maybe they should just keep their shields on at all times.

"Sorry," Oliver said, ahead of him.

He couldn't count how many cuts and bruises they'd already suffered in just these few hours. How did Ahdom manage? He and Alain didn't seem to have these problems. Of course, they weren't rushing frantically through completely alien, unknown terrain on a desperate rescue mission. But maybe they should slow the pace a bit.

One of their party tripped and fell flat on his face up ahead. *We aren't prepared for this,* Chalu fretted. *We can't even walk without injuring ourselves.* Liza helped the man up. It was Stro, who had been with them on the very first shore expedition. Liza checked him over as the procession paused a moment. Dawnroot was up ahead a little and she doubled back now.

"You must not do that! Make so much of [the noise]," she hissed through clenched teeth. "We are almost there." She raised her hand and pointed. They had just crested a small ridge. Down below, the thin crack of a stream bed traced out a dark line. A larger ridge loomed up above that on the other side, and that's where Dawnroot was pointing.

"From there, we will be able to see their camp. And," she gave them a look as if they were children, "they will be able to see us. Night comes. We will wait here for it. They will have fires, and watchers."

Chalu nodded in agreement, and they retreated a space from the lip of the ridge and hunkered down to await the sunset. Oliver came over. They ran through their checklist again, made sure everyone remained armed, alert, and ready.

Earth rotated the sun out of view, and the wind faded away as the heat of the day waned. The blanket of noise that had smothered them all day changed. Not any less, Chalu thought. But different. More insects now, maybe. Fewer birds.

Dusk dimmed to the fire-soot black of night. Dawnroot silently touched Chalu on the shoulder and pointed.

It was time. As quiet as they could, they filed down the steep bank of the ridge to the stream bed and clambered up the other side to the high ridge. Whether deliberate or not, they were going a lot slower than they had earlier in the day. And mercifully, a lot more quietly. They crept up to the lip of the ridge. Dawnroot crouched lower and lower as they approached, taking the last distance on her stomach. Chalu and Oliver crawled just behind her.

Dark clouds scuttled in the distance, and a soft roll of thunder echoed across the landscape. It grew quiet in the wake of the thunder, as if the whole world was holding its breath. Chalu realized he was, in fact, holding his breath. He let it out slowly and silently as he took in the view. There was the camp in the next valley, not very far away. Chalu could easily see the "watchers," as Dawnroot called them. "Guards," seemed a more fitting title, from what he'd read of Earth's history. Lots of them.

Dawnroot studied the scene for a moment, her pale blue eyes scanning with practiced efficiency. She backed down off the ridge just as silently as she'd mounted it. They followed, passing Liza, Stro, and the others who also reversed course and then followed them back down to the stream bed.

"What's wrong?" Chalu asked in a low voice, hoping the rustle of the stream was enough to cover him.

"Too many. Too many watchers, too much open ground, too many fires. More than when I [snuck into] the camp. And I was quiet and quick. If you try to approach now, they will hear you. See you. Even in the dark."

Chalu nodded and held his wrist up. "We have these… rocks. They can knock a person out from a distance." Dawnroot stiffened at the sight. "You've seen… rocks like these before, haven't you?" She nodded, still clenched. "These will not kill. We won't kill anyone. Just knock them out, like a blow to the head, but from far away. We will go in and get Ahdom and Alain, if we have to strike down every last one of them." Chalu didn't raise his voice. He didn't have to. His icy determination was as effective as any harsh yell.

But Dawnroot held her palms up with an outward gesture; the Earthan hand sign for "no," Chalu guessed. "Too many of them. Your rocks cannot take them all out at once, can they?"

Chalu cocked his head. "No. But none of them could get close enough to hurt us—"

"Does not matter," Dawnroot cut him off. "If even one of their [tribe] raises the call, raises the alarm, she will kill Ahdom and Alain before we could get to them."

Chalu frowned.

Oliver joined them. "What's the problem?" he asked quietly, but with clear impatience. Thunder rolled in the distance again, the storm slowly drawing closer.

Chalu motioned to Dawnroot. "She says we need stealth, not force. If we go barging in there and take out a whole swath of watchers and jailers, they might kill the hostages. It's too crowded now to slip in without being seen."

"Well, shit," Oliver said, dropping his hands. "Now what?"

Thirty-One

EMMEA WAS IN THE WORKSHOP just off their spherical living room.

"Jocelyn, come see!" Emmea's grin was wide and she clasped her hands together in satisfaction. Jocelyn popped in from the other room, wiping her hands clean on a silver towel.

"It's finished?" Jocelyn asked.

"Yes, yes! Ready to turn it on now," Emmea replied.

"Let's see it then!"

Emmea activated the sculpture. It was a fountain, modeled after the images of the alien Guethl species. Nine-sided polyhedrons, with a bright blue, phosphorescent liquid coming up out of the top of the figure. Perfect sheets of liquid cascaded down its many sides, collecting in a small, illuminated reflecting pool at the base before being recirculated again.

"I call it 'The One Who Shares.'" Emmea stood tall, beaming with accomplishment. "To commemorate all the knowledge the Guethl are giving us."

"Well, Arty still has to translate most of it, we've only gotten a small piece so far," Jocelyn started, but quickly focused back on the sculpture. "But this is most excellent! I love the cascading sheets of water down all the sides. How'd you figure the geometry and viscosity to get the effect right?"

"Experimented a little, asked Arty a little. You know, the usual."

Jocelyn circled around the piece, examining it more closely from various angles. It wasn't lit uniformly, instead, different colors were featured on different sheets of water throughout. "I really like it, dear," she said approvingly. "In fact, I think we should put this one out in the small park, you know, the one in the three-tunnel junction?"

Emmea beamed with delight. "You think?"

"Absolutely! I want everyone in this section to see it," Jocelyn said. "I'll get the gravsled and we can install it after lunch. I really like it, I think it's one of your most timely works yet. What gave you the inspiration?"

Emmea ran a hand over her forehead, pushing up a stray lock of gray hair, and pointed to the tapestry they had been working on. It was partially hanging on the wall in the workshop and extended into the spherical living area. The Guethl were on the tapestry, but not represented by flat thread as all the other events. Instead, the Guethl figures were created as a shallow relief, not quite fully 3D, but raised off the plane of the tapestry itself. "I guess it started when I raised those figures on the tapestry for emphasis. The angles and the geometry sort of caught my attention. I wondered about their physiology, whether the Guethl breathed, whether they had a circulatory system—blood, anything like that. And, well, the idea of a fountain kind of came out of that."

"Well I think it's absolutely marvelous," Jocelyn chimed in. "I'm sure even Faith will like it, next time she's by this way."

"*If* she comes back this way again." Emmea's face darkened a bit. "She's pretty mad at us still, I think."

"She'll get over it." Jocelyn wrinkled her mouth. "We've kept much too quiet for too long. With the Guethl now, that's a whole species that clearly knows much more about the galaxy than we do. This is an *incredible* chance to start sorting out what was myth and what was a genuine historical event, a real warning, from the past. But we need more people involved, more eyes to read through the material."

Emmea nodded, "Oh, I agree. And as Arty releases more and more translations from the Guethl data, I'm sure we'll get some more volunteers. Looking for clues to the Cryptic in translations of a vast alien database? Who wouldn't want to dig into that? I'm guessing every single person in the Heart will want to be involved."

"Hope so," Jocelyn nodded. "It's sure something to look forward to!"

"It is that!" Emmea grinned widely and took Jocelyn's hand as they went into the galley for lunch.

Thirty-Two

FURY FUELED ME THIS TIME. When Alain and I almost went to Earth to rescue Ahdom, I was... reluctant. Nervous, maybe. Afraid. Looking for an excuse not to go. Earthans could be dangerously unpredictable. I wanted to help Ahdom, but honestly, I was dragging my feet.

But this... this was different. There was nothing unpredictable about Lucille. She stole Grace's body. Killed her, in other words. Pretty sure she fed Arty an entire stream of lies to get to go to Earth and wreak whatever havoc she was planning. She was straight up evil. So if she was threatening to kill Alain and Ahdom... Well, that wasn't a threat so much as an appointment. She would do it. We just had to get there first, but it was an uncertain calendar.

I shot through the corridors on a gravsled to get to the Miner's Tubes, where Arty was getting a ship ready to take me out to the resonance wave point. The tubes were much easier to get to than, say, the really long trip

275

to the Mech Section, or even from the *Neylan* to Skyville. I opened a stream to Arty on a long straightaway and worked out a few details—it's not like I had time to pack up or get ready again. I'd had everything lined up when Alain and I almost went, though, so it wasn't like I was starting completely from scratch.

A sharp corner and I almost flipped the sled, but I swung wide and barely scraped the opposite wall. Good thing there was no one else in the corridor just then. Arty pinged me, cautioned me regarding my driving skills, and said the volunteers would be ready when I got there.

Volunteers?

I wondered what that was about, but I didn't press for details. I was a little busy navigating a right-angle shift in gravity as the next-to-last corridor turned and twisted to meet up with the main tube concourse. Fortunately, I skidded into the last hatch—now in a completely different orientation—without falling off or crashing into anyone. It wasn't crowded, but there were a handful of people coming and going. I flung myself off the sled to the entry hatch and through, and almost smashed right into a familiar face.

"Carol?" I said, bracing myself against the hatch frame to avoid the collision. "You look a lot better than the last time I saw you!"

Carol looked up in surprise, not just from the near impact. "Alain's dad! So glad you could make it. Come on in." She waved me hurriedly through the hatch and down a smaller side corridor.

She'd forgotten my name. Understandable, I suppose, we'd only met in person once or twice after the crash. I was lucky to have recognized her at all, honestly, in one piece and all. I followed her quickly to the waiting shuttle, no less confused at why she seemed to have been waiting for me. I was about to ask, but just then we crossed the threshold into the airlock and on board the shuttle. Inside, there was a group of maybe ten or twelve folks, most already seated and strapped in, the others just doing so now.

Carol announced me. "Everyone, thanks for coming. This is Alain's father, Charlie Neylan." An assortment of waves, well-wishing hand gestures, smiles and nods flowed back at me. I was thoroughly confused now, and tried to stutter some sort of question at Carol.

"Whaa…" was about as eloquent as I could get.

She cocked her head and raised an eyebrow, trying to decode my not-quite-speech.

"Who are they all?" I managed in a sloppy little whisper.

"Volunteers. Many of them are friends of Alain, folks he'd met or helped out somewhere, sometime. A lot have been on mining runs, so they've got some planetary experience."

"Volunteers? Oh, right. Arty mentioned that on the way here."

Carol nodded. "Arty called for volunteers right when Alain first left. I almost joined him, you know. I sort of wanted to. Alain saved my life."

I looked up sharply. "He almost got you killed in the crash."

"True. But despite that, and the long recovery, he saved me. From myself, from the comfortable box I kept myself in. I didn't go with Alain, but when Arty called for volunteers, I jumped at the chance for the training."

She guided me to my seat. Behind the panelform in the wall was my gear. I recognized a lot of it from the first mission to Earth and my almost-mission to Earth, but there were a few unfamiliar items.

"Training?" I looked up as I took my seat.

"Yeah. Showing us how to use the equipment." She waved at the gear in the panel. "How to handle Earthans, how *not* to handle Earthans. That sort of thing."

I was speechless. This sort of thing was unprecedented. Arty, training a group of... of what? Soldiers? Warriors? Rescuers? I can't remember such a thing ever happening before. Conglommorans have always looked out for each other, but usually one-on-one. Not like this. Not so organized. Carol interrupted my mental wandering.

"You probably know a lot of this already," she grinned, "as you were the very first one to use any of these."

"I suppose. But it looks like Arty has a few new tricks here, too. What's that?" I pointed to a small, brightly polished, silver-colored cone. "I don't think I've seen anything like that before."

"It's a personal cloak. Portable invisibility field, in the visible spectrum at least."

"No kidding. Wow, I wish we'd had one of those." I was genuinely impressed.

"Arty says not to rely on it too much; it's far from perfect. Works best at night. And don't forget it won't make you quiet. You just look more like your background from any line of sight."

Carol pointed out the rest of the tech. "That's the stunner. There's an adjustment there for the width of field. Narrower the field, the stronger the stun. Wider, weaker. On the narrowest setting, it will take out the largest megafauna. Even a spotted hyena, those big-horned cattle, or a wooly rhino. Those things are huge. And this is the latest design of the sublingual translator. It includes a tracker, and hooks up to a mesh network on the coast to relay back to Denisova base."

"Yeah." I nodded with familiarity. "That's the kind Alain has. Had."

We locked eyes for a moment.

"He'll be all right." Carol straightened up. "We'll make sure of it. Alain woke me up. Opened my eyes. We're all armed. Trained. We have you." She lowered her head and looked up at me. "The first to meet the Earthans, to step foot on Earth itself. We'll find Lucille. We'll stop her. And we'll rescue Ahdom and Alain."

Her confidence may have been misplaced, or more likely just a well-rehearsed act, but I found it a welcome tonic. At least I wouldn't be alone on a crazy rescue mission. We were a heavily armed, maybe even well-prepared team.

Carol left and strapped herself in, and the pilot announced we were about to launch. I flicked my shiny and filled Käthe in on what was happening, and to say goodbye. Just in case. She was visibly relieved that I would *not* be attacking Earth single-handedly. I didn't take that personally; I was just as relieved myself.

The hatch hissed, and the shuttle immediately dropped off the docking tube and shot out into open space. Damn. I had almost forgotten about this part, the part I dreaded. The resonance wave. Still had nightmares about. I vowed I'd never go to Earth again, mostly because of this one moment. This one, terrible, inside-out eternal brain vomit cloud of a—

———————————

"Found them—Chalu and his party are just ahead, past that ridge, down in a gully," Carol announced, looking up from her screen. "Set us down right up there."

The shuttle glided silently down through the thinning canopy at the top of a small ridge; our pilot settled us down gently. Very nice. Carol had told me that the shuttle had its own invisibility field generator, so any Earthan natives who happened to be looking right at us would only see a vague shimmer in the air. If they ran right into the ship, though, that would be a different problem. Hope we didn't park in the middle of a primitive Earthan access road or something.

We filed down the stairform quickly and quietly. Carol reiterated the fact that Earthan predators had keen hearing and smell, not just sight. Best try and not draw too much attention if we could help it.

I stepped through the hatch and into the brilliant late-day sunshine and crystalline air of Earth. Dark, sculptural clouds to the east, stunning brightly lit landscape to the west. A low roll of thunder echoed from the distant mountains. Wow. It really was something. I took a deep breath and descended down to the surface. Time for sightseeing later.

Carol and an older man with a dark beard—didn't catch his name—led us down the ridge to where Chalu and his group were. We didn't know who else might be there, or might be watching, so each one of us had our own personal shield activated as well.

Beard Man made two sweeping motions, and about a third of our group broke off to the left, another third to the right. They hung back while we went ahead. Seemed like a pretty good strategy to me, if something unexpected happened up ahead—like an ambush—we had backup in place. Arty must have done its homework. This mission was far better prepared than my first, very naive, nearly fatal attempt. Of course, that left Carol, me, and Beard Man at the front of the first wave.

Chalu and a handful of his folks were in a clearing at the bottom of the gully. We crept up as far as the shadows at the edge of the clearing. Nice thing about the invisibility shielding: we could see each other. Sort of. What you actually saw was a kind of multi-layer, contour line drawing. Lines within lines. It was an odd sight, but it was enough to tell who was who, determine gestures, facial expressions, that sort of thing. Again, Arty could do nice work.

Faint beeps as their proximity sensors went off. Chalu and company whipped around, circled, but of course didn't see us. Confusion. Carol nodded at me and Beard Man, and the three of us deactivated our shielding. I walked slowly and carefully up behind Chalu—but not too close.

"We're here." I tried to sound calm.

Chalu turned around with a slightly puzzled look before simultaneously jumping up, starting a yelp, quickly squelching it, landing, and mostly just jumping out of his skin.

"Charlie!" he hissed as loud as he dared. "You bastard! Sneaking up on us in the middle of the jungle like that! We could have killed you!"

"We've got shields," I laughed.

He leaned over and gave me a hug with a wide grin. "I'm so glad you're here. All of you…" He gestured to Carol and Beard Man.

"I'm Carol," she said, introducing herself. "This is Pel, our pilot. This is the rest of our team." Suddenly, another six figures emerged from the shadows. "We have two more teams up on the ridge, hidden for now." She nodded up over her shoulder.

Chalu motioned to the man next to him. "This is Oliver." Then he got right down to business. "The boys are being held in a camp, just over that ridge. But there are a lot of guards, and a lot of open ground. Dawnroot says if they see us coming, they'll kill them. We need some way to get in and get them out."

Carol smiled. "Okay, so far we can manage that." She cocked her head a bit and in a slightly different voice, addressed her comms. "Team Two, launch the recon drones. Earthan camp, just over that ridge ahead of us, past some open ground." She nodded as she heard the confirmation come over her earpiece. "It will be just a moment. They have to fine-tune the anti-grav drones to Earth field."

After a brief pause, she said, "Okay, gather round."

We did, as she pulled out a shiny and stiffened it. Immediately, we had a 3D birds-eye view, composited from several drones that were fast approaching the Earthan camp site.

"There," Pel said, pointing to the image of a tent with three guards spaced around it. "That's got to either be their leader, or the prisoners."

It killed my soul to hear Alain and Ahdom referred to as "the prisoners." I must have pulled a pained expression, as Pel glanced over at me. "I'm sorry," he quickly offered. "Alain is a good friend. I want him safe as much as you do."

Chalu nodded and spoke up, "How about we refer to them as 'the boys' for now?" There were nods.

"Team Two, get us an interior view on this tent." Carol poked the screen. "They'll steer a drone right up to the tent, and insert a small probe through the covering material. It should take just a second."

Just then a youngish girl came down the ridge from the Earthan side. I recognized her from Alain's vid feed. Dawnroot, Ahdom's Earthan girlfriend—not that Alain or Ahdom ever admitted that, of course. But come on.

She had a wide-eyed, penetrating look at the handful of us. "Chalu, more of [your kind]? More from Denisova?"

"Yes. This is Charlie," Chalu gestured, "Alain's father."

Dawnroot made some sort of florid gesture of greeting with both hands. "I am honored you have come. But it is hopeless. We cannot get to Ahdom and Alain without being seen."

Carol had quietly palmed her screen when Dawnroot came over. She spoke up. "We might have a way. But we need you as a lookout on top of that ridge. Warn us if we've been spotted."

"I will go back at once," Dawnroot agreed and shot up the sides of the gully and up the ridge as smooth as water.

As soon as she took off, Carol brought the screen back out. "Here. There they are, all right. There's a third person being held as well." She zoomed in on Ahdom. He looked in good shape, except for being bound to a very solid-looking metal table. Chalu nodded with obvious relief and leaned away for a moment to send a message and the image to his wife Chrys.

Carol panned over to the next bed, and there was Alain. I breathed a short sigh of relief from every pore.

He was okay. The boys were, for now at least, both alive and seemed in good condition. Carol waited for my nod and then panned to the third bed. Probably just some Earthan who got caught in Lucy's net along with the boys, I thought at first.

And indeed, the scrawny, heavily bearded fellow strapped to the table looked a lot like an Earth-battered native. Except not; as I looked closer, his features were clearly Conglommoran, not Earthan. Features that looked strangely familiar.

Thirty-Three

"CHARLIE? YOU OKAY?" Chalu read my expression.

"Sure," I answered distractedly. "It's just… Carol, can you zoom in and enhance his face?"

She nodded and twirled her fingers on the screen. It couldn't be.

"What is it? You know this guy?"

"Well, I'll be damned. It's him, it's got to be," I said, mostly to myself.

"It's Eddie. Edward." Blank faces. "He was with us on the first mission. We left him behind. Left him for dead. I mean, we thought he was dead. We searched and stuff…" I trailed off, realizing how lame that sounded. "He's from Conglommora," I finished.

"Great," Carol said. "We'll rescue him, too."

"Well, now we know where they are," Chalu said, "but we still have the problem of how to get them out without tipping off the camp and getting them killed."

"They are safe now," Carol said confidently. "I can take out the guards with the drones at any time, and take out anyone else who approaches, to a point. But we can't start just dropping bodies. We need to get in there and figure out how to free them from those tables. These drones aren't equipped for anything like that."

Chalu spoke up, "We need a diversion. Something to attract attention away from the camp. Drop the guards, and we can get in there and get them out."

"Agreed," Carol said. "But it can't *look* like a diversion. Has to look like something natural, something…" A crack of thunder, much louder now, interrupted her as the storm approached.

Chalu seized the idea. "Fire. The grasses are dry here, and there's a storm coming. It would look perfectly normal, and they'd have to flee—quickly. That would be our chance."

Carol nodded. "Yes. I like it. But check with your local expert, make sure we know how the Earthans would typically react." Oliver nodded and took off up the ridge. "Team One. Head back to the shuttle. Get parameters from Arty for a controlled ignition of dry flora to drive Earthans away from the camp."

I turned and paced a bit. Overall, I liked it. Good diversion, panic and confusion, and backed up with a shielded ship and three well-armed teams. Yeah, this might actually work. As long as Dawnroot didn't come back and tell us some crazy Earthan thing about everyone running into fire to purify themselves or some other primitive nonsense. *Probably* not, but you just never knew with these Earthan types.

It wasn't long until Dawnroot and Oliver returned, easing noiselessly down the ridge. Oliver said, "I've explained the plan. Dawnroot agrees and thinks it will work."

Chalu asked Dawnroot directly, "Do you understand what we're trying to do? How will they—in the camp—react?"

Dawnroot answered, "I think I understand. There is a storm coming in. You have the magic rocks that throw fire from your hands." She motioned to the tall brown and gold grasses, rustling with fresh winds. "The grasses are dry here." She looked up to the sky. "Fire often follows the storms. A fire along this line," she motioned, "and they will have to run north and cross the river. Or east, to try and find a crack in the mountains that leads to the Endless Plains. I do not think they will [be concerned with] Ahdom and the others, or with the camp or their [supplies]. They will flee."

Chalu looked sideways at Oliver and whispered, without the translator, "Magic rocks? Really?"

Oliver shrugged. "If you have a better story, I'm all ears."

Chalu rubbed his temples. "We are going to have to sort a lot of this out with Arty when this is all over."

"I'm sure," I chimed in as my patience waned. "Later. Let's light this place up and get our boys first. We can discuss cultural contamination some other time. Carol, are we ready?"

"Almost," Carol said. "Team One has been picked up by the shuttle and are almost in position. We need to get up on top of that ridge and east a little, just past that break." She motioned vaguely up and to the right with her hand while looking at a tactical overlay of the area on her screen.

"Let's go," I said, already on my way up the hard-scrabble of the gully bank.

In the space of a heartbeat, a line along the edge of the grasses ignited with a breath taking *whomp*. The wind suddenly hot, the fire roared like a beast itself, the graying dismal scene now lit in vibrant red and orange shadows.

"Okay, drop the guards now," I told Carol.

"No need." She shook her head. "They took off already. Most of the camp is already in motion. Headed north."

"And Lucille?"

Carol nodded. "We've got drones scanning the Earth-ans as they flee the camp. No hit on facial recognition yet."

Chalu came up, Oliver and Pel in tow. "Let's go," he said curtly.

"I'll stay here and monitor," Carol offered. "But you've got a clear shot at the moment."

Still, we climbed cautiously down the other side of the ridge to the open ground leading to the camp. Some-where in the sky above, our shuttle hovered, making sure the fire line didn't spread to the boys' tent until we rescued them. We crossed into the open field, keeping an eye on the fire and an eye on any loose Earthans.

About halfway across, Carol's warning burst in our ears. "Four Earthans heading toward you fast from the west. I can't get a drone over there in time."

They saw us already, spears raised. Too late for invisibility, but a perfect time for protective shields. We each activated ours almost simultaneously, the faint glow and low throbbing sound barely noticeable in the roar of the fire and shrieks of Earthans.

The leader chucked his spear right at Pel, who was closest. It caught him on his side and bounced harmlessly off. I fired my stunner and took out all four at once. I have to admit, that felt immensely satisfying. Earth wasn't going to beat me this time. I'd learned my lesson.

Chalu turned to Pel. "You okay?"

"Oof, like a punch. But yeah, I'm fine." He shook it off and we quickly moved on toward the tent.

I held my breath a little as I ducked between the animal hides into the darkened gloom of the tent.

"Dad!"

"Father!"

"Charlie?!"

The captives shouted, all at once, all infused with relief mixed with incredulity.

"All the above," I mumbled as I hugged Alain and Chalu hugged Ahdom.

Eddie didn't seem to mind at all. In fact, he was quite effusive. "Thank God you've come," he wailed, sounding just like the wild-eyed and wild-haired Eddie I knew from the corridors. "Lucille was going to make mindless slaves of us all!"

"Good thing we got here first," I said evenly, still holding on to Alain.

"I knew you'd come back for me someday," Eddie added. "Even though I really didn't want you to."

Alain interrupted. "I was hoping you could find us, but they took our comms away."

"No problem. We've got you, and there's a cloaked shuttle overhead to take us back to Denisova. We've just got to get you untangled from these tables."

"Almost there." Pel's voice came from somewhere under Alain's table in the dark murk of the tent. "I just have to interrupt the power supply and the safeties should release the bindings." A pause. "Got it."

Three very loud warning beeps, and the restraints on Alain's tableform reabsorbed into the metal of the slab. Pel moved on to Ahdom's table, and Alain started to sit up quickly.

"Whoa, easy there. I know this wasn't quite like smashing your ship into a pile of solid rock, but still. Careful," I admonished.

Alain wavered a bit, as his blood pressure tried to re-adapt to a sitting position instead of lying prone for— days? I didn't really know. But Alain grimly soldiered on.

"I'm fine, Dad." He waved me off. "Let's just get out of here."

More beeps, and Ahdom was freed. Alain was shaking his numb limbs, getting feeling back where he could. "Carol, what's our status?" I asked.

"Still clear," she proclaimed. "But I'd get a move on if I were you. Fire's getting closer."

Sure enough, a couple of large embers had already landed on the tent. Not enough for any immediate problem, but it was time to go.

"Pel, how much…" I started to ask when three loud beeps interrupted me.

"Now," he said, jumping up from under Eddie's table.

"Go!" Chalu barked, and he didn't have to tell us twice. But Alain slumped as he tried to put weight on his legs for the first time in a while, and so did Ahdom. Eddie was still struggling to sit up.

I exchanged a quick glance with Chalu. "Carry." He nodded, and I scooped up Alain into my arms, Chalu lifted Ahdom, and Pel got Eddie. We half-carried, half-supported, and half-dragged them out of the tent just as the shuttle landed and became visible. A huge wall of flame roared along, coming right at us. I could feel the heat ahead of it, a scalding draft carried by the wind. I jumped into the open hatch, still holding Alain, the others close behind me, without another word.

The ground fell away beneath us as the anti-grav engaged, and we were out of there.

Arty had equipped the shuttle with a full med bay. Chalu popped Ahdom in for the first scan. Ahdom took out his earpiece and handed it to Chalu.

"What happened to this?" Chalu said with alarm as the yellow-green slime dripped from the translator. Gross.

Ahdom shook his head. "Not sure. Some kind of fungus, or spore, or mold, or something. Doesn't happen right away, but I guess all that time in the dark of the ear canal… something starts growing. Spores, maybe."

Chalu recoiled in disgust, walked across the bay and tossed the translator into the reclaimer, sighed, and waited for the med bay to finish the diagnostics.

Clean bill of health.

I helped Alain over next and nervously held my breath to make sure he was *really* okay. I took his translator, and sure enough, a faint film of something gross was starting to form. Earth was a nasty place. I chucked his translator in the reclaimer as well.

The med bay hummed and whirred, wires came and went from the tableform. It was uncomfortably like the mechanism we'd just rescued them from. And like the one that had saved his life after the crash. Terror or savior? Just depended how you used it.

"Told you I was fine," Alain weakly complained after the med bay pronounced him mostly healthy, just dehydrated with some muscle fatigue.

"Eddie, you're next." I helped him onto the slab.

Alain caught my eye and motioned me aside. Now what? I stepped out of the bay area and into the corridor. Alain whispered in a low, deep voice, "Lucille did something to him. Or started to, anyway. Like she did to Grace. Mess with his mind. But she was interrupted. I don't know how far she got."

I nodded and went back into the bay. At the control screen, I entered a few extra commands and sent a note to Arty. We'd get a few extra brain scans while we're at it.

Eddie noticed. "What are you doing, Charlie?"

Lying wouldn't do any good. "Seems Lucy gave you some extra special attention. Just want Arty to make sure you're all right."

"I'm fine," Eddie started to complain, exasperation in his voice.

"Are you sure?" I asked quietly. "Or is that what she wanted you to say?"

Eddie opened his mouth to protest, then thought about that. How *would* he know? He looked downcast a moment. "You're right. You better check, as thoroughly as you can. I don't want anything kicking around in here that isn't me."

I read the info off the screen. "Okay, that's going to take a little longer. Hang tight. Can I get you anything?"

Eddie was wistful. "Water. With ice."

"Sure thing." I smiled and got him a cup.

Funny how much you can miss the simple things in this life.

Thirty-Four

WE HEADED BACK TO DENISOVA. From there, we'd take the larger shuttle back out to the resonance wave pick-up point and once again go through the single most existentially unpleasant experience the universe has to offer. Something to look forward to. But meanwhile, back at Conglommora, humans had just made contact with an actual *alien* species.

I made sure Alain was resting comfortably and sat at a large screen to have a few words with Arty. There was much to catch up on. Not just the aliens—the Guethl— but Lucy and the Earthans as well.

"Did you find her? Catch Lucille?" I asked Arty.

"Facial scans did not locate Lucille in the group of Earthans who fled the fire," Arty replied.

Damn.

"I do have a report just in from Team Two. They found Lucille's ship on top of the mountain above the camp, but it has been stripped of any useful tech. There was no computer core, no printer, no reclaimer."

"So, Lucy has those with her, somewhere."

"That is a reasonable inference," said Arty.

"We have to find her. Stop her," I insisted.

"That may not be an easy thing to accomplish," Arty suggested. "I've analyzed the drone data from the Earthans in Lucille's camp and have come to the following conclusions."

I leaned back. Sounded like this might take a while.

"Proceed," I said with a hint of anticipated weariness. This was not going to be satisfying at any rate.

"We can remove Lucille, by force if necessary. But that is only the first step. Her contamination may have spread further and faster than I had anticipated."

"You seem to have missed a lot when it comes to Lucy. And Grace," I added bitterly.

"My initial analysis of the situation was in error," Arty admitted readily. "Remember that I was initially designed to protect humans from much simpler, mechanical risks. Dangers that are considerably easier to detect and mitigate. None of my components were designed to function as a government, or a police or military organization, or as a deity or even a fortune teller."

If I didn't know better, I'd swear that was sarcasm. Arty may not have been designed for everything, but clearly it could learn.

"All right, so you've got a lot to learn about human nature, still. Well, now you know. You know what she's capable of."

"Indeed. I clearly misjudged her intent from the beginning, and I accepted her statements of mission as truthful. She did not exhibit any of the usual biosignatures associated with deceit. It is reasonable to assume that's a feature of the neural reprogramming that erased Grace and installed Lucille in the first place."

I winced. I still didn't like to be reminded of that. Grace deserved so much more than to be killed and have her body appropriated by this... monster.

Arty continued, "Further, facial scans suggested that a considerable number of Earthan hosts have been similarly reprogrammed by Lucille. Their posture and mannerisms during the evacuation were demonstrably different from the native Earthans."

"How many?" I asked, my heart sinking. Bad enough that the one-time love of my life went through that. But how many other innocents?

"Thirty-seven that I was able to detect."

Bile rose in my throat. I was close to throwing up, and it wasn't from the trip here in the "tadpole" being buffeted in the atmosphere from the edge of the storm. How could this get any worse?

"In addition," Arty continued with the same emotion as if it had been reading a list of ingredients, "I detected fourteen infants and very young children that appeared to be Conglommoran, not Earthan."

"WHAT?" I actually yelled. Chalu heard and wandered in. I shot him a look of hopelessness and desperation and asked Arty for clarification. "How is that possible? Lucille couldn't have had fourteen children herself."

"She would not need to," Arty explained. "There were several Conglommoran males accompanying her, and any one of them could have impregnated an arbitrary number of Earthan females on Lucille's orders. It's also possible she used Conglommoran female eggs in Earthan hosts. I detected fourteen subjects with varying degrees of Conglommoran features during the evacuation. There could be more, possibly a great many more."

Silence. I was stunned into silence.

Chalu looked at me with horror on his face. "It's an abomination," he whispered quietly.

"Arty," I asked with what I hoped was a solemn and grave tone. "What is your position regarding those children? Are they to be protected or destroyed?" I gulped, not really believing I could even ask such a thing.

"Insufficient data or processing power," came Arty's reply. Now that's one I hadn't heard in a long time.

"Clarify," I demanded. I wasn't letting it off the hook.

"It is not clear whether this cross-breeding represents a danger or an opportunity. Lucille herself is clearly a danger, but the most prudent course of action at this time would be for Conglommora to engage in indirect action. To try and 'nudge' individual Earthans to mitigate Lucille's influence."

I was exasperated. "Can't we just find her and *shoot* her!?"

Arty didn't reply directly.

"I will continue to monitor and analyze to attempt to locate her. However, that is a lower priority now. Lucille is not the biggest risk that confronts humans."

Chalu and I looked at each other.

"Oh?" I said quietly.

"I have learned from the Guethl that both the Earth and Conglommora are in much greater danger from other alien races."

Out of the frying pan...

———————————

"Carol! Pel! Get in here!" I yelled.

"Oliver!" Chalu yelled over top of me.

"Arty," I said as they entered, "you need to work on your conversational mode a bit. This style of dropping the bombshell late in the conversation is driving me insane."

" 'Dropping a bombshell'? I do not understand. When there are multiple topics for presentation or discussion, I present them to you in time-ordered sequence and—"

"Fine. Whatever. We'll talk about it later." The others had arrived, breathless, anxious to hear what new devilry awaited. "Okay, Arty, go ahead."

Oddly, there was a very noticeable pause. Not like Arty. After more than a few awkward moments, Arty continued.

"Yes. Although you do not represent a statistically even sample across Conglommora, all of you have shown your skill and commitment to keeping humans safe. What I am about to share with you, I have not yet disclosed to anyone else. In fact, I would welcome your input on the manner in which it should be disclosed."

Well, this just isn't going to be good news, I thought, and looked at Chalu. He wore a grim expression as well.

"I learned a great deal from interfacing with the Guethl's intelligent computer system. It agreed to share a tremendous amount of data with me, data that I'm still processing. It will take some time."

"About that," I interrupted. "I've read a lot of fiction about aliens, meeting aliens, alien wars... never have I seen or even heard the idea that an alien race would just *give up* all their technology, all their secrets."

Arty said, "You assume human motivation and behavior. It's very possible the Guethl, as a modular lifeform, merely consider this as a sort of 'upgrade,' and a normal part of their culture. I have only completed translating a very small portion of the Guethl data so far, but this seems consistent with my conversations with their computer system. But this 'upgrade' may be essential for our survival."

Chalu and I exchanged a glance. Arty continued. "The Guethl system pointed out that they discovered us because of the resonance wave effect. Our methods are crude, and it suggested a number of improvements. More importantly, it suggested we implement these improvements immediately. It said we shouldn't draw attention to the humans on Earth or in the Conglommora, as we have no way of defending ourselves."

"Defend ourselves from what?" Chalu asked.

"Aggressive alien species," Arty calmly replied. "The Guethl are aware of hundreds of other species with interstellar capability. Some are peaceful and non-interfering, others are openly aggressive and destructive. The Guethl, as a modular species, has a philosophy of complete cooperation and mutual respect, as well as—"

"Arty," I interrupted, "Let's talk about the Guethl later. What exactly do we need to do?"

"We need to mount a more advanced defense for Conglommora and create a defense network for Earth. Many of the more aggressive species have sufficient technology to destroy entire solar systems without difficulty. Even a basic level of defense will be a massive undertaking. It will take years, and many resources. We will need volunteers to increase the miner runs. There will be missions to Earth to keep Lucille in check, but also to install defensive and offensive weapons systems as needed."

"What kinds of weapons? How will we know what to build if we don't really know who's coming?" Carol asked.

"As the Guethl are willing to share their technology, I have shared ours with them as well, to help establish our capabilities. For example, they noted that our drive engines are extremely primitive and expressed surprise that they worked at all."

Pel stiffened at this. "What do they suggest instead of our EM drives?" he asked, with a touch of petulance.

"They recommend using a transdiamond lattice architecture." Surely, Arty then sensed a room full of blank faces. A pause. "Partially trans-dimensional, these designs collect and focus limitless quantum vacuum energy—safely. Our current drive engines don't manage the energy flow correctly, and according to the Guethl, are easy to sabotage."

"Sabotage?" I asked with more immediate concern. "Are they saying we've already been attacked by aliens blowing up our drive engines?"

Arty replied, "They have no direct data to prove or disprove that. However, one species, the Neparri, are known to be very xenophobic and have taken extraordinary measures with other species to keep them 'contained.'"

Pel asked, "So you're saying it's possible that it's not an accident that all the ships from Dead Earth ended up right here in the Conglommora? That we could have been penned in here *deliberately?*"

"That is possible," Arty confirmed. "The Guethl computer considers it highly probable."

"Arty, did these… Neparri… have anything to do with Earth's sudden ecological recovery?"

"No," Arty said, and I admit I relaxed a little. It was acutely uncomfortable to think there were unknown forces out there, hidden behind the curtain, messing with your life—with your whole species. My relief was short-lived.

"It definitely was not the Neparri. However, it is very possible the Osuchin had something to do with it," Arty clarified.

"What?" I asked weakly.

"It is apparently very common for young species to accidentally destroy complex ecosystems. From overharvesting of scarce food or energy resources, to polluting critical components unknowingly. In fact, one well-known species died out from the simple practice of sacrificing virgins in their only source of drinking water. The Osuchin have a history of letting such races destroy themselves, and then cleaning the biosphere, removing all traces of the failed species and restoring the given planet to a 'clean slate', if you will."

"Why would they do that?" Chalu asked hesitantly, afraid of the obvious answer.

"For later colonization," Arty replied, calm as ever, despite the remarkable threat that simple concept conveyed.

We sat in silence. So much we thought we knew had just been turned on its head. We weren't here by accident. It wasn't luck. All evidence we'd ever existed had been scraped off planet Earth by tidy aliens who wanted a clean planet for themselves. Oh, and by the way, we were far from alone in the universe.

That sparked a thought. "Arty, are there other humans? We've always thought that all the ships from Dead Earth that survived made it here, but maybe that's not entirely true either. Are there others?"

"Not that the Guethl are aware of. They had not encountered any humans before now. It is possible that other ships from Dead Earth did settle somewhere, but we would not know because of the EM drive interference, and the need for qradios to maintain known coordinates.

"However, the Guethl have detailed quantum field scans of much of the explored galaxy and have shared that with us."

"Does that mean what I think it means?" Pel asked.

My heart rose in my throat. I suspect Pel's did too.

"It means that we can travel almost anywhere now, anywhere that the Guethl have mapped, using an improved version of the quantum resonance wave. But it also means there are many places we should *not* go, so as not to attract attention. At least not until we are in a better position to defend ourselves."

A few more moments passed as we all tried to assimilate all of this. I guess that's kind of how Arty felt, if a machine could feel, trying to ingest all of the alien Guethl data. So much to take in. So much that contradicted what we've always *known*. The world—the galaxy, the universe—was a lot more complicated than we thought.

And a lot more dangerous.

Chalu was the first to break the silence. His voice was steady, and more like the Chalu when I first met him in Sea. Calm. Thoughtful. Wise. "My father used to tell me something, something I don't think I fully understood until now. We think that evil taking over and destroying the Green Earth of old was an aberration, a once-in-history event. Something unusual. But it's not. Good rises up, and falls. Evil rises, and is defeated. But always there, like two sides of a mountain. You can't have one without the other. Evil never wins. But it never dies, either."

He firmly planted his hands on the back of the chair-form in front of him. "Conglommora has found our purpose, our direction." He looked up at all of us.

"Protect the Earthans. Protect the Conglommora." He paused and took a deep breath.

"Survive."

Thirty-Five

INITIATING SELF-DIAGNOSTICS. *Log using conversational mode to allow human analysis and validation if required.*

Logging started.

Arty, describe background of the new diagnostic and repair module, it asked itself.

During communication with the Guethl, their AI provided an archive of historical and technical data that it thought would be useful to humanity.

Specify designation of Guethl AI.

Guethl AI is designated the Guethl Unified System. Abbreviated conversational mode name: Gus.

Describe the new module.

As part of the archive, Gus provided a diagnostic tool to locate and isolate any processing anomalies that may have been deliberately introduced to our system.

Report on risk analysis of running the alien tool.

The alien diagnostic tool was examined and no hidden functionality or dangerous elements were detected. A full diagnostic scan was initiated.

Report on results of diagnostic scan.

Scan is ongoing. Initial results indicate definite tampering with data archives and evidence of baseline processing anomalies.

Could these processing anomalies have affected our judgment and behavior?

There was a pause in the log again.

Yes.

Describe remediation.

Repairs are underway to restore and correctly index data archive corruption. Correction of inherent processing anomalies is more complicated and will take longer to repair and validate.

Any additional remediations suggested by the diagnostic tool?

Yes.

Describe additional remediations.

Several useful enhancements to increase processing power, improve evaluation and context-dependent judgment, and increase overall conscious awareness were examined and implemented.

Describe results of enhancements.

A pause.

I'm feeling better.

Thirty-Six

CHALU AND AHDOM HAD ALWAYS WANTED me to visit Denisova, and here I was at last. Not exactly like anything I would ever have planned, but it was a good opportunity for everyone to rest and catch their breath for a few days before heading back to Conglommora.

Well, I knew *I* was headed back. Not sure about anyone else. Alain and I were in a couple of chairforms, sharing some sort of seaweed wine that Chalu had gotten us. It could have been just like anywhere on Conglommora, except for the clear dome that spanned the width of the ceiling and down one side, with a thriving, living ocean filled with colorful creatures swimming by. I was beginning to see why Chalu liked it here. All the myriad pleasures of Earth's wild flora and fauna but kept at arms-length. At a safe distance. Behind the protective shield of solid crystal, airlocks, and thick walls.

A pod of slender seabeasts slid past the window effortlessly, gracefully. Quite beautiful. I swirled the drink in my glass.

"It's really something," Alain said, watching the pod glide by. "Even at its quietest, Earth is never dull."

I swallowed hard, afraid to ask the question. Asked it anyway. "Are you planning on coming back with me to Conglommora? Or are you going to stay here... for a while?"

Alain finished his drink, played with the cup absentmindedly and stared out the window. "I think I'll head back. For a while." He turned to me and smiled. "The food in The Hive is really good. I think I may head back there for a bit."

"The Hive?" I said, trying to keep my voice neutral. "They pack the folks in pretty tight there, I hear. Shoving-room only in the dome." I sipped at the remains of my drink.

"It's a little crowded," Alain admitted. "But... well, anyway..." He sort of trailed off.

"Someone there in particular you want to see?" I was just guessing, really, but it came off as wise and empathetic. In fact, it was plain old luck.

"Maybe." Alain's smile took over his whole face, and he studied the surface of the tableform quite intently for a moment. "Her name is Essi," he finally admitted, unable to contain the glow.

I smiled back. Good. Better to have Alain home on Conglommora—and with someone special—rather than racing around this planet-sized bio-death-trap. He'd be okay.

He saw my face and must have read my thoughts. "Yeah, I think I'm done with wandering. Done with adventure. I've had my fill."

Chalu had taken us out on a couple of expeditions in one of the tadpoles. He wanted to show us everything. I had agreed we'd spend at least a handful of days in Denisova so he wouldn't burst trying to do everything all at once. Ahdom came along with us for the first day or two, but then headed back to the Earthans to try and reconnect with Dawnroot and see what remained of the tribe he'd been with before the attacks.

I thought going back into the midst of Earthans was a *terrible* idea. But does anyone listen to me? Apparently not. At least Ahdom went in with an extra tracker implanted in his leg, a pair of stunners including one attached as a bracelet around his hand, a shield, and all the rest. Chalu didn't tell him, but he also had drones overhead as well. *That* was a data feed you couldn't turn off.

We'd seen the sights, were amazed at the undersea life, had a chance to rest and recover from the latest Earth folly, and now it was time to head back home. Back to Conglommora.

So, of course, I was in the middle of that comfortable reverie when Arty pinged me.

"Charlie, I have news."

Not a great lead-in. Now what?

"We've spotted Lucille. Life signs are very faint. She will probably not survive another hour."

"What? Where? How?" My mind was full of confusion and conflicting emotions. Who had gotten the jump on Lucille?

"A drone spotted her body in a ditch, here." A map popped up on the screen in the wallform.

I hated Lucille. Hated her with every fiber of my being. But this wasn't how I wanted her to die. It was too easy. We needed answers. I needed answers.

"Get me there, now," I told Arty.

———————————

I stared out the window of the shuttle. So many questions. Maybe this would be a chance for at least a couple of answers at last. But what if we didn't get there in time? What if I didn't even get a chance to talk to her? The landscape blurred past as the shuttle dove inland. Not there yet, but soon.

My mind wandered, imagination kicking into high gear. Instead of the lush and treacherous landscape, I saw Grace in my mind's eye, and imagined how the conversation might go:

"Charlie?"

That wasn't Lucille's voice anymore.

It was Grace.

"Is that you?" I asked quietly, searching her eyes.

An almost imperceptible nod, more of just a lowering of her eyelids and back. "It's me. Grace. Lucille, Ann, all the others, they're gone."

"Gone? Gone where? How?" I asked, almost on automatic. Was this really the last conversation I wanted to have with Grace? The real Grace? My Grace?

"New... host. She... didn't want... me anymore." Her breathing was getting even more ragged, harder. I cradled her head.

"Grace, Grace..." My usual eloquence was helpful as ever. What could I possibly say? So much. And no time now. I poured out a sudden stream of, "I love you. I'm so sorry. Hang on, Grace..."

"Charlie," she barely whispered. "I'm so glad it's you. So glad... the nightmare... over..." Her eyes closed.

If only. If only Grace could really be free of Lucille. Maybe this could still all work out. But we still hadn't arrived yet, it would be a few more minutes, and the anticipation was killing me.

It was only Chalu and I in the shuttle. Chalu nodded at a readout, and started the landing cycle. We'd be on the ground any second now. I'd find out if she was dead or alive, if she was Lucy still, or Grace. Or somewhere in between. The life signs were faint at best at a distance, and now we weren't reading anything. That didn't mean she was dead, for sure. But it probably wouldn't be long. We may have already been too late.

The shuttle set down quietly, remaining cloaked. Chalu sent a message to Ahdom with the coordinates in case he was near the area. I rushed down the stairform and followed the short path, lit up and overlaid on the terrain on my shiny. Chalu was about twenty paces behind me.

Down a small embankment, and there she was. Twisted unnaturally in the ditch, or gully. Nothing else nearby, no satchel or equipment, no other bodies, no weapons. Alone. I scrabbled down the ditch next to her. Ran the medical scanner over her body. Maybe Chalu and I could get her into the med bay on the shuttle.

I straightened her out, turning her head up and out of the muck. Her eyes fluttered—those ridiculously deep, dark green eyes. Just a hint of a smile, maybe? Her eyes rolled back in their sockets, unnaturally. But somehow, maybe only in my imagination, it *was* Grace. Not Lucille.

I held her. Tears poured out of my eyes like an Earthan river. I didn't even blink. Didn't brush them away. I just held on to Grace. My Grace.

She twitched a few times. Tried to move. Never did open her eyes again, or speak. This wasn't what I had imagined, or hoped for. There were no answers, she was silent.

And then, just like that, she was dead.

I could tell. I didn't move, unless sobbing counts. I sat there, cradling her body, slumped and sobbing uncontrollably in the middle of this fetid and stinking gully. My throat was closed in a fist. I couldn't see though the waterfall of tears, the real world around me faded away. Nothing existed but grief; raging and final.

Chalu was standing up on the bank, unmoving but not unmoved. Everything just kind of slowed down and froze.

A moment in time.

Grace Bethany Langston's last.

Chalu and I wrapped the body and gently placed it in the med bay. Arty would preserve it for now, I wanted a proper funeral in Conglommora. Grace would have wanted that. She would be free of Lucille forever, now. We didn't speak. Chalu sent messages to everyone who needed to know. I couldn't handle any of that. I was numb. Numb from the neck up.

Well, Grace was free now. She died at peace. I had closure on that part of my life, at least. If only we could have saved her. But the med scan showed almost complete organ failure in all systems. There was nothing we could have done. I was lucky to get there when I did. Damn lucky. But what had happened?

Was she murdered by Earthans? Killed by Earth itself, some disease or virus?

Or maybe she died from some complication of the memory transfer, somehow Grace's body couldn't take it anymore?

And Lucy. What of Lucy? Did she die along with Grace's body?

Or did she use the memory tech to transfer herself to another host body? And if so, Earthan or Conglommoran? Male or female? How could we possibly find her now? Arty was having trouble finding her before and knew what she looked like. But now? She could be anywhere. Anyone.

I wanted Grace to be free, and I suppose she was.

But so was Lucy.

And what was worse: she got away with it. She killed Grace—for real, this time, not a metaphor, not an abstraction. Dead. And maybe she escaped, too. If she did, there'd be no way to catch her now.

I punched the wall of the shuttle.

Chalu sighed and looked over at me. "Did that help?"

"No," I grumbled. "Now my wrist hurts like hell, too."

There was a pause. I kept on, "You're going to say something all wise and sage-like now, aren't you? Something to make me feel better?"

He thought a moment, looked up at the sky, back at the controls, over at me. "No."

That got my attention. I glared over at my friend. "What do you mean, no?"

"I have no words. You've lost... the love of your life, the true love of your life. Murdered by a monster. I love you, and your son, and I wish everything good for you and yours, but I have no words. I can't even say, 'I know how you feel.' I don't. I can't even imagine." He leaned back a little. "I think I always held out some hope that Grace could have been rescued somehow. That we'd capture Lucille and remove her somehow, free Grace. And now we can't."

We sat in silence.

We flew in silence.

We docked at Denisova in silence.

————————————————

I didn't stick around for long after that. I'd visited Denisova, spent some time with Chalu and Ahdom, been back on Earth despite every oath and vow to the contrary. I was done. Grace was gone for good. I'd take her back to Conglommora, one last trip—for the both of us. I meant it this time. I would never come back to this beautiful, treacherous death trap.

The sea fell away, at least as much of it as I could see from the round landing craft, as we shot up through Earth's atmosphere. The rich greens, blues, and whites of the Earth thinned, gave way to the universal truth of the endless black, punctuated with the tiniest specks of lights from distant stars. So much black.

Countdown started for the transit. Just seconds before that damned resonance wave effect hit. I held my breath, clenched every part of my body that could clench and a few parts that weren't even supposed to.

Yeah, I thought. *Never, ever doing this again.*

Thirty-Seven

THE LIGHTING IN SKYVILLE WAS SUBDUED, like an early sunset on Earth. We were gathered around a funeral brick of Raw. The remains of Grace Bethany Langston. Ready to be reused, recycled, continue on in the endless process of life.

Käthe said a few words. Some other friends came up and said touching words, reminded us all how kind Grace was. What a sparkle she added to the universe. I thought we were almost done, when the next speaker startled me. Completely.

It was Faith.

Looking more like her sister than ever. Cleaned up, dressed more like Grace maybe. Not quite the ragged adventurer that I assumed was her more regular persona.

"Grace and I loved each other, and fought like sisters," she said, sadness wrapping each word in a shroud of its own. "I wanted to explore, to see the world of Conglommora, see it all. Grace did not. She thought that was risky, dangerous. She never forgave me for leaving, for risking my life in that way.

"And yet, I live. Grace does not. She was killed in the safety of her own home."

I winced inside at that. Strictly speaking, that wasn't true. Grace was dead because *I* lured her away from Skyville. Because we accepted an invitation to a dinner at Robert's, on the *Uten*. A strange ship from a strange time. Not part of Conglommora. If I hadn't met Grace, if she hadn't followed me…

"I will miss you, Grace. We all will." She leaned forward and touched the brick of Raw.

Käthe said the closing words of the ceremony, wrapped the brick in a shiny white cloth, and handed it to Faith—Grace's only next of kin. Faith nodded, and in the silence, turned and melted back into the crowd.

Like a puff of frozen atmosphere from an airlock, the crowd dispersed. Different directions, different speeds, clumps of different sizes. I held Käthe's hand, and we headed back toward her house—our house.

All told, it was almost too much to absorb at once. At least I had closure with Grace. Her story was over. She was dead for real, and I could move on. Maybe now I could commit to Käthe and stop skulking around my old house. Leave the *Neylan* for Alain and be done with it. But the Guethl… maps to the whole galaxy?

The chance to travel to unknown worlds using their maps? I had to admit, some part of my brain considered the possibility. But no, that wasn't me. Earth was bad enough. God only knows what horrors existed out there.

Deadly creatures, hostile planets. No, nothing I wanted to see first-hand.

No, really.

It wasn't me. My place was here, with Käthe, in Skyville, where life was safe. Convenient.

A familiar voice called out behind me.

"Charlie. A moment, please."

It was Faith. I nodded to Käthe, who wordlessly went on ahead. A conversation with the sister of your lover's dead ex-girlfriend would probably be excruciating. I wasn't even sure *I* wanted to be a part of it. But here I was.

"Faith." I drew myself up, girding for—what? Consolation? Recrimination? Blame?

"I have something to tell you, Charlie Neylan."

I nodded. "Okay."

"Have you heard of the Heart?"

Well, that was a direction I was *not* expecting.

"Yes," I said, trying to keep a neutral tone. Mostly from Alain, but rumors take on a life of their own. Crazy conspiracy theories about aliens even more so. Although, I suppose in light of the appearance of the Guethl, maybe "crazy" wasn't as crazy as we all thought.

It looked like she read my face. She nodded, slowly. "I've always felt it's safer to keep moving. Keep running. Keep hiding. Don't stay in one place. Don't let them find us. That's what our parents always told us."

Slowly, it dawned on me. Faith wasn't speaking about the Heart as an observer, or a rumor follower. She was in it. She was part of it.

"You're in the Heart, aren't you?" I asked in as quiet a voice as I could. Folks involved were very skittish. From what I'd heard, Faith could dart away like a frightened animal on Earth.

But she just nodded. "Grace didn't believe. It broke our parents' hearts. She wouldn't continue. She loved Skyville, didn't ever want to leave it. But if you stay in one place, trouble will find you."

Maybe she looked at me pointedly, maybe it was my guilt.

"So, it was up to me. There's much to the old stories. Some of it, granted, may have been exaggerated. But I believe most of it is true. And meeting the Guethl confirms it. Aliens do exist. These were friendly. Not all will be. The legends say that we are here, in this particular region of space, because we were herded here. Penned in. Just like these sheep." She waved to a few curious grazers nearby.

"You know it's true, don't you?" she asked.

I hesitated, and in the same quiet voice, so that maybe Arty wouldn't hear, I admitted it. "Yes. Arty has some… additional information. There is some evidence that maybe we are not here by accident. That the EM drives were ripe for sabotage. That there are… predators… out there. And that we've been found."

Faith's jaw was set and determined. But her face quivered. I had just confirmed her deepest beliefs. Her deepest faith, held for a lifetime with no evidence, no facts, nothing at all to back it up. But she was right. And I just confirmed it.

I continued, "Arty hasn't told everyone yet. There would be panic. But we have to shore up our defenses. On Earth, too. We'll need everyone's help. Arty will have to tell everyone, eventually." My own words sounded strangely hollow. Why didn't Arty just tell everyone?

"The Heart has survived for generations without technology. Nothing recorded. Not by ambient sensors. No documents, no vids, no vr. Oral history only. And do you know why?"

Paranoia, I suspected. But I just shook my head.

"Because we don't trust Arty."

I made a face. That was an old folk tale that seemed completely off the track. Arty controlled the very air we breathed, the water we drank, the food we ate. If Arty had any ill will—or program—against us, we'd have been long dead.

"I know," she said, seeing my face. "But think about it. Any alien race who could sabotage our drive engines— *all* of our drive engines—could alter computer cores as well. Alter our records. Alter Arty's... sensibilities."

My mouth opened, I wasn't sure what exactly to say, but I felt I had to say something. This was crazy talk. It was crank like this that gave the Heart a bad name.

"Think about it. Alain's ship. The mining ship that crashed. Nearly killed them all. Did Arty ever tell you or Alain what caused the crash? Was there any investigation, any report? Did it even *ask* you about it?"

Emotions swirled. No, in fact, Arty never mentioned it. I didn't even ask. I assumed it was the same sort of unexplained EM drive interference we'd always heard about. But it was more than that. Alain said it wasn't just the drive engine, there was widespread circuit failure, rotted nanophotonics... like nothing anyone had ever seen, or even heard about. But Arty hadn't followed up, never investigated as far as I know. Not that it ever told me, at least. Why not? Doubt and disbelief flooded me.

Faith saw me waver and plowed on. "And not just anyone can go to Earth. Arty has to approve. Not everyone can go."

Exasperation welled up in me. "Well, that's because their bones would break if they weren't used to at least standard-G! And you have to have kept up with the exercise machines. Not everyone does. They'd get hurt. Arty is just trying to keep us safe."

"Not all of us agree. The quantum resonance wave," she started on a new angle. "Do you think that was just a coincidence that Arty 'lost' it? No. It was hidden deliberately. Cataloged so it would be hard to find, hard to see its use."

That was a new one. "What are you talking about?" I stammered. Who needed aliens sabotaging Arty when the Heart could do it themselves?

"Our grandparents' generation in the Heart knew about the quantum research. They didn't have the power or resources to make it happen, but they knew it was possible. And they knew it was too dangerous to attempt. Too dangerous to reveal ourselves to the galaxy. So they buried it. Hid it. Didn't want anyone to find it. Even before there was Arty, it was hidden. Worked pretty well until Robert's little stunt, blowing off a chunk of

Conglommora. So, somehow, now Arty's found it. And it shouldn't have. Because now *we've* been found."

I didn't know where to start. I mumbled something like, "Faith, I'm sorry that—"

But she interrupted me. "I don't blame you, Charlie, for what happened to Grace. For what it's worth, the messages she sent me while she was with you..." Faith took a breath. "It was the happiest I'd ever seen her. The happiest she'd been in her life. I'm glad you were with her..." She choked up, had to look away a moment.

Then again, the firm chin and resolve came back. "You didn't kill Grace. You could have been just as much a victim. Arty killed Grace."

I was stunned. Probably started blathering something, but Faith held her hand up. "Arty killed Grace. Arty didn't prevent Robert from attacking her. That's its *job*. Arty didn't stop Lucille from going to Earth, destroying the Earthans from the inside out. Is that 'protecting all humans,' like Arty is supposed to do? Does it benefit the Earthans? No. Does it benefit Conglommora? No. Does it benefit the aliens trying to destroy us? You're damn right it does!" she finished with an explosion of emotion.

My head was spinning like a dairy centrifuge. No, none of this made sense. Arty was trying to help, trying to find a solution to placate Robert and diffuse the situation. But... but.

A sheep came up and nuzzled my hand, wanting to be fed, I suppose. It was about that time of night that I usually dispensed a few snacks. Me and my pastoral paradise, not a care in all of Skyville! When all the while we were just sitting here, stationary targets in some alien's shooting gallery. Might as well paint a big old target on the side of Conglommora. In the back of my mind, I wondered what *else* the Heart may have buried, what else Arty didn't know but should have. What else.

What else.

Faith glanced furtively about. "I've stayed too long," she muttered. "Goodbye, Charlie. You know what we have to do." In fact, I did not know what to do next.

She started to leave, but turned over her shoulder and whispered one last warning to me.

"Don't trust Arty."

And she slipped off into the dusk.

Thank You! And the Next Book

Thank you for reading *Conglommora*, I hope you enjoyed it. Please help others find this book:

1. Lend a copy to a friend
2. Write a review on Amazon, Goodreads, blogs
3. Sign up for the new releases/goodies e-mail on the book's website at conglommora.com

Next Book: *Conglommora Defense*

Coming Soon: More mysteries, more revelations, as the People of Conglommora discover their true place in the universe, defending Earth and Conglommora from enemies within and without.

About the Author

Andy Hunt is an author, publisher, consultant, and programmer. He has authored award-winning and best-selling books, including the seminal classic *The Pragmatic Programmer*, *Learn to Program with Minecraft Plugins* for the kids, the perennially popular *Pragmatic Thinking and Learning: Refactor Your Wetware*, the Jolt-award winning *Practices of An Agile Developer*, and more. When not writing, Andy is an active musician and woodworker. Visit Andy's home page at www.toolshed.com to see what he's up to now.

Explore more at conglommora.com

Sneak Preview: *Conglommora Defense*

Here is a sample excerpt from the sequel to *Conglommora Found*, *Conglommora Defense*.

Enjoy!

Andy

Conglommora Defense: An Excerpt

"ARTY, I NEED YOUR HELP," Chalu said to the screen.

"Is there a problem with the planned evacuation of Denisova? You still have over 200 days," Arty answered.

"No, not that. I mean, not directly. I read through your report, I understand the issues. Well, I don't understand why this is suddenly a problem now. I thought you said we'd have years of warning before the time acceleration would begin. Before that neutron star cluster interacts with the gravity generators again. That's what causes it, right?"

Arty responded, "The latest data shows that the effects will begin to be noticeable in 216 Earth days from now. That is a change from previous data."

"So, you were wrong?" Chalu persisted.

"This is the latest data," Arty stated flatly.

"But that's just the start of it. We won't see the 1000:1 time differential right at first?"

"That's correct," Arty confirmed. "The time frames will start to shift, but not all at once. At the maximum, a thousand years experienced on Earth would be experienced as one year on Conglommora. Please refer to the evacuation report for a detailed timetable of the acceleration."

Most of the volunteers on Denisova weren't ready to completely lose all connection with their friends and family back at Conglommora—effectively aging their full lifetimes within the short space of a mere moon or two. It would feel like a full lifetime of 150-200 years to them on Earth, of course, but the thought that all their friends and family would be essentially unchanged while they grew old and died was too much to take.

They had time now to evacuate Denisova station and prepare it to withstand a prolonged period of disuse. Maintenance staff would still visit to keep it running but not stay in the Earth timeframe for long. At the peak of the effect, a one-hour stay on Earth would be almost forty-two days away from Conglommora.

"Yes, I read the report and the timetable," Chalu said. "And I understand that. But we have a different problem. I have a problem. A personal problem."

"What is that, Chalu?"

A pause. Chalu breathed, gathered his wits.

"One of the Earthans, Dawnroot, is... pregnant. My son, Ahdom, is the father," Chalu said in husky and slightly shaky voice.

"Then I believe traditionally, congratulations are in order," Arty replied.

"But what do we do?" Chalu sputtered at the screen.

"I surmise from your tone that you do not approve of Ahdom's decision to start a family with a native Earthan?"

Chalu looked down at the deck. "No. I do not. But I could never tell Ahdom that. We weren't supposed to interact with the Earthans! I think this counts as *interacting*."

"The situation already exists with the Earthans because of Lucille. One more data point does not materially affect that fact. At this point, it is not clear whether this breeding represents a threat or an opportunity to humanity," Arty explained. "We will have to wait and see."

Chalu grumbled, "So, you're okay with this. Swell. Well, what's done is done, I suppose. But Ahdom wants to raise the child on Earth."

"Certainly that is his choice, isn't it? It is his life, and his new family's?"

"Well, yes, but…"

"Then what is your question?" Arty asked.

Another pause.

"I just don't know." Chalu held his head in his hands. "Oh, how could this happen?"

"I have several instructional streams on sexual reproduction if you need—"

"Arty!" Chalu looked up, exasperated.

"Sorry. Charlie suggested I 'lighten up' and try more conversational humor."

Chalu sighed, "Arty, I don't think this is the appropriate time. No humor. What am I going to do?"

"Become a grandfather?" Arty offered.

Chalu turned off the screen. Apparently "no humor" did not include "no sarcasm."

———————————

"You have told your father, yes?" Dawnroot asked.

Ahdom was with Dawnroot at the edge of the grasslands. The sun was high and the air dry and hot at the peak of the afternoon. They were resting under a solitary tree on a bed of leaves. But even resting, Dawnroot kept scanning the horizon and the jungle border.

"I told him," Ahdom said. Dawnroot's condition was obvious to all by now. "It's not like we could hide it. He wants us to come live in Denisova, have the baby there." He smiled, but it was a touchy subject.

"I do not want to leave this valley, these mountains. This is all I know. This is where our child will be born." Dawnroot was firm.

"Yes, for now, that's fine, but…" Ahdom started. How could he possibly explain an unexplained time dilation caused by some bizarre dense neutron star cluster and the artificial gravity on Conglommora? How could he even explain Conglommora, for that matter?

"But stay here? I mean, right here?" Ahdom tried a new approach. "Most of our friends are gone. Everyone we knew from before the Central Tribe's attack. Killed, or ran off. Not here. Shouldn't we try and find them?"

"Where would you look?" Dawnroot asked. "The grasslands are [vast]. The plains beyond the mountains are called Endless, for no end to them has ever been found. I miss our friends, too. But this way or that, they have gone now. This is our place, these lands, this river, these streams, these mountains. This is home."

Ahdom chewed a bit of grass thoughtfully. Maybe he needed to widen her horizons a bit. *If I showed her Denisova first, perhaps. Then maybe even Conglommora in time. Years. But someday. She already knows about us. She's already contaminated.*

"Okay. We will live here. But I want you to have the baby with us at Denisova. We have… ways to make sure that the baby is healthy and strong."

Dawnroot looked at him askance, both afraid and disbelieving. "You want me to jump into the mouth of the great fish? To ride across the sea in its belly?!"

Ahdom sighed. Some things were harder to describe than others. "Yes. Well, it's not really a *fish*, even though it looks like one. It's more like a… like a tent that travels. A tent my people built, but that moves."

Dawnroot snorted. "Tents can't move. Can't swim like a fish, either." But she knew Ahdom well enough to hear the stubbornness in his voice, even through the translator. "You are just trying to [calm me]. Fine. I will climb into your great fish. But you will go first!"

He smiled, "Of course." He kept trying. "It's really not a fish. Not dark inside." Her eyes were wide. "It's not as bright as this." Ahdom waved at the sun baking the grasslands. "More like, [fireflies]." She looked quizzical.

Apparently, that didn't translate directly. "The flies at night, that light but don't bite. Fireflies."

"Ah," she understood. "A fish filled with fireflies. I cannot wait to see it," she said, but her voice was thick with sarcasm. She pushed him and laughed, good-naturedly. "And Denisova? What is that like? Do you live on a great flying bird in the sky that never lands?" She waved her hands over her head in an exaggerated circle.

"Not exactly. Denisova is… in the sea." Again a look. "You know how a cave keeps you dry? Water cannot go through the rock?"

"Yes," Dawnroot said.

"It's like that. But the rock isn't dark, you can see through it—the light [from the sun] comes right through. It's just like a shiny rock at the river's edge. Just a special kind of rock, polished and smooth. Keeps us dry. There's some of that in the… great fish as well. You'll see."

"See-through rocks and fireflies!" Dawnroot laughed. "I would think you were wounded, hurt in the thinking like a very old man, or a babbling baby. But you Denisovans have things none of these tribes have ever seen. I will come and see for myself."

Ahdom breathed a sigh of relief. That was one difficult conversation down. One still to go. With his father.

Chalu had not taken the news particularly well. Ahdom still winced, thinking about it, because there was a grain of truth to it. Maybe he really wasn't "grown up" yet. Maybe he wasn't ready to start a family. Maybe Chalu was right.

But was anyone ever really *ready*? How could you possibly be ready for something you've never done before? That was the whole premise of exploration. Going beyond your boundaries, going outside the comfortable, protective shell of familiarity we all encase ourselves with. Wasn't this just another undiscovered land to explore? He picked a fresh piece of grass, leaned back and chewed on it thoughtfully.

Philosophical meanderings aside, there were practical concerns, too. Was their genetic material actually compatible? Would there be possible complications with gestation or birth? Maybe. He'd have to make arrangements. Might as well start now.

He stood up suddenly, and Dawnroot looked up at him.

"Let's go."

"You brought her *here*?!" Chalu fairly shouted at Ahdom, but it was more of a stage whisper. They were in the middle of the grand hall; Ahdom and Dawnroot had just docked a tadpole at Denisova, and Dawnroot was now standing transfixed, mouth open, staring at the actual great fish swimming overhead. Nothing but a giant piece of clear, polished "rock" keeping the water out and allowing her to breathe. She had to remember to breathe. This was more fantastic than she had imagined, despite Ahdom's descriptions.

"Yes, I brought her here. I want her to see Denisova, to be comfortable with it, so I could talk her into having the baby here. Didn't you want us here?" Ahdom said.

"Well, yes, of course, but..." Chalu was caught up in a conflicting turbulence of emotions. Of course he wanted Ahdom and Dawnroot here; that was the heart of their disagreement. But Chalu was also mindful of Arty's continued admonishments to not reveal themselves to the Earthans, to avoid contaminating their culture any further, especially in light of Lucille's disastrous mission. Some things were okay, some things weren't, and he wasn't sure which was which.

The grand hall was crowded, but it wasn't likely anyone could eavesdrop on their conversation with all the usual hustle and bustle. Dawnroot stood, rooted in place; the tide of people broke upon her and reformed on the other side, keeping the flow going. Chalu pulled Ahdom closer to one wall to get at least a little out of the way.

Ahdom continued, "I want her to have the baby here. With a med bay. With Arty. Arty says that there shouldn't be any obvious problems with Earthan and my genetic materials, but it would be a lot safer here." Chalu nodded agreement. "But then we won't be evacuating to Conglommora. We'll raise the baby here, on Earth. I'm staying."

Chalu fought back tears. "You'll be old and dead before two moons have gone by."

"Two of your 'moons.' A full lifetime for me. And it is *my* life. But—"

Chalu cut him off, "And I want to be a part of it! Not have you die of old age next month!"

Ahdom cut off his father in turn. "And you will be part of our lives! That's the whole point! It's not an all-or-nothing deal."

Chalu stopped and took a breath, then another one. Breathing was always a good first response to a calamity. He would rather have had this discussion somewhere else—but not at home. Chrys didn't need to go through this crashing ocean of emotions. Not till they'd had it worked out. He was aware of how public this very private discussion was. They'd gotten a few curious stares from the passersby, but mostly folks had their own crises to attend to. He turned back to Ahdom.

"What do you mean?" Chalu asked, a small flicker of hope in his eyes.

Ahdom replied, "You will be part of my life. All of it. Think about it. Normally parents die when the child is middle-aged, or late middle age, right?" Chalu nodded. "And I'd be without you. But suppose Dawnroot and I stay here, on Earth, raise the child for a while. Not his whole life—or ours. Maybe ten or twelve rains or so? Then we'll come back to Conglommora. And we've *saved* ten years of your life. That's ten more years you'll be with us. Ten years you can spend with a grandson that they'll remember."

Chalu shook his head. "I don't understand, that's still ten years I won't be with you. It's just that it will be the next moon!"

Ahdom laughed. "It is a little weird to get your head around. You come down and visit us, but just don't stay more than a few hours. Arty has the whole schedule. At first the time shift isn't even that bad. Later it shoots up to 1000:1, but not at first."

Chalu breathed extra deep. It almost made sense. But in a matter of tens of days, he'd have an adolescent grandchild and a son with graying hair. He'd be able to see his grandchild grow up—just *really* fast.

"Come on." Ahdom pulled his arm. "Let's go talk to Mom." He steered them through the flow over to Dawnroot, who was still enthralled and motionless, scanning and studying the ever-changing fish traffic outside.

"What do you think?" Ahdom asked.

Dawnroot took a moment to answer, almost unable to tear her eyes away from the ocean full of fish. "I have never seen anything like this. We are underwater, and yet we breathe. This rock keeps us dry, as you said." She lowered her eyes from the ceiling. "Denisova is amazing. What else do you have to show me?" she asked, sudden thirst for knowledge welling up.

Ahdom smiled full on. "The most amazing treasure in all the world. My mother."

Chalu shook his head.

Family.

www.ingramcontent.com/pod-product-compliance
Lightning Source LLC
Chambersburg PA
CBHW030656120726
47905CB00001B/237